No Revenge So Complete

ALSO BY SARAH FOULGER

Yards of Purple

No
Revenge
So
Complete

SARAH FOULGER

brook street press
SAINT SIMONS ISLAND

Brook Street Press
www.brookstreetpress.com

Brook Street Press is a trademark of Brook Street Press LLC

First Edition

Library of Congress Cataloging-in-Publication Data

Foulger, Sarah M. (Sarah Marguerite), 1955–
    No revenge so complete / Sarah Foulger.— 1st ed.
        p. cm.
    ISBN 0-9724295-1-4
    1. Married people—Fiction. 2. Adultery—Fiction. 3.
Sisters—Fiction.   I. Title.

    PS3606.O84N6   2003
    813'.6—dc22

                                            2003017010

Jacket and text design by Charles Casey Martin

Printed in the United States of America

10 9 8 7 6 5 4 3 2 1

With deep and abiding gratitude,
I dedicate this book to my husband, Russ,
who is my rock;
to my sister, Alice,
from whom I always expected great things;
and to my friend, Jim,
who in following his bliss,
brought this book to life.

There is no revenge so complete

as forgiveness.

—Josh Billings, 1818–1885

CHAPTER ONE

The First Monday in May / *Helen*

IT WAS STILL DARK WHEN THE phone rang. Somewhere in the murky continuum between twilight and pitch.
Just enough scattered particles of light that with a minute of
adjustment, familiar territory is negotiable. Helen was the
only one to hear it. At first the ringing phone entered her
dream world. In the dream, she was in her own home, except
that all of the furnishings were missing. It was empty. She was
weary. So very weary. Yet, as she wandered through her sub-
conscious house, she could not find a single chair in which to
sit and rest. The walls were emptied of all pictures. She

searched for the annual family Christmas portraits. These should have been hung chronologically around the living room walls but she did not see even a faded mark on the walls where the portraits belonged. A phone rang somewhere in the house. As she searched for the phone, consciousness overtook her dream state. She stumbled out of her bedroom into the Cimmerian hall to an unrelenting telephone from the waking world. "Hello," she answered, clearing her still sleeping throat. The jarring edge of a female voice demanded to know, "Who's this?"

"This is Helen." She stopped herself from delivering the question in kind and employed a well-practiced politeness laced with curiosity. "May I ask who is calling?"

"This is Nadine and I need to speak to Steve right now, do you hear me?"

"Steve?" she asked, startled and intrigued. "Just a minute."

Helen let the black receiver dangle from its cradle on the wall. Slowly, she headed down the long hall to her parents' bedroom. Steve. How very odd. Never before had she heard anyone refer to her father as Steve. He was called Mr. Quintal by almost everyone; in rare instances, Stephen. Her mother called him Stephen. The call, however, must be for her father. Who else would it be for?

Her parents were sound asleep, curled in opposite directions. It seemed to Helen that her mother's face held a strained smile, while her father's relaxed mouth released methodical snores. Gently, she tapped her father on his silk-covered shoulder, whispering, "Dad. Dad. It's the phone. Dad. Someone's on the phone for you." He bolted upright like some ashen creature from a horror film arising precipitously from the realm of the dead. A suburban Dracula. The bright red numbers on his bedside digital alarm clock read 4:32 A.M.

"What is it?" he whispered brusquely to his youngest daughter, sounding more than a little annoyed. She felt terrible about waking him but did not know what else to do with the woman on the phone. Had Helen been more conscious, she might have taken a message for her father. It was too late for that now. Now her father was staring at her with unmistakable irritation, waiting to hear why his youngest daughter had so boorishly cut short his sleep.

"Someone named Nadine is on the phone and would like to speak to you."

"Shhh," he whispered urgently, his eyes widening, unwittingly betraying their unconditional panic. Her father was distinctly awake now.

Her mother stirred, rolling over to ask her husband what the matter was.

"It's nothing," Stephen lied, "just someone from work."

Stephen Quintal insisted his daughter go back to sleep as he fled downstairs to the privacy of the phone in the den. Helen scurried to the telephone receiver in the upstairs hallway. She knew she should replace the receiver and return to bed as instructed but, like a mouse clinging to the shadows, she sat down on the floor, her tired back resting against the wall. She listened intently, trying neither to breathe nor to reveal her pounding, spying heart.

"Nadine, it's four-thirty in the morning. What are you doing?" she heard her father ask with an edginess in his voice that was recognizable to Helen.

A now whimpering voice replied, "Is it? I've lost track of the time. I've been up all night. Actually I haven't slept much for three days and I don't think I should be the only one losing sleep, Steve. Listen." Helen heard the woman on the phone take a deep breath. "You know how you told me you couldn't have kids? Remember that? Well, something is definitely not right here, because I am pregnant, Steve, and, there is . . ." The woman stopped. Helen thought she heard a stifled whimper. After a long pause during which Helen was afraid her father might hear the hammering she could feel in her chest, the woman continued, "There is no one else. You know there's no one else. That makes you the father. You!" The woman stopped to take another deep breath. Her father did the same. The woman continued, "Do you want to tell me what's going on? I think I deserve an explanation. I need some sort of explanation here, Steve."

Helen screamed silently, "You need an explanation!" What was happening here? Was she still dreaming? Was she really hearing what she thought she was hearing? The woman sounded sincere enough. Angry and upset but disturbingly sincere. Her father, on the other hand, was oddly unresponsive. When he did speak, he did not sound exactly like her father.

"Steve. Steve? Are you there?" the woman asked.

"Of course I'm here," he assured her. His voice was calm yet Helen could tell he was aggravated. "Nadine. I need you to calm down. Listen, I will meet you this afternoon at five o'clock at The Captain's Folly. I'll fix everything. I promise. But I have to get off the phone now and I need you not to call me here again. Not this morning. Not ever. I thought you understood that."

The woman hung up but Helen could still hear her father breathing, air rushing back and forth through outraged nose hair. She thought she could hear the rapid pulsing of her own veins until that was interrupted by a flat dial tone. Helen waited for her father to hang up before doing the same. She was shocked, bewildered, and shamefully interested in what had just happened. Nadine's voice sounded young and vaguely familiar. The more she thought about it, the more certain she was that she had heard this troubled voice before. But where? And what was going on here anyway? Was this true? Was some apparently young woman pregnant with her father's baby?

Such an affair was unimaginable to Helen. She did not think her father could possibly do anything like this. Her father have an affair? She could not fathom it. She could not picture her father doing anything that messy with her own mother, let alone anyone else. Certainly not with someone who sounded like this rude person. And then there was the accusation of deceit. Her father was not a liar. Of this much, Helen was confident. There had to be an explanation. She heard her father shuffling up the steps and hurriedly tiptoed back into her bedroom. She was wholly awake, trying to make sense of the contemptible yet fascinating drama she had just overheard. As Helen wandered through her neural networks, she located an intersection that placed the name "Nadine" among her sister's acquaintances. Now that would be something. That would really be something. But that would also be impossible. Helen was embarrassed by her own curiosity.

Her mind was spinning so fast Helen nearly felt dizzy, though she was flat and motionless in her bed. She began to doubt what her ears had absorbed. Her father was not the sort of person to get involved with another woman and certainly not with someone as young as Jane's friend, Nadine. She knew her father to be a morally upright man, a good man who had, as she well knew, no patience for lies. Helen recalled a time when she told her parents that a special necklace had been stolen. This was a beautiful necklace, a gold pillow heart that hung from a delicate chain. Her father had given it to her four years ago on the occasion of her tenth birthday. It was a gorgeous gift and she loved her father for it. She felt special when she wore it and, until it disappeared, she wore it all the time.

One day at the beach during a particularly hot summer following her eleventh birthday, Helen wore the necklace right into the surf, where it disappeared into yawning ocean sands. She felt so stupid that day. Lying there in the dark, trying to make sense of her father's words on the phone, that same debilitating sense of idiocy revisited her afresh. When she confessed to her parents that the necklace was gone, stolen right out of her beach bag, she could tell by the look in her father's discerning eyes that he did not believe her. Her guilt-ridden face flushed as her father asked, "Are you sure that's what happened, sweetheart?" At that point, Helen had come clean with the truth. She remembered her father's tender reaction, how he had held her to his warm chest and said, "You can tell me anything, Helen. But don't lie. Don't ever lie."

The worst part of the whole experience was not the lie, however, nor was it the awful discovery of the lie. It was how extremely small she felt for having disappointed her father. It was the dreadful numbness in the pit of her stomach when he insisted on taking her back down to the beach and determinedly tried to help her find the spot where the precious necklace was forever lost. It was the hopelessness that prevailed as she watched him dig uselessly for more than an hour in the slippery wet sand beneath the shallow rolling waves. It was the fact that he went out and bought her a second gold pillow heart necklace the next day. It was the realization that he could easily have lost his temper, as he had many times before over disappointments far less serious, especially with her sister, Jane, yet this time he did not. It was understanding that she had shirked the responsibilities that go with being daddy's little girl. It was the knowledge that, while her father had gone the extra mile in attempting to make things right again for her, she could never wear the replacement necklace. It was not the same. The new necklace was a ruthless reminder of her plain failure as a daughter. It sat inside an antique Spanish leather jewelry box in the back of her top drawer alongside another gift from her father, a stopwatch she used when she was trying to improve her speed on the soccer field. The box seemed to hold nothing but souvenirs of her inadequacy.

Her father's expectations were a funny thing, Helen reflected. They were not universally applied. They were distinctly tied to individual persons. He expected thoroughness and optimism from her mother, perfection and success from her sister, but what, other than being a good girl, did he expect from her? When she was active in sports, there were a few years of somewhat inflated expectations in that one area of her life, but since then Jane was definitely the high focus of her father's expectations. In some ways, this made Helen's life simpler. Less pressure. Less yelling at her. But it also left her feeling incompetent and obtuse sometimes. What did Jane have that she did not?

Helen was sure her father had gone back to bed but now she heard his bare feet padding quietly into her room. Through deliberately closed eyelids, Helen could see the day brightening rapidly and, as she lay in perfect physical stillness, pretending to sleep, she hoped her father would not see how fully awake she truly was. He whispered, "Helen?" She did not answer. "Sweetheart?" She did not stir. He seemed to stand there for an inordinately long period of time during which she felt increasingly culpable. Finally, the feet padded back down the hall. She heard her father turn on the shower in her parents' bathroom and felt safe enough again to open her eyes. She checked the time. It was now 5:52.

Helen tried to distract her electrified mind with a book she had just started reading, *The Bell Jar*. Her older sister, Jane, had recommended it. Helen was intensely interested in this story of a deeply disturbed young woman but could scarcely concentrate on it now. She tucked it back beneath her pillow and retrieved a half-empty bag of chocolate chips she had pilfered from the baking cabinet in the kitchen and had carefully stored in a plastic container beneath her bed. She sat up in her bed eating one small chip after another, allowing each bittersweet piece to dissolve lovingly on her tongue before adding another. She felt nervous, guilty, and stupid.

Helen looked around her pale pink room. Everything was in its proper place. Her desktop was clean but for a neat pile of schoolbooks on the right side and her completed math homework on the left. Her closet door was closed. A poster of a humpback whale breaching the surface of the ocean was carefully tacked to the wall above her desk. More than a dozen framed photographs of soccer and softball teams, for which she had played from the age of five, hung on the wall in straight rows, like squares on a monthly calendar. All was as it should be; yet everything felt alarmingly disorderly.

AT SIX O'CLOCK HELEN HEARD the alarm clock begin its disagreeable beeping next door in her sister's room. There were two ways to get from her room into Jane's—through the hall or through the bathroom they shared. She sneaked in through the bathroom. That way her parents, especially her father, would not know she was talking to Jane. Not that chatting with her sister was unusual in the least. The sisters were close. They were in one another's rooms all the time. This morning, however, Helen did not want her father to think she was up to anything. Once in Jane's room, Helen hit the snooze button on the noisy alarm. How could her sister not hear that annoying beeping? How could it not wake her? Seeing Jane's eyes blink open, Helen placed a plump vertical finger to her own lips, letting her sleepy big sister know she had an important secret to share.

A few minutes later, through a face full of fine, light-brown hair that did not seem to know where to go, her very stunned sister asked, "What are you saying?"

"I'm saying that someone named Nadine is pregnant."

"Oh my God, Helly!"

Jane had an odd smile on her face. She proceeded to laugh with greater than usual intensity and threw her full head of disheveled hair back. Helen witnessed a wild combination of disbelief and delight in her sister and understood entirely. She watched as Jane filled her lungs and let the air out slowly through pursed lips and puffed cheeks. Helen considered her sister, Jane, to be one of the most beautiful girls on the planet. Jane got all the pretty genes. She was petite, had straight, silky brown hair and striking gray eyes like their father, whereas Helen was big-boned and overweight, with uncooperatively wavy hair and plain blue eyes. Helen said nothing more as she waited for her lovely sister to finish reacting.

"It can't be. And it can't be my Nadine," Jane said, shaking her head and scrunching her forehead.

"You do have a friend named Nadine, don't you? She's the one with the red hair, right?"

"Nadine Aiuto. But she . . . she's gay. She's a card-carrying lesbian. Everybody knows that."

"You positive?" Helen was privately appalled by the idea.

"I'm pretty sure. She used to have a boyfriend but that ended when she met this girl a few months ago. Some girl from another school. Now she claims she gay. She's real open about it."

"Jane, how many Nadines can there be in this town?"

"Are you kidding me? There must be dozens. Well, at least a few anyway. And Dad's Nadine doesn't have to be from this town, Helly. 'Dad's Nadine.' That sounds sick. What did this Nadine say? I want to know everything."

"Well, she called him . . . Steve." Helen produced her most disgusted look, a look that was strictly reserved for the most repulsive information.

"Steve? Dad? No way."

"Way! Steeeve," she said, over-enunciating for effect.

"Dad? Are you sure? This is like something you'd find on a tabloid: 'Hopeless Geek Sires Child of Teenage Lesbian.' Holy shit, Helly!"

"Also, she made it sound like Dad lied to her. Like he told her he couldn't have kids anymore. I have a hard time believing that."

"Wow." Jane sat there shaking her head in disbelief. "I have a hard time believing the whole thing."

The two of them stared at one another with widening eyes, then burst into hysterical laughter. They laughed so hard tears ran down their pale cheeks. It took them a few seconds to notice that their eavesdropping mother had opened the door and was standing in the doorframe looking terribly pleased with her obviously happy daughters. She must have heard them laughing all the way down the hall. She probably thought they were celebrating something. Mom stood there looking utterly angelic, with her sapphire eyes and ever-grace-filled posture, her naturally loose ash-blonde curls framing a sweet oval face. A soft blue robe was zipped all the way up to her chin. A contented smile completed the serene picture that stood in Jane's now wide-open doorway.

"I love to hear you girls laugh," she said. When they responded with what must have looked like blank nods, she asked, "What's so funny?" Without skipping a beat, Jane answered, "Helen has an amusing imagination."

"That's true," their mother responded with a wispy chuckle that emerged from her lungs like a little feather escaping from a down pillow. She continued, "Remember that time Helen thought she was a professional basketball player? And all she would wear was shorts and a jersey? And she carried a ball with her everywhere she went? Even to bed? Remember? She even slept with the ball! Remember?"

"Yes," Jane replied with a giggle.

"Mom," Helen pleaded, "I was five years old."

Rescuing Helen from their mother's embarrassing babble, Jane interjected, "It's getting late, Mom."

"Go get ready, then. See you downstairs," she said, gliding toward the steps. Their mother's oblivion drove the sisters further into fits of wild laughter to the point at which Jane began to look a bit sick to her stomach.

Helen wanted more time with her sister but Jane suddenly seemed in a great rush, dressing quickly, skipping breakfast, leaving for school early. Helen was surprised that her sister's interest in what had transpired early that morning was so short-lived. Apparently, Jane just wanted to get to school and get on with her life. As if nothing at all had happened. As if the most shocking news of their lives had not just flashed across the screen. The worst part now was that, with Jane gone, there was no one with whom to share the full weight of the secret. Her father had also left early, but there was nothing unusual in that. He was a very hard-working man with an important business to run. Anyway, as much as Helen loved him, this morning it was a relief to have her father out of the house. Helen was sure that, if he got a good look at her eyes, he would see that she knew something. He would recognize her guilt. She was not ready for that.

HELEN SAT AT THE BREAKFAST TABLE with her mother, eating toaster waffles with raspberry syrup. For a relatively quiet woman, Corinne Quintal could softly talk up a storm. Sometimes that drove Helen crazy. This morning, however, she welcomed mindless chatter about her mother's plans for the garden. "Most plants are very resilient given the fickle weather of spring." "Manure works miracles." "Bulbs need room." Corinne had an especially soothing voice. It almost did not matter what she was saying. Form can be as comforting as substance. She had a good voice for mothering and a helpful voice for medicine. Helen's mother, Corinne Quintal, was a pediatric nurse and, most often, the monotonous blather was about her young charges. The children's names changed but their stories were always the same. It was all about disease or mishap or, sometimes, even death. Helen was glad this morning for the emphasis on gardening. Blah, blah, dahlias. Blah, blah, roots. Blah, blah, mulch.

Helen appreciated her mother but had difficulty connecting with her. Sometimes her mother seemed to care more about her patients at the hospital than she did about her own daughters, to know more about the lives of those sick kids than she knew about what was happening in her own home. The refrigerator carried more artwork from the pediatric ward than products of their own family life. Helen's last report card, laden with lovely praise from her English teacher, was up there on the front of the refrigerator but was covered by strange and colorful drawings by young ailing artists from the Grace Memorial Pediatric Unit. Sometimes Helen felt taken for granted by her mother.

Helen looked like her mother and she knew it. That was not all bad. Her mother had a plain-vanilla prettiness that was lasting longer than what she saw of other kids' moms. But her mother was also a little overweight. Helen, at the age of fourteen, had bigger bones than her mother and carried more weight, a problem that developed when she hit puberty, slowed down, and abandoned athletics. Whenever she complained about these facts, her mother tried to reassure her with unsatisfactory adjectives like "statuesque" and "sturdy." Her father was far more truthful. Her father used words like "diet" and "exercise."

Helen noticed a lull in the gentle breakfast prattle and looked up at her mother who had, apparently, asked her a question. "I'm sorry, Mom, what?"

"I was just wondering if you should be on your way to school by now."

Helen looked up at the kitchen clock and snapped out of her disjointed thoughts. When did it get so late? Now, she would probably miss the bus. "Why didn't you say something sooner?" she asked her mother.

"Sorry. I guess I lost track, Helen. My mind is obviously somewhere else this morning. I can give you a lift. Go get your things, Pumpkin."

Helen wanted to say, "So, what else is new? When is your mind not somewhere else, Mom?" But Helen's own mind was not a paragon of clear thinking this morning either. With her mother's help, she arrived at school on time, but forgot to bring in her math assignment, which was, undoubtedly, still sitting squarely atop her desk.

IT WAS DIFFICULT FOR HELEN to concentrate as she moved from one classroom to the next through the well-established pattern of her school day. As if on a sickening ride at an amusement park, her head would not stop spinning and kept coming around to the same view—the speckled blue carpet of the upstairs hallway where she had sat listening to her father talk to a mad woman named Nadine. A woman who declared she was pregnant. Helen was glad not to have any exams with which to contend today and could not wait to get home again. She spent much of the school day wondering what that terrible phone call meant for her family. If this Nadine person were really pregnant, her parents would not get divorced, would they? Her father would not go off with this other woman, would he? It was unthinkable. Helen wanted to feel the floor of her own home beneath her feet again instead of the buffed gray tiles of the middle school. She needed tangible assurance that life at home would remain the same.

At the end of the day, the bus ride seemed endless. Helen's friend, Elaine, kept trying to talk to her about their "dumb" science teacher and his "dumb" atomic models project. Helen gently sucked on her upper lip, massaging it with her tongue and tasting its metallic flavor. She pretended to listen, nodding strategically from time to time, but she did not look at Elaine. Instead, Helen stared out of the dirty bottom pane of the window next to her seat on the bus. She reviewed each store, each house, each familiar site as it passed. The big new bookstore that carried more books than the town library. The brick bank where she kept her savings account and where they kept a large pewter dish filled with wrapped lemon drops on the high countertop. The card shop that also sold fresh fudge. The little jewelry shop where her father had purchased not one but two gold pillow heart necklaces.

Perhaps for the first time in her life, Helen saw how very flat everything was. There were no hills in this town, not one. Everyone lived at about the same level. Most of the dogwoods were the same height. Each suburban house was a bit different in color and detail yet they were more or less the same. Three bedrooms, more or less. Two bathrooms, more or less. Four family members, more or less. She thought she knew this town like the back of her hand. Today, however, on this cloudy spring day that had started so abruptly and abnormally, Helen felt like a tourist, a stranger, someone who was looking from the outside in rather than from the inside out.

She got off the bus but did not immediately go home. Instead, she ran two and a half blocks, not looking back and not stopping until she reached her destination. Fifty-seven Reed Lane. The home of her good friends, Duke and Earl. Duke was a retired taxicab driver who called himself a Buddhist. Helen was not sure about the Buddhist part but she knew that Duke had an uncommon amount of common sense. He was the wisest person she knew. Earl was Duke's beloved dog, a smoky-gray cockapoo, part cocker spaniel, part poodle. He roamed the neighborhood freely and most neighbors did not seem to mind. He was a quiet, friendly dog and Duke had trained him to do his business in his own backyard. Earl loved Helen, often greeting her as if she were the lost sheep he had just found. Every one of Helen's entrances was a celebration to that wonderful dog.

Duke and Earl always seemed to have time for Helen. She did not ever feel out of place or in the way at 57 Reed Lane. A visit with Duke and Earl made her feel special again. Not so plain. Not so plump. Not so callow. She could talk about real things with Duke, about how people should spend more time being good to one another. Duke always had some meaty thought for Helen, such as, "Your worth, Helen, always belongs to you. Nobody else can tell you who you are." A bit of wisdom that was offered regularly was some version of "It's not about yesterday or tomorrow. It's not even about today. It's about this moment. This very moment is what's real."

She needed Duke and Earl right now. She needed some insight and understanding. She needed to be in a place free of judgment. They did not disappoint her. When she knocked on the door, Duke opened it ceremoniously, announcing to his four-legged companion, "Look who's come to visit. It's our princess, home for a rest from her royal obligations." Earl licked her hand. Duke motioned her into the kitchen where he poured her the usual, a tall glass of pink lemonade. "Good for the soul," Duke said. Helen loved how the cold rim of the glass felt against her bottom lip. Duke's kitchen was her sanctuary. The sweet lemonade was sacramental. Duke's house was dark, with narrow, draped windows and heavy Italianate furnishings. It felt mysterious to Helen and yet, she always felt safe there.

Helen told Duke she had a secret. She could not tell him what the secret was, only that it was bad. Really bad. He sat across the kitchen table from her and listened intently. Then he closed his eyes in silence. Duke was big on silence, very often followed by profound advice. Helen wondered what he would say this time. Perhaps something about truth or being honest with yourself. After a pause big enough to pack a hearty lunch in, he looked deeply into Helen's anxious eyes and told her, "Patience is the key." She was not at all sure what he meant. She nodded, however, as if she did. As if she understood the full import of those few powerful words. Right now patience appeared to be far removed from her predicament. Helplessness was more like it. Helplessness laced with guilt. Helen left Duke's appreciative, nevertheless, of his steadfast support and dependable interest in her life.

WHEN SHE WALKED THROUGH THE FRONT DOOR of her own home, Helen was relieved to see that nothing had changed while she was gone. The dark green plush couch in the living room was right where it should be. The paisley wing chairs sat opposite the couch, lending their customary symmetry to the room. The bright brass clock on the polished oak end table read 3:37. The family pictures were all in place. The house seemed oblivious to her secret, blissfully unaffected by it. Perhaps she had misspent her day overreacting to matters she simply did not understand.

She ran upstairs and opened the middle drawer of her desk. A mess of small objects lived in that drawer. Scattered pens and pencils. Scraps of paper. Hair accessories. And in the back right-hand corner, a stash of gummy bears. She opened the crackly cellophane bag and counted out ten. Breathed in their comforting sweet aromas. Put a red one in her mouth. Let it roll around the middle of her mouth. Wondered if, at this very minute, her father might be meeting that woman and telling her to get out of his life. Her father was a smart man. Surely he knew that a young woman like that was not to be trusted. She was like Thomas Hardy's Bathsheba, self-serving and without principles. He must know that. Helen bit down on the middle of the gummy bear, severing it into two sticky pieces and skillfully moving them to either side of her mouth where they continued a slow delicious disintegration.

Music drew Helen to the den, where she found her sister, Jane, on the blue plaid couch. Jane was never home this early. Never. Her sister's eyes were closed. Her face, pale. Her arms, folded over her belly. Like a sleeping maiden waiting to be kissed by a prince. Why was she home? And why was she listening to a crooning lovesick balladeer, saccharine full orchestra in the background? The kind of music they usually made fun of behind their mother's back. Jane, sensing Helen's presence, offered a weak, gravelly, "Hey, Helly." Her eyes remained closed.

"Why are you listening to this crap?" Helen asked with a tone that conveyed her revulsion. No response. "Did you hear me?" She put another pliable gummy bear in her mouth. This time a yellow one.

"Gimme a break. I didn't look before I turned on the CD player. Apparently, Mom was the last one in here." Jane opened one eye. Through it, she hurled an imaginary dagger at her big baby sister.

"Okay. Okay. I'll leave you alone," Helen said, quickly discerning that this was one of those times when sisterly jabbing was, for whatever reason, unwelcome. Greedily, without thinking or checking for color, she stuffed two more gummy bears in her mouth. This meant there were three in there altogether, which affected her speech, giving her a gluttonous lisp. "You look white as a ghost. You sick or something?"

"I think I have a hangover."

"What?" Helen nearly choked on the bears. A hangover. Jane had been drinking. In the middle of the day.

"You heard me, punk."

"Hey! What did I do wrong?" Helen asked in an injured manner.

Jane took a deep breath and apologized, "Nothing. Nothing, Helly. Look, I've just had a really bad day. That's all."

"Gummy bear?" Helen offered, holding out a palm that held a small pile of sticky bears of various colors. She could tell now that the newcomers to her mouth were both, unfortunately, green, her least favorite flavor.

"Please get those away from me, Helly," Jane pleaded with a groan.

"Does this have anything to do with what we talked about this morning?"

"Does this have anything to do with what we talked about this morning," Jane mimicked. She sounded all beat-up inside.

"Don't tell me it's the same Nadine. Did you find out? Is it? Is it your Nadine?" Helen looked into her sister's eyes with a solemnity appropriate to secrets that go to the grave.

"Yes," Jane said, "but you have to swear you won't tell a soul!"

"I swear. Cross my heart and hope to die, stick a needle in my eye," she whispered, drawing a cross on her chest with her right thumb and aiming an imaginary needle at her right eye. Then she fell into the end of the couch where Jane's feet were curled and tried to find a place to put this fresh and terrible information. She filled her mouth with the remaining cluster of sticky sweet bears.

Helen started nodding her head up and down like a bobble-head doll on a dashboard. The sisters sat there in silence, listening to one sentimental tune after another. As much as Helen detested the singer, the soulful tenor seemed to be singing all the right words for this somber moment. "Why have you done this to me," he moaned, "Why, oh, why?" When the CD was finished, Helen just waited. She knew from experience that her sister would, eventually, convey the rest of the story. She had more than enough information for now.

"Can you turn on the TV?" Jane asked.

Helen complied. Talking heads broke the silence like unsuitably raucous voices in a library.

"Too loud. Too loud!" Jane complained.

Helen made the adjustment. An in-your-face talk show was on. Ordinarily, the sisters wallowed in these nearly predictable performances in which frenzied argument was brought right up to the brink of bedlam. The unqualified dumbness of such shows appealed to them. Today, the talk show provided petty noise as a backdrop to a very serious conversation. As strangers squabbled with one another in front of an audience of millions, Helen dared to ask, "What is Nadine going to do? Did she say?"

"She says she's getting rid of the baby as soon as possible."

"Abortion?"

"Yeah."

"But that might be our little sister . . . or brother, for God's sake."

"Well, I don't think Nadine has thought of that, Helly. Jesus, I still can't believe it. Dad and Nadine. This is so wrong. So wrong."

"What are we going to do?"

"We are going to stay out of it, that's what!"

"Yeah, I guess. I guess we don't have much choice."

"She's the one who doesn't have much choice, Helly. Think about it. What would you do? What would you do if you were just finishing high school, just getting ready to start the rest of your life, and you found out you were knocked up?"

"Don't say 'knocked up.' It makes it sound so . . . so violent. And I don't know, Jane. A baby wouldn't be so bad." Helen openly imagined their maybe sibling. What would it look like? A stunning sister with red hair like Nadine's? A little geek who looked just like Dad? Jane told her to stop being ridiculous. It was out of the question. There would be no baby. There would be no sister or brother. It was painfully apparent to Helen that Jane did not wish to talk about the baby. Biting the skin around the nail of her right index finger, Helen leaned toward her sister and asked, "So what's the deal with the lesbian thing? Is she or isn't she?"

"No, she isn't. That was just a cover. She didn't want anybody thinking she was, you know, with a man. A married man."

"That's so stupid." Jane did not react to her comment. Apparently, her sister was now buddy-buddy with Nadine. "How'd you get the hangover?"

Never before having seen her sister in such a sorry state, Helen was curious. She knew Jane had drunk alcohol before. But always at a party. In the evening. When Jane left the house this morning, she seemed not to care very much about the phone call. She gave no indication that she was upset about it in any way. Helen, however, had been entirely wrong about her sister. It was all an act. Jane cared. She cared herself into cutting out of school. She cared herself right over to Nadine's house. And she cared herself into a throbbing hangover. Evidently, Jane was taking the news of their father's affair far more personally than Helen. Jane asked Helen for a glass of ice water, which Helen obediently retrieved. As if it were strong medicine, her sister took tiny sips of the chilled water and recounted the regrettably illuminating reconnaissance mission.

WHEN JANE ARRIVED AT ALQUOT HIGH that morning, she waited near Nadine's locker. "You should see it," Jane said, "It's covered with magnets." Nadine's locker advertised everything from AIDS awareness to monthly chocolate cravings. A large pink triangle commanded the center of the locker door. Only seniors were allowed to decorate their lockers. It was a privilege most seniors relished. Jane had time to memorize Nadine's locker as she watched hundreds of schoolmates come and go to their respective homerooms. Eventually, the halls emptied to the point of conspicuousness. When Nadine did not show up, Jane left the school.

"You just walked out?" Helen asked in astonishment. This was unusually irresponsible for her sister.

"I decided to go find her. I had to know, Helly. She didn't come to school. Why? I had to find out." Jane described how, with great stealth, she walked down one corridor into the next and stepped out the front door without anyone stopping her.

"You went to her house?" Helen asked with wide incredulous eyes. "You've never been there before, have you?" Jane shook her head earnestly. "Were you scared?"

"A little. I mean, what was I going to say to her? That's what I was wondering the whole way over there. I had no idea what to say. You can't just ask somebody if they're having an affair with your father! You can't just slip a 'By the way, are you pregnant?' into a conversation like you're talking about the weather. Sure I was scared. First I was scared she wasn't going to be home at all. Then I was scared she was going to be home but she would be nasty to me or something. And then I was afraid I wouldn't know what to say."

Helen thought her sister was very brave to have left school just like that. She couldn't imagine cutting out of school without permission. The idea of heading over to Nadine's house without knowing what would happen was beyond her. Jane had guts. Helen knew that. Anybody who could get up on stage like Jane did had real guts. But this was different. This required uncommon courage. Helen knew she never could have done it. And she wanted to hear all about it. Every outrageous detail.

Jane explained that she had never been inside Nadine's house before but knew where it was. It was one of the big ones on the water. Helen wanted to know which one and her sister described the house without any trouble. Weathered cedar shakes accented by clean white trim. Budding rosehips lining the slate path to the front door. Helen knew the house. She had ridden her bicycle that way countless times. All the houses down there were beautiful but the older ones, like Nadine's, were unquestionably the loveliest. Her father always said as much.

Jane told Helen that, when she arrived, the house looked empty. Nervously, she knocked on the door but there was no answer. Cautiously, she walked on old moss-couched slates around to the back of the house, then stepped up onto a magnificent deck overlooking the calm waters of the bay. But for the stubborn clouds of the day, the deck was positioned to be sun-drenched. Jealously taking in the salty view, Jane heard a door slide open behind her. She turned around. Nadine walked out onto the deck and peered at the water without acknowledging Jane's unexpected presence. Jane was relieved that it was not Nadine's mother or father who emerged from the house. She would not have known how to explain herself.

Jane watched as Nadine fell back limply into one of four teak deck chairs that formed a semicircle off to one side of the cedar deck. Her normally exquisite face appeared misshapen by distress. Jane knew that Nadine was aware of her presence but was choosing to ignore it. She could feel her face turning red and was glad Nadine was not looking at her. Was Nadine angry? Should she turn around and leave? She did not wish to upset Nadine any more than she appeared to be already. Also, she did not want her suspicions to show. Jane closed her eyes and willed herself to clear the flush from her face, to rid the concern from her eyes, and to expel any residual apprehension from her appearance. She put on her best devil-may-care persona. Tossing her hand toward the bay, she said, "A little cloudy but it's way too nice to be in school today. I needed a break." Without waiting for an invitation, Jane nonchalantly plopped herself down in a deck chair next to Nadine and, with her, stared out at the still ocean water.

They sat there in uncomfortable silence and, at one point, Jane thought that Nadine had, perhaps, fallen asleep. Once again, she considered leaving. Maybe this really was none of her business. But then, in a fragile voice unlike the one Helen had described earlier in the day or the one typically heard in the halls of Alquot High, Nadine asked, "You want a drink or something?" Encouraged by Nadine's muted hospitality, Jane replied that she would, thank you very much. She followed Nadine into the kitchen.

Not only to fill the awkward lull in what was hardly a conversation but also because she was so taken with it, Jane told Helen she did not think she had ever seen such a perfect kitchen. It was strikingly and delicately beautiful. The whole room was painted a soft yellow, the color of the palest of their mother's trumpet daffodils. Small tiles hand-painted with grassy sea-green leaves drew a border around the sink and countertop. Jane felt as if she were standing inside an exquisite Dutch kitchen. Like a modern version of Hans Brinker's cottage kitchen when it was all cleaned up at the end of the book. The sweet smell of lilacs permeated the house, Jane said. Her nose drew her to a tall clear glass vase spilling over with budding tresses of blooms. It sat directly in the middle of a counter extension that was surrounded by oak barstools, each one topped by a round embroidered pillow. The pillows looked as if they had been hand-stitched to match the decorative tiles.

Jane watched as Nadine opened a high oak cabinet. It held an assortment of small appliances from which Nadine selected a blender. Faintly, she asked, "You like margaritas?" and without waiting for a response, she proposed torpidly, "Let's make margaritas—big, icy margaritas." "To drink?" asked Jane, surprised by Nadine's suggestion. She was not certain she had heard her hostess correctly. Nadine stopped and, for the first time, looked directly into the face of her guest. Jane felt stupid. Of course the margaritas were to drink. She did not realize, when Nadine made the offer, that she had meant alcohol. It was still early morning. Just past nine o'clock.

Regaining her composure, Jane said intrepidly, "Why not?" She tried to sound savvier than she was. Actually, she thought a drink might cut the frayed ends from this already ragged day. "Well, alright," Nadine said decisively, with a little more vigor in her voice. As she removed an icy can of drink mix from the freezer and proceeded to dump it into the blender, Nadine seemed to shake loose the sullen posture in which Jane had found her. Adding ice and tequila, Jane observed the surfacing of Nadine's famous smirk, a look Jane had seen many times in school. Nadine asked her to grab a bag of pretzels out of the bread drawer next to the sink.

Nadine created a blender full of the pale green drug. They consumed it as if they had just emerged from a week's journey in a dry desert. It was delicious. Sweet but acidic. Ice cold yet warming. The salty pretzels were a perfect complement. They talked about the weather. How warm it was last week. How little sun was predicted for this week. They spoke about friends they held in common. Lindsay. Maureen. Jack. They reviewed bits and pieces of their senior year of high school, now nearly completed. The homecoming dance. The faculty talent show. The senior video, now, according to reliable sources, in the final stages of production. About an hour into the pleasant but immaterial chitchat, Nadine confessed what Jane already knew. She was six weeks pregnant. She would not say who the father was, only that he was "a toad from hell, a liar, a slimeball, and a creep too." Jane held her tongue, not an easy thing to do with a belly full of high-test tequila.

"What are you going to do?" she asked.

"I guess I have to get rid of it. I don't know what else to do. I can't be pregnant. I can't have a baby. Not now. Not like this. My father would have a heart attack and my mother would kill me. There's a place in Amityville that Cassie Ranger went to last year when she got knocked up."

Jane nodded intently, pretending to know all about Cassie's unfortunate experience.

"You knew about Cassie?" asked an amazed Nadine.

"No," Jane answered, surprising herself with her own honesty.

"Well, there's a lot you don't know," Nadine murmured. Jane thought she saw a wince. Maybe Nadine was wishing she had not spoken those last words. Jane returned a smile for the wince and offered, "I'll go with you if you want."

"You mean to the abortion clinic?" Helen asked. "You wouldn't really go, would you?"

"I FELT SO BAD FOR HER, Helly. I mean, we're finally finishing high school. Everything is out there ahead of us. I can't believe Dad did this to her. She hates him. She really hates him."

"How can she say that? I think this is her fault. How does she even know who the baby's father is? Somebody like Nadine is . . . "

"Is what, Helly, is what?" Jane was clearly angry at the tack she was taking. Helen continued her course of thought anyway.

"Well, she's sort of a slut, isn't she?"

"How can you say that? She's only seventeen, Helly."

"Yeah, but she's not exactly innocent."

"Would you say that if it happened to me?"

"It wouldn't happen to you, Jane. You know that. This isn't Dad's fault. I don't see how she can blame him. And I don't see how you can blame him."

HELEN COULD SO EASILY IMAGINE Nadine luring her father into something he would never otherwise have done. There was no other explanation. It was like putting a kid in a toy store and expecting him not to touch anything. She did not really know Nadine. Had only seen her from a distance. But she knew her type well enough. The kind of girl who wears tight clothing and wiggles around asking for it. She went looking for trouble and her father simply got sucked into it. Nadine must have known what she was doing all along. The only problem was that she had not been careful enough. Helen was outraged that Nadine had been so thoughtless. So reckless. So devastatingly selfish. Clearly, she had not thought about where this might end or who could get hurt. Undoubtedly, Nadine knew her father had a family. How could she have overlooked that unalterable fact? Helen knew her father through and through. He was an honorable man who loved his family. Who loved her. She wished she had not finished the gummy bears so quickly and started to chew the skin around her right-hand middle finger.

"Listen," Jane interrupted her thoughts. "That's your opinion, Helly. I'm not going to try to change your mind. I don't care what you think. That's not true. I do care what you think. But the most important thing right now is this—I promised Nadine I wouldn't tell anyone. You have to swear you won't tell anyone. Nothing we've talked about leaves this house. Swear it, Helen. You won't tell anyone." It felt like Jane was attacking her. Helen could not imagine sharing this awful secret with anyone. How could Jane not know that?

"I swear. It's our secret," Helen replied. She felt hurt by the entire conversation. Helen was not used to disagreeing with Jane. Nor was she accustomed to the painful lack of trust implied in her sister's remarks. Jane was her role model. Confidant. Primary source of both comfort and comic relief. Helen counted on her sister for support, for guidance, for defense. Jane was her stronghold. In one day, this stupid affair with Nadine was threatening the most important relationship in her life.

Shortly after five, their mother stepped through the front door carrying two bags of groceries. "I'm home!" she announced cheerfully. No response. "I have all the pizza fixings!" Silence prevailed. She found the girls sitting in the den watching an early edition of the local news with the sound on the television turned almost all the way down. As if they were trying on the experience of profound hearing loss. "Hi!" she tried again, rapping on the doorframe to gather their attentions. "Oh, hi, Mom," Helen answered dimly. Jane forwarded the necessary lies.

"Mom, I came home from school early with horrible cramps. I just couldn't stay. I didn't even make it to homeroom."

"How are you feeling now, sweetheart?"

"A little better. I'll need a note for tomorrow."

"Next time, call me, C.G. I'll be happy to bring you home. Would you like something for the pain?" It bothered Helen when her mother or father called Jane "C.G.," short for "Clever Girl." They called Helen "Pumpkin." Because, insisted her mother, she was so cute. Like a pumpkin. Helen did not think pumpkins were especially cute. They were big and blobby. Helen refused to call her sister anything but Jane.

"I already took something for the cramps," Jane lied again, pulling a blue throw pillow over her stomach.

"Oh, by the way, Dad called," their mother continued. "He's stuck with a client and won't be home until late."

"I'll bet!" Jane said, under her breath.

"What was that, honey?" asked their mother sweetly.

"Nothing."

Their mother sat down with them on the edge of the couch and earnestly explained to the girls that their father had been working extra hard lately. They all needed to be a little more patient and understanding. Helen remembered Duke's advice, "Patience is the key," and wondered again what that meant. Her mother continued, "Running your own business isn't easy these days. Dad has to attract all his own customers and then he has to keep them. It's a lot of work."

"Okay, Mom," the girls said, nearly in unison. But it was not okay. She was not okay. Their mother sat there explaining the situation to them, asking them to be patient and understanding, but what did she know? Did she have any idea what was really going on in this family? Or how confusing it was? Helen noticed a weird paper shape stuck in the back of her mother's hair. "Mom, what is that thing?" she asked, pointing at the object with a look that defined her disapproval.

"Oh, this. This is a present from a patient." She unfastened a paper bow decorated with a crayon rainbow. She had bobby-pinned it to the back of her head and Helen thought it looked ridiculous. A little patient had, of course, given the peculiar hair accessory to her. Their mother began to prattle about a girl with leukemia. Helen and Jane exchanged furtive glances, as if to say "Here we go again" to one another. At least, thought Helen, Jane and I are on the same page again. Taking the hint, her mother seemed to abandon all thought of her small hospital artist, whoever it was. She asked Helen, "How about you? You have a good day?" Her youngest daughter nodded dismissively, adding a "Fine, Mom."

"Well, you won't believe how beautiful the organic eggplant is. Someday, I'm going to have a big vegetable garden and we can try growing our own eggplant." With that, their mother skipped into the kitchen where they could hear her unloading groceries. Their mother could be so random, Helen thought. So flighty. Like a delicate butterfly flitting from one blossom to the next. One subject to the next. Helen thought her mother was not much like other mothers. Plenty of other mothers worked. That was not it. It was as if her mother were not quite there. She could be in a room and yet not quite be in the room. Like a television with a loose wire. A picture that fades in and out.

Monday was always make-your-own-pizza night. The ingredients changed slightly, depending on the season and what was fresh. Tonight's toppings included red bell pepper, fresh basil, thin slices of prosciutto ham, and, not to anyone's amazement, organic eggplant. The girls usually enjoyed pizza but the situation was more difficult this evening, more complicated. Helen noticed that Jane barely touched her supper. She was still feeling a bit queasy and continued ice water therapy. Helen ate her pizza slowly and meticulously, finishing it down to the last crumb of crust. Then she picked at Jane's generous leftovers. She had to admit, the eggplant was pretty good. Her mother had sliced it thin, breaded it, and sautéed it in olive oil and butter.

After supper, Helen took a turn at stretching out on the couch in the den. She had consumed a hearty supper but now nibbled thick curly corn chips from a bag that her mother handed to her, saying, "Try these." She dipped them in heavy sour cream mixed with salsa and shredded cheddar cheese, a recipe Helen adored. It was nice of her mother to fix this for her on the spur of the moment. Was she being especially kind because she could sense something was going on? Could her mother see how shook up she was? She hoped not. She drank Coke directly from a two-liter bottle, letting the bubbles tickle the insides of her cheeks before swallowing. Then, when her mother was busy in the laundry room, she sneaked into the kitchen and stole an old piece of frozen lemon cake from a plastic container in the back of the freezer. She allowed each bite to melt in her mouth like cold sweet butter in the bottom of a warm pan. It felt wonderful.

Helen returned to the couch and lay there worrying about everybody. Jane. Her father. Her mother. Why was Jane taking Nadine's side? Could she not see what a tramp Nadine was? If she really was pregnant, was her father even responsible? And what would he do now? How could her father get rid of Nadine? What would happen if her mother found out? Her mother would not leave him, would she? No. Where would she go? It was inconceivable. She could not imagine her mother without her father. Her mother was responsible for surface responsibilities, for the dry cleaning and the groceries, but her father provided the solid backbone of the family, their standards and principles. Her mother could not survive without him. She would never leave. Even if she found out. And how would her mother find out? Helen was certainly never going to tell. Anyone.

It suddenly occurred to Helen that, as unlucky as she was to have been the one to answer the phone this morning, it was a good thing her mother had not been the one. And Helen was, for once, pleased about her father's rule that there be no telephones in the bedrooms. Many times had both Helen and Jane wished for phones in their rooms. Most of their friends had them. Many had their own lines. Their own phone numbers. As a way of controlling the amount of time his teenaged daughters spent on the phone, Stephen Quintal had restricted the phones to three: one in the kitchen, one in the den, and one in the upstairs hallway. If the girls wanted privacy, they could shut the louvered doors of the den and call their friends from there. That was the house rule.

Helen was reluctantly compelled to draw another corn chip from the bag, even though she felt as if she might blow up. In fact, she wanted to. She wished she had not eaten so much. What was wrong with her anyway? Why was she always hungry? Helen's mind rattled. She thought she could actually feel her brain jumping in her head. As if she were in the back seat of a bus traveling too quickly down a bumpy dirt road. She had heard of a mind spinning but this was nothing like that at all. It was more like popcorn in a microwave. Small thoughts kept popping open, filling her with head with exploding bits of anguish. Helen had always thought of secrets as being precious pieces of information that functioned as a bond between friends. For the first time, she was experiencing secrets as shackles.

Jane was up in her room, presumably navigating her brain around the remains of the hangover and through fresh waves of calculus homework. Helen wished her sister would blow off the homework just as she had blown off school. She wanted her sister to come back downstairs. To sit with her so that she would not feel so alone with the secret. She fantasized Jane walking back into the den and saying, "I understand why you're sticking up for Dad," or "You might be right about Nadine." Eventually, however, she abandoned the fantasy. Turned on the television again to lessen the sense of isolation.

Helen watched a show about the glittery lives of professional models. They were all so beautiful. So skinny. So nauseatingly sure of themselves. How did they get that way? Were they born so stick-framed? Did they all have plastic surgery, like her friend, Elaine, said? Why did she have to be so big? So chunky? Sometimes Helen felt like a freak. This was one of those times. She could not watch anymore. Her left hand palming the top of her head, as if to keep a lid on it, Helen closed her eyes. Fell asleep. Still listening to the sickeningly confident voices talk of travel. Of boyfriends. Of clothing. The hand was still there when she heard her father come through the front door. And she was still afraid that, when he looked at her, he would see she was carrying the secret.

Helen checked her watch. It was almost ten o'clock. She had been on the couch for much of the evening. Her father would definitely not approve. She jumped up. Turned off the television. Smoothed out the couch cushions. Returned the four blue throw pillows to their proper positions at either end. The bag of chips, greatly diminished, still sat on the floor. She kicked it beneath the couch. The dip dish had been removed, undoubtedly by her mother. She was grateful for that, as she hurriedly attempted to make the den look like she had not been loafing there uselessly all evening. She did not want her father to think anything was out of the ordinary.

Helen heard her father kiss her mother. She heard her mother say how glad she was to have him home. She listened as her mother asked in her own uniquely lyrical tones, "Have you had anything to eat, Stephen? Can I fix you something?" The voices sounded nice. Normal. Like people who care about each other. Like people who would never leave one another. This detestable affair with Nadine was all a big mistake. Her mother need never know. Perhaps Nadine had set out to ruin her father but it was not going to work. It was never going to work. Surely, her father would see to that. Her mother said, "You look a little ragged, Stephen."

"Tough day at the office," he said, "tough day."

Helen opened the computer cabinet and started it up. She could pretend she was working on a school project. That way, when her father came into the den, as he almost certainly would, Helen did not have to look up at him. She could act as if she were knee-deep in a paper. She did, in fact, have a poetry assignment due on Friday, as part of a segment on iambic pentameter. Maybe she could actually get it started before he made his way to the den. Why was it taking so long for the computer to boot? How long did she have? She heard her parents proceed to the kitchen. One room closer. As soon as the computer was ready, she started typing furiously:

> I wish the day could start again for me.
> I wish my ears were not so sharp and quick.
> I wish the morning could be taken back.

Steps came toward the den, as she knew they would. Without looking up, she said, "Hi, Dad."

Hi, sweetheart. You're working late."

"Big project due."

"Oh?" He came up behind her. Put his hands on her shoulders. Leaned in to see what she was writing.

Helen covered the screen with her sizeable hands, saying, "You can't look."

"Can't look at what?"

"Can't look at this. I just started writing a poem and it needs a lot of work. It's just not ready to be seen, Dad, that's all." She could not look up at him.

"Okay, Pumpkin. I won't look then," he replied respectfully. "You have a good day?" Was there any suspicion in his voice? It was impossible to tell.

"Sure, Dad, great. I don't mean to be rude but I need to have a first draft ready to hand in tomorrow morning and it's already ten o'clock."

"Yeah, sorry I'm late. Things are crazy at work right now. I promise I won't look," her father reassured her. "Just be sure to get enough sleep, Helen. I want you in bed with your teeth brushed before eleven."

"Before eleven," she parroted and her father went back the way he came.

She had dodged another potential confrontation but she needed, she thought, to prepare herself for the next one. For now, however, as long as the computer was up and running, she free-associated a few more lines. The way they sometimes did in class. Without worrying about grammar or segues or spelling. It was a way, said her English teacher, to "heat up the creative stew."

> A secret hanging by a little thread.
> It threatens to fall down, to injure me.
> O why, O Why, is this all happening?

Her words poured out sloppily onto the digital page. Nothing rhymed. Nothing flowed. At quarter to eleven, she saved her work. Turned out all the lights. Headed for bed. The house was utterly quiet. Just as it had been right after the phone call and, unquestionably, before it. Suddenly, the world was defined by Nadine's phone call. It was a dividing wall. There was everything before the phone call. And there was everything after it.

HELEN THREW ALL OF HER CLOTHES into the wicker hamper in the bathroom that sat between her room and Jane's. She lifted a baggy pale pink T-shirt from a hook on the bathroom door and pulled it over her head. She took her time brushing her teeth. Then she leaned close to the other bathroom door, the one that lead into Jane's room. A thin strip of light at the base of the door indicated that Jane was still up. She longed to feel close to Jane again. The way she felt before the phone call. Just as she was about to open the door and peek into Jane's room, she heard her father's voice and drew back. Her father barked, "Listen, Jane, just because your senior year is almost over doesn't mean you can start slacking off."

"What are you talking about, Dad?"

"Mom tells me you got a C on your last chemistry exam."

"Dad, this is not a good time to talk about chemistry."

"Jane, you can do better than this. I know you can."

"Dad, listen, it's only a freaking C+."

"Don't get rude with me."

"Dad, I'm serious. This is not a good time."

"Well, when is a good time?"

Helen knew where this was going. Her father could be a pit bull, sinking his teeth into something, then, not knowing how to let go.

"Dad, does it really matter? Does it? It's not like I'm going to Princeton. It's not like I'm going to Juilliard, even though that's what I wanted and you know it. No. Where am I going? Nassau Community. And then if I'm lucky . . ."

Before she could complete the stinging sentence, her father broke in, "You're lucky they took you at Nassau Community with a C in chemistry. It's a good school and it's not so far from home."

"Yeah, I know. You don't have to tell me again, Dad. I have the speech memorized. 'The city is a dangerous place for a young lady on her own. We want you to be closer to home. Nassau's a good place to prove yourself.' I know all your reasons for wanting me to go to Nassau. But they're not my reasons, Dad. They're yours."

"Do you actually think they would have taken you at Juilliard? Think again, C.G. Think again."

"It was a C+, Dad. And that's not my grade in chemistry. That was just a test. A little test. It hardly counts. I'm probably getting a B in chemistry."

"You could be doing a lot better."

"Look, if you want to know when a good time to talk is, then come home on time, Dad. You can't do this to me. You can't walk into my room at eleven o'clock at night and do this to me. I've worked my ass off for you. And for what? That's what I want to know. For what?"

"I just told you. I won't tolerate rude language."

Helen could no longer stand what she was hearing. The assault was on Jane yet she felt each blow intensely herself. She knocked on the door lightly but loudly enough for them to hear. Politely and without opening the door, she asked, "Can you talk about this tomorrow? I'm sorry to interrupt but I really need to get some sleep."

"Sure, Pumpkin," her father replied. "We're not finished with this chemistry issue," he concluded to Jane.

Jane and her father were so much alike and yet, they were as oil and water. They knew how to take one another on, how to push one another's buttons. Helen was relieved that her little rescue effort was successful. Once her father was clearly gone from the vicinity of Jane's room, Helen entered and whispered to her sister, "Are you okay?"

"No, Helen, I'm not okay," Jane whispered back. "I can't take it anymore. I don't deserve this. I have worked so hard to be the kind of daughter he wants me to be. The kind of student he wants me to be. Hell, the kind of person he wants me to be. What does he expect, anyway? I can't be perfect. He's obviously far from perfect. I can't take it anymore. Not from him. Not anymore."

Helen hugged her sister, as if to reclaim her. Neither daughter spoke. Their silence was soon interrupted, however, by more yelling down the hall, this time in their parents' room. Apparently unsatisfied by his row with Jane, their father had moved on to their mother and was now yelling at her. "This is your fault," they heard him say. "She is lazy and vulgar because you let her get away with it."

"She's a teenager," their mother responded.

"She's almost a grown woman," he said, "or at least she's supposed to be."

"You're right, she's a young woman, Stephen, but I don't know how to get through to her," Corinne answered. "Honestly, I don't. You are much better with her than I am. You always have been. Maybe I would have been better with boys. My friend, Marilyn, has three teenage boys and doesn't have a minute of trouble with them. Well, maybe a minute, but not much more. Teenage girls always hate their mothers. The other day I was reading an article that said it's actually good for teenage girls to hate their mothers. It helps them figure out who they are or something like that. Anyway, Stephen, you know she loves you. You're her father."

Her mother humbly stole her father's thunder, effortlessly commandeering the conversation and removing it into her own world, her own field of vision. The focus was no longer Jane. The focus was Corinne Quintal. She was so good at this, thought Helen. Jane could learn a thing or two from their mother about how to deal with their father. "I have to get some sleep, Jane," she said, "I'm wiped out."

"Thanks, Helly," came the sincere reply.

Settling herself into bed again, Helen took the book out from beneath her feather pillow and read hungrily. She knew she should try to sleep but was manifestly wide awake, alert like a goalie when the other team is converging, ready to make a shot. Helen used to play in goal. Back when she played soccer. It could be a very lonely position, especially when the defense broke down. Knowing that her mother could not be a helpful ally, and having witnessed the defection of her sister to an unexpected point of view, Helen felt exceptionally alone. Nadine was only a team of one but, right now, she seemed to have the advantage.

Eager to give her conflicted mind a vacation from her troubles, Helen opened up *The Bell Jar*. If she could lose herself in somebody else's problems, maybe she wouldn't feel so bad about her own. Maybe. Jane had just finished reading Sylvia Plath's most widely read work, and had gone on and on about it. She said it was all about how easy it is for a woman to go crazy in this world and what they used to do in the old days to a woman who went crazy. She told Helen that Plath knew what she was writing about because she had gone crazy herself. As an eighth-grader, Helen was thrilled at the prospect

of reading "senior" material. Esther, the main character, fascinated her.

Helen found the first-person storytelling to be very
appealing, almost as if Esther were right there in her room
talking to her, narrating the dire account of her life. She
understood fully why Esther was so jealous of Doreen and so
captivated by her as well. Helen knew what it felt like to be
eclipsed by beauty. The only people who had ever made Helen
feel beautiful were Duke and her father. The poor girl in this
book did not have a father. Helen did not wish to lose hers.

CHAPTER TWO

Tuesday / *Stephen*

LIKE A PATIENT FACING AN UNCERTAIN procedure the next day, Stephen slept fitfully. He spent his insomnia managing uneasy thoughts and counting long minutes. Until yesterday, he had not seriously considered how content he might be in his own home. In his own bed. With his own wife and his own children. All of that seemed threatened by Nadine. She called dreadfully early yesterday morning. Stephen felt reasonably confident that she would not call him again at home. Yet, as the scarlet numbers on his bedside clock climbed slowly but steadily toward 4:32, he became increasingly anxious. Like a man afraid he is being stalked.

Stephen rolled over and studied his wife. She slept on her side, curled up slightly, facing away from him. In the barest illuminations of first light, she looked painfully familiar. Soft. Plump. Like one of the pleasant round women painters seemed to enjoy so much. But with more tiny spreading lines around the far side of her eyes than such artists ever allowed. Her right arm was exposed, holding the blanket in place along the crescent line of her hip. Just above the elbow, a long white wrinkle sliced through her pale skin. Corinne had aged poorly in the last few years. The force of gravity was beginning to catch up with her, causing everything to droop a little. Tissue was not clinging to bone as well as it once had. The shifting metabolism of middle age had contributed a few inches to her waist and hips. Light brown spots were forming on her hands. But she was pretty. There was no denying that. And she was still his wife, the mother of his daughters. He made a commitment to Corinne almost twenty years ago. He fell in love with her, promised her the rest of his life, and never once considered reneging on that pledge.

When Stephen first became involved with Nadine, it seemed a manageable crime. Like eating an extra piece of chocolate cake. He was able to keep the affair in a separate place in his mind. As if what happened with Nadine happened in another country altogether. On the other side of an ocean. His family had no reason whatsoever to visit that country. Things happened all the time in a man's life that his wife and children need never know. A man might purchase an expensive antique clock, for instance, and, not only because that clock was an office expense but for the very reason that he was the one paying the bills, his family was left out of the decision completely. Men are accustomed, reasoned Stephen, to living in separate realms.

Strictly as a precautionary measure, Stephen slipped out of bed and took a defensive position by the telephone in the kitchen. He did not want his daughter, Helen, answering any more unexpected, far too personal phone calls. She acted a little odd last night when he came in, not even peering up from her homework. He fervently hoped Helen had not overheard anything. That would certainly make matters worse. How could Nadine have called him at home? He had made it perfectly clear to her that she was never to interfere with his life outside of their planned "dates." He felt his pulse race as he searched desperately to find the appropriate file in his mind for this unplanned event. Where could he place that wild and troubled voice that had interrupted his household in such a base and untimely fashion?

Well, if Nadine called again this morning, he would be ready. He would take control of the situation. Actually, he almost wished Nadine would call. They needed to discuss her situation. The sooner, the better. Last evening, he waited for her at The Captain's Folly for more than three hours. It was embarrassing. The waitress kept asking him if he wanted anything else. Stephen sat there through six cups of coffee, three English muffins, and a shift in waitresses. Eventually, he ordered a cheeseburger platter, picked at it, and when, by eight-fifteen, Nadine still had not arrived, he started for home. Angry. How dare she play games with him? How dare she waste his time like that?

Stephen first met Nadine in the bar of The Captain's Folly. He remembered that mild December night as if it were magic, a rousing dream disconnected from the real world. He had gone to the bar for a Bloody Mary, hoping it would smooth the sharp corners of a difficult day. He could have fixed one for himself at home but for the fact that his wife did not tolerate alcohol well. Having grown up with a chronically inebriated father, Corinne did not understand moderation. It was all or nothing with Corinne. Every once in a while, therefore, he went to the Folly where he could enjoy a drink without the burden of her fear or the nuisance of her judgment. That day had been particularly trying. People in general and clients in particular were often stressed out before the holidays. A stressed-out client sometimes justified a drink at the end of the day. Corinne never had to know.

Stephen was very disciplined about these occasional drinks. Seldom did he order more than one. This was not only a way of adapting to his wife's anxiety; it was who he was—an exceptionally controlled person. This particular December evening, however, turned out to be unpredictably different from the others. Just as he was finishing his one end-of-a-bad-day indulgence, a lustrous redhead walked into the bar, looked at his glass, and ordered the same thing. She was the kind of girl who shows up on catwalks. Who knows how to move. How to strut. How to puff out her lips and stick out her chest without even thinking about it. That night, she was wearing a short black skirt and a tight green blouse. Stephen was instantly thrown into a testosterone rush. She was the most attractive thing he had seen up close in a long time. Throwing his trademark caution to the wind, he piped up, "That one's on me, young lady."

"How nice," the girl responded without any apparent hesitation. "Extra horseradish, please," she spoke sweetly to the bartender. And then, just like that, she moved her form-fitting skirt over to the bar stool next to his. "Thanks," she said in a low mesmerizing voice. "Happy Holidays," she added seductively. The young woman sharply clinked her glass against his, almost to the point of shattering. Then she took the leafy celery stalk out of her glass. Twirled it expertly on her tongue. Stephen offered a single rigid chuckle in response to the stranger's blatant invitation to trouble. His next Bloody Mary had plenty of horseradish in it and he found himself wondering how he ever could have ordered it any other way. Three biting Bloody Marys later, Stephen Quintal and Nadine Aiuto were kissing playfully in a corner booth. Stephen ran his left hand over her compact, gravity-unaffected breasts as Nadine gently walked her fingers up his right leg.

"Just a minute," Stephen said, struggling to breathe normally. Awkwardly, he slipped out of the booth, heading for a payphone near the back door of the diner. He could tell she had seen the plain gold wedding band on his finger. She must have guessed, therefore, that he was calling home to say he would be late. She did not seem to care. From the phone across the room, he could see her conspicuously leafing through his leatherbound planner. Under most circumstances, he would never allow a perfect stranger to look through his personal effects but, in that moment, nothing in the planner seemed to matter. He had not been instantly captivated by a woman since he was seventeen. The girl looked up at Stephen and licked her lips as he offered his wife the first deceit. That should have been the most difficult part, the dishonesty. Stephen held little tolerance for lies, yet he found it remarkably easy to justify his mendacious behavior. The truth could only hurt Corinne, reasoned Stephen. He did not wish to hurt his wife.

Stephen sat at the kitchen table remembering exactly how this relationship with Nadine started yet wondering, all the same, how he could possibly be so ensnared in such a predicament. Nadine was beautiful. Thrilling. In the grand scheme of his life, however, how much did she really mean to him? She was a fantasy, albeit a very pleasant and comforting one. She was an exciting afternoon twice a week. She was part of his routine. Two days earlier he could not have imagined thinking of Nadine primarily as "part of his routine." She was, of course, more than that. But she was only nineteen years old, for Christ's sake. He and Corinne had not used any birth control for years and, in all that time, there were no more pregnancies. How could Nadine be pregnant? Did she seriously think their relationship had a future? What was he thinking when he got involved with a girl like that?

For more than four months now, Nadine and Stephen had met on Mondays and Wednesdays at the Drift Catcher, a motel three blocks from The Captain's Folly. For more than four months, Stephen had lied to his family about a hot new client who was reorganizing a bankrupt chain of motels. From the start, Stephen was not especially interested in making sense of this new relationship. From time to time he thought that he should, perhaps, feel guilty. But he did not. He welcomed what had become for him a refreshing release. He knew with flesh and blood certainty that this felt great. It was exhilarating to make love to someone so eager, so responsive. He had all but given up on Corinne several years ago. She was so predictable, so mushy. Nadine was an eager learner and he was a willing teacher. Nadine made him feel energetic, renewed. When he was with her, he could not remember feeling more alive or more creative.

Why had she not shown up last evening? Over the phone, Nadine was insistent about talking to him. Rudely insistent. Almost hysterically insistent. Now she was ignoring him. Stephen could well imagine Nadine off somewhere brooding all by herself. This thought made him angry. He did not have time for her moody behavior. If she were truly pregnant, and he had his doubts, she needed to deal with it. Nadine had to get rid of it. There was no time to waste. There could be no baby. Stephen was not enthusiastic about abortion but in this case, there was no alternative. There could be no living evidence of his indiscretion. In fact, there could be no more indiscretion. He would not jeopardize his family life any longer. As he sat there, the fact that this relationship must come to an end, however abruptly, became more and more clear to him. He felt like he had been slapped hard in the face.

Stephen's immediate problem was that he had no way to contact Nadine. From what little he knew about her, and he had to admit to himself that he knew shockingly little, Nadine still lived at home with her parents. He could not simply show up on her doorstep with the possibility of her parents standing right there beside her. Nadine once told Stephen how upset her father would be, were he to discover she was seeing a man more than twice her age. No. Going to her house, in reality her parents' house, was out of the question. Stephen knew where Nadine worked, however. That was a possibility. Nadine worked right there at the high school. In the library. As a library assistant. Stephen could probably find her there. In such a quiet public space, she would not make a fuss. They could speak reasonably. Sort out a plan. At least find a time when they could meet to sort out a plan.

The thought of having to face Nadine's parents caused Stephen to remember his own father and mother. Michael Quintal was an ambitious man and a hard worker. He owned a little repair shop in New Jersey, specializing in small appliances, and it was his good fortune to be living in the midst of an appliance explosion. His father was a genius at fixing things, a gift Stephen could only wish he had inherited. The repair business was successful enough that both children, Stephen and his sister, Jane, were able to attend a local community college. Michael Quintal's goals were not limited to business and family successes. One of his great ambitions was to eliminate any trace of ethnicity from his personal presentation. He married a woman with Northern European genes, adopted a Jersey accent that was indistinguishable from any other, and legally changed his first name from Miguel to Michael. The only evidences that his father was not descended from the Mayflower were the wonderful Spanish-Mexican dishes his mother learned to prepare and a few family heirlooms of strictly sentimental value. Stephen was grateful for his father's strictness. While he sometimes missed him terribly, he was glad his father knew nothing of the mess he was in now.

Restless with wondering how to proceed and what might happen next, Stephen wandered away from the kitchen into the living room. The phone was not going to ring after all. Nadine had, apparently, learned her lesson. He need not have worried about that. His eyes scanned the walls of the living room. They were filled with framed photographs of the family. Memories of Decembers gone by. All of their family Christmas portraits hung on those walls in strict chronological order. He reviewed them systematically, starting with the most recent and remembering each year in turn. The fact that, in each picture, they appeared progressively younger was inescapable. The photographs filled him with longing for the family they had been, for the father he once was.

When he began to analyze the five-year-old portrait, he noticed a problem. The upper right-hand corner of the frame was beginning to separate. There were, apparently, no fasteners securing the frame. The glue was giving up and, if that was happening in one corner, it would not be long before the other corners weakened. Stephen immediately took down the defective frame and brought it to the basement where he kept a tidy workbench. There, he took the whole frame apart, assuming he could do a more thorough job of fixing the frame this way. But when he found the bottle of wood glue on its appointed shelf, he discovered it was quite dried out. Worthless. Stephen held the frameless picture in his hands and stared at it more closely under the bright fluorescent light suspended above the workbench. The picture made him feel old. Five years ago, he had no gray hair. Five years ago, the skin around his jaw was tight. But what was truly amazing was how young the girls looked. They were still girls then.

Not any more. Helen was enormous, tall and ungainly like Corinne's father, and still growing. Jane was now a beautiful young woman. There was no turning back.

The photograph called to mind the memory of a holiday dinner shared at a fancy restaurant up on the North Shore. Jane ordered a stuffed trout. Stephen remembered being amazed at his daughter's courage in trying something entirely new to her. There was an adventurous spirit in that kid. Helen, on the other hand, was more of a "meat and potatoes" kind of kid. Like her father, he thought. As sadness crept into his heart unaware, his eyes began to sting. He rubbed them with the bony knuckles of his index fingers. Gingerly, he laid out the pieces of the frame on a newspaper and covered the whole project with a clean rag. He would get back to it after he could locate some new glue. It must be getting late anyway.

Back in the kitchen, the clock read 5:51. Not as late as he thought. His head still flooded with tender family memories, Stephen suddenly had the idea that he could make a big family breakfast. Every Sunday morning, they used to share a big breakfast, just the four of them. His teenaged girls were not as interested in this tradition any more. Not Jane anyway. Most days, she was not willing to wake up in time for toast. She was, in every way, becoming more and more frustrating. Helen, at fourteen, could still pack away the pancakes, but she was not far behind Jane in conforming to adolescent behavior. Nevertheless, influenced unavoidably by memories of more cohesive family days, Stephen took out the big cast-iron skillet and started to make French toast. Surely, if only for a few minutes, they could share a meal.

No one appeared more surprised than Corinne by Stephen's sudden domestic impulses. She was the first to come down the steps. "You're inspired this morning," she said. He wondered about that. Was it inspiration? Guilt? Regret? Longing? Did it matter? He wanted to sit down to breakfast with his family. With all of them. What could be wrong with that? He answered her, "Yes, I was. I noticed that one of the picture frames in the living room was starting to fall apart. I guess the picture got me thinking about those amazing breakfasts we used to have on the weekends. Remember those?"

"Yeah. You used to go all out for breakfast. Want help?" Corinne asked.

"I think I have things in hand, Cory. Maybe you can convince the girls to come down and eat this French toast with us."

"I can give it a try. No guarantees."

"Thanks, Cory." When was the last time he had intentionally thanked his wife for anything? Not the automatic thanks that is offered as a matter of course but the thanks that has real thought behind it, genuine gratitude. He could not recall. He needed to be appreciative. Corinne was always there for him. Always. It was essential for him to reciprocate, to make up for his recklessness.

She was not long in asking the girls about breakfast and came back with hesitant findings. "They seem confused," she said with a little lilting laugh. "We haven't had breakfast together as a family in a long time and it is a school day after all. It's hard to get Jane anywhere near the kitchen on a school day. She's preoccupied. You remember what it's like at the end of your senior year. There's a lot going on. She's got the play and she has the prom to think about. I know there's plenty of studying left and it's so hard to concentrate when the weather gets nice. Although it's cloudy today. More cloudy than yesterday. But, hey, I think it's great, you making breakfast and all."

"They'll be down," Stephen said, referring to the girls and cutting Corinne off with his confidence in their daughters. He watched as Corinne poured out four small glasses of orange juice. Set them on the table. Removed a vitamin bottle and a medicine bottle from the cupboard nearest the refrigerator. Popped the round plastic caps from the familiar bottles. Took the two pills, easing each one down her throat with a swallow of juice. Replaced the caps. Returned the bottles. Let out an audible sigh.

"You sure you don't need help?" she offered.

"No, this is coming along nicely." The stack of French toast was growing visibly.

"Do you mind if I check the garden then?"

"Everything's under control in here," he answered, giving her permission not to assist him. "Everything's under control," he murmured again, wishing his words to be true.

A full glass door led from the kitchen out to Corinne's amazing garden. Through this door, Stephen watched his wife pull tiny weeds as his inspired stack of French toast continued to swell. From a distance, Corinne's flabbiness was not as evident. She was still attractive. Matronly but nice-looking. Sadly, she could never be to him what Nadine had been. As he thought about it, Corinne had to hold some blame for the mess he was in. If she had taken better care of herself, perhaps they would be closer. He would not have been so tempted. He caught this ugly thought and jabbed at it with the sharp realization that reclaiming his marriage was not going to be easy. This was not just about Corinne getting more exercise. Somehow, he was going to have to change his own mind-set.

Twenty-one years ago, Stephen met Corinne in the hospital, Grace Memorial, where she still worked full-time. Stephen was there to visit his little nephew, also named Stephen, the son of his deceased sister. Poor little Stephen was in the hospital to have his bothersome tonsils removed. He was four at the time and had lost his mother to cancer two years earlier. Young Stephen was all grown up now and living in Florida, but back then Uncle Stephen felt a special responsibility for his little namesake. He should really give his nephew a call sometime soon, Stephen thought to himself. They had once been so close.

A lovely young nurse, Corinne Turner, treated his recovering tonsil-free nephew like a prince, bringing him charmed

Popsicles and cheerful children's books. She offered both Stephens a fresh supply of enchanted reassurance with each visit. He fell in love with her extraordinary kindness. She was pretty, with a gentle face and lovely eyes. She had an appealing ability to be what others wanted her to be. She became deeply interested in whatever others were talking about. She seemed to agree with everyone. She was like an intelligent piece of clay. With her cooperation, other people created who she was. Corinne formed a perfect shape around his personality.

On their first date, she wore a soft blue blouse that made her eyes shine supernal. He was smitten. She was not the most exciting lover (in this regard, her kindness was not attractive to Stephen), but she tried to please him in her own comfortable and dependable way. They were married within the year. It was a small traditional affair, which took place outdoors on the beautifully manicured lawn of her Aunt Laura's North Shore home on a bright Saturday afternoon in June. Aunt Laura was not a true aunt, but rather a childhood friend of Corinne's mother. She had come to the rescue of Corinne and her mother many times as they battled what Corinne called "the demon," referring to the alcohol. She outdid herself in making Corinne's wedding a lovely event. The only disappointment of the day was Corinne's father who, as Corinne's own mother had predicted, drank too much. Stephen was horrified by the drunken spectacle but Corinne did a marvelous job of ignoring his impolite remarks. She dismissed his behavior with offhanded "He gets like this sometimes" and "Isn't he having a good time today!" comments to the guests.

When Corinne first told Stephen they were expecting a child, he was terribly frightened. Fatherhood was beyond his imaginative capabilities. Marriage suited him. Becoming a parent was another matter altogether. Children were noisy. Children were time-consuming. Children were expensive. Much to his surprise, however, he enjoyed being a family man. And, while he had originally wanted boys, he grew to like having such industrious and beautiful daughters. What had felt like an intrusion into his early marriage had become a source of pride and, he dared to think, happiness. Lately, it was much more of a challenge, but those first ten or twelve years of being a father were, Stephen considered, the happiest years of his life.

Breakfast did not progress as Stephen planned. Jane stayed only long enough to eat one piece of French toast politely. He could tell she was still mad about last night. She excused herself in order, she claimed, to finish preparing for a quiz. Helen ate well but had nothing to say and, but for brief glances accompanied by short answers, generally "Uh-huh" and "Nope," she would not look up at her father. He tried not to read too much into Helen's behavior. Furthermore, he was disappointed by the overall response to his breakfast effort. He blamed Corinne. She could have injected more enthusiasm into the meal. He had witnessed her cheerleading skills on many occasions, but this morning she was disappointing. She could be such a marshmallow. She did not discipline the girls well enough. She did not set sufficiently high expectations from them. She was too understanding. Too absorbed in her work. He probably should have insisted that Corinne stay home after the girls were born. His mother had never worked outside of the home.

There it was again. His rotten attitude toward his wife. Here she was busily cleaning up the kitchen while, in his own mind, he was deriding her. She was not the one who fell for Nadine. She was not the one who got Nadine pregnant. This was not her problem. Well, not directly. And it was not her fault. He went over to Corinne. Kissed her on the cheek. She looked up at him with profound surprise. Stephen thought he might have seen a wave of suspicion wash over her face and disappear again as she responded with a kiss of her own. This one on his lips. He wished he might turn into a prince for her again. He hoped she could not see how awful he felt. How shamefaced he was on the inside.

Everything was such a mess. It was as if he had been sitting blissfully on a warm, sunny beach with a soothing tide licking his toes when, without warning, a rogue wave had blown in to clobber him. Jane was still cross with him. Helen was barely speaking to him. Nadine was clearly enraged. Corinne remained, thankfully and unsurprisingly, in the dark. Somehow he needed to set all of these women aside and get to work. He could not afford to be overwhelmed by the unforeseen surge of their impulsive reactions. The relative peace and order of his work life awaited him.

STEPHEN QUINTAL RAN HIS OWN BUSINESS and was quite good at it, not by his own accounts alone but according to the owners of many businesses he helped to streamline. He had started out in accounting and, after a few years of working for someone else, decided to start his own company. Slowly, the accounting end of things stretched into recommendations for increased efficiency and productivity. Eventually, he expanded the scope of his trade, taking in clients, mostly small businesses, who wanted or needed to improve their bottom lines. Among other strategies that were obvious to him but astonishingly unclear to small businesses, Stephen taught his clients how to consolidate job descriptions, eliminate unnecessary staff, develop programs for staying within acceptable salary limits, cut the fat from corporate expenses, utilize tax-benefiting business practices, and perhaps most importantly, take the long view. Stephen was always telling his clients to "take the long view," advice that was refreshingly opposite what many consultants were dishing out.

His own office was rather small and economical. It was up on the third floor and had one large window that looked out over a busy highway. He leased all of his equipment because he could afford better technology that way and because, in the event of equipment failure, the leasing agent repaired or replaced everything fairly quickly. His office furnishings were sparse but of high quality. He had a gorgeous Bukhara rug in browns and greens, four beautiful silk-upholstered French arm chairs, a glistening maple coffee table without a scratch on it, and, his newest acquisition, an antique Boardman and Wells eight-day clock, with a reverse-painting of Brownsea Castle in Dorsetshire, England. Lumpy chairs and tacky pictures did not attract new clients. Quality invites quality, his father always said. Appearances can be crucially important.

Stephen was a one-man show who enjoyed not having to negotiate decisions with anyone else. He did, however, have one full-time secretary, Florence, who was very good at what she did and was handsomely paid for her loyalty. Effective business practice did not always mean lowering salaries. In the long run, it could be far more expensive to train someone new every few years only because another employer was offering a better compensation package. Florence was a good buy. She was not only efficient and dependable; she brought a certain warmth to the office. Florence had, for instance, taken it upon herself to make the office look a little more comfortable. Friendly. She brought in leafy plants and lace curtains and kept a porcelain dish filled with fancy butter-mints on her desk.

When Stephen walked in on Tuesday morning, Florence was already diligently word processing. She was an older woman, probably mid-sixties, although Stephen would never have dared to ask. In the twelve years she worked for him, Florence had been sick only three times. Never had she been late. But the best thing about Florence was that she never took anything personally. When Stephen was upset and ranted and raved a bit, as sometimes happened, like a boulder sitting in midst of a fast-flowing river, she simply channeled his temper to either side. She was able to brush off words that would, instantly, have brought tears to Corinne's sensitive eyes. On top of all that, Florence made great coffee.

As usual, she greeted him with a very professional, "Good morning, Mr. Quintal." Carefully budgeting her words, Florence brought him up to speed with regard to correspondence and calendar. She told him that, as requested, she had rescheduled the "Cosmetic" meeting he missed yesterday afternoon for early next week. A small Long Island manufacturer of skin creams was attempting to upgrade their facility and had hired Stephen to assess their growth potential. Stephen told her he would, unfortunately, have to leave early again today. Since Nadine did not show up as planned, he had missed yesterday's meeting for nothing. Of course, Florence was completely unaware of these matters. He asked Florence for the "Airline" file.

Last week he had won a new account with a small airline based in New Jersey that was near bankruptcy. Stephen was certain he could streamline their organizational structure significantly but he had to be honest with them. He was not sure restructuring alone could pull them out of their financial woes. The troubles they faced were industry-wide. He took the file to his end of the small office, an area that was partitioned to conceal his large gray desk. There within the consolations of his self-made world, he pored over pages and pages of information that had been faxed to him by the debt-besieged airline. Very quickly, it became clear to Stephen that, like so many businesses, they were top-heavy. They had too much higher-paid management. When they did pare down their work force, remaining employees would need flexibility training, in order to cover all jobs previously divided among a larger workforce. He spent the morning drafting an organizational plan to take with him on a site visit next week.

Try as he did to banish his personal plight from the haven of his office, two overlapping clouds shadowed his thoughts: a deepening worry about his family and the persistent and consuming irritation he held toward Nadine. His failed attempt to bring his family together at breakfast made him feel as if he had already lost his girls. Then there was Nadine. He never intended to hurt her but it would have to happen. He would have to dump her. He would do what he could to help her. But she had to go. It had to end before anyone found out. Before any real damage could be done. Stephen stared out of the window, not looking down on the traffic or the commerce but looking up into a graying sky. It seemed to him a warning sign. He made a few phone calls. Found a doctor who could take care of Nadine before the end of the week.

By mid-morning, unable to give reasonable attention to his work, Stephen made the decision to attempt contact with Nadine at her place of work. He skipped lunch, addressed the most pressing tasks, then left Florence with a fresh pile of phone calls to make and letters to write. He was not sure of Nadine's hours but he knew the school day ended at around three o'clock. Beyond that, how long the high school library remained open was an unknown. He thought, therefore, that he should get there before the end of the school day. Stopping briefly at the bank to withdraw enough cash to cover Nadine's procedure, he did, in fact, arrive, a full hour before the last bell rang.

STEPHEN HAD VISITED ALQUOT HIGH SCHOOL many times in the four years Jane was a student there. It was hard to believe she would really graduate in a month's time. As he walked through the main entrance of the school, students were herding themselves through cement hallways covered with high-gloss paint. Prominently displayed around the administrative offices were poster-sized pictures of students running across the soccer field, students playing their band instruments, students creating clay sculptures, students on stage in costume. Curiously, Jane was not among them. Stephen had hoped the halls would be clear. He imagined slipping into the school quietly, going straight to the library, and finding Nadine there.

Perhaps they would find a corner of the library where they could talk calmly, reasonably. It was not ideal but how else was he supposed to connect with her? How else was he supposed to help her? When he arrived, however, the halls were not clear at all and, as he bravely entered a stream of students who were aimed, roughly, in the direction of the library, he was stopped by a hard tap to his right shoulder.

"Good afternoon, Mr. Quintal," the vice-principal welcomed him brightly. "How can I help you?"

This interruption was not part of Stephen's intended scenario. He clutched the money envelope more closely and replied, "Oh, hello, Mrs. Stewart." He was flustered. At least he recognized her. Clearly, she knew who he was. What should he say? How could he excuse his way into the library? Before he could come up with an idea, Mrs. Stewart asked, "Do you need to see Jane? I can get her for you."

Stephen looked down at his shoes, searching for a way out of this embarrassing quandary. The eager vice-principal mistook his gesture for a nod. Without waiting for confirmation, she replied, "Come on in. You can wait in my office." He did not know what to do. He had been caught in an unexpected undertow and was being dragged into Mrs. Stewart's hole of an office. "Have a seat," she said and before he could resist in any way, he was sitting in a small stainless-steel office chair fitted with scratchy fire-red upholstery. "I'll be right back," she said. Stephen did not know how to respond. What should he do? Should he simply leave? Should he now pretend, as Mrs. Stewart herself suggested, that he needed to see Jane? What would be the purpose of their meeting? He was not thinking quickly enough. Clearly enough. He felt trapped. Stuck in that little room like a criminal on the hot seat waiting to be interrogated. He had to get out of there.

The vice-principal's desk was a mess. Papers were strewn everywhere. This made his situation seem all the more chaotic. He put the envelope for Nadine down on the floor by his feet and frantically searched the desk for paper and pen. All he needed was a blank piece of paper but he could not find a single scrap. He was shamefully aware that, if Mrs. Stewart returned, she might think he was rifling through her things. He gave up on the cluttered desk, removed a discarded flyer from a small, cracked plastic trash basket, turned it to the blank side and, with a fat red marker that stood like a beacon above the disorder on the desk, Stephen began to write a note to his daughter.

> Dear C.G.,
> I was in the neighborhood and came by to find out
> how things are going.
> See you later. Love . . .

Before he could print the D in Dad, Mrs. Stewart was back and, right behind her, a very red-faced Jane. Quickly, he grabbed the money envelope from the floor in front of him.

Jane looked him right in the eyes and shook her head surreptitiously. She was visibly embarrassed that her father was intruding. Stephen could tell Jane was still very upset. The tension between them obvious as a black eye, Mrs. Stewart said, "You can talk in here," and without further inquiry, she left her own office, closing the door behind her.

"What do you want?" Jane asked, standing over him while he remained planted in the uncomfortable seat.

"Well, you were so angry last night," he replied, "and you left in such a hurry this morning." Perhaps he could pretend this was all about her, that he was there only because he cared so much about her. That would not be difficult to pretend. He did, indeed, care about his daughter. Deeply. More than he could express. More than she could know. He continued, "C.G., I know I was a little hard on you last night. I came to apologize."

"Dad, you're not here to apologize. I've never heard you apologize for anything." Jane had never spoken to him like this before. He was shocked. Where was his sweet, approachable little girl? Who was this strident young woman standing above him, confronting him?

"Jane," he spoke her name, and was about to suggest that this was neither the time nor the place for a heated conversation, when his daughter took another tack altogether.

"I know about Nadine, Dad. I know what you've done. I went to her house yesterday. I had lunch with her today. How could you do this? She's my age, for God's sake."

"Well, not quite," her father answered, offering what he knew to be a pathetically puny defense.

"So she's what, four or five months older? Big deal, Dad. She's a high school student. Now she's a pregnant high school student. How could you? How could you do this to her?"

Stephen was stunned. Nadine was not a high school student. What was his fuming daughter suggesting? "She is not a student, C.G. She works here in the library."

"No she doesn't. Where did you get that ridiculous idea? She's a student. She's in my chemistry class, Dad. The one you think I'm failing. Nadine graduates in four weeks just like the rest of us."

Stephen closed his eyes. It was his turn to shake his head in disbelief. He had been duped. Was Nadine even "legal" when the affair started? A student. He was having an affair with a high school student. He was genuinely shocked by this revelation. Nadine lied to him. This infuriated Stephen. As far as he was concerned, lying was the worst thing one person could do to another.

"She told me . . ."

"I don't care what she told you. And what does it matter anyway? Does it really make a difference if she's eighteen instead of nineteen or twenty or even twenty-one, Dad?"

"To me it does," he answered.

Jane shook her head slowly, her revulsion glaringly evident. "Dad, I have to go. I have a class."

Jane's judgment poured over him like hot tar, painfully searing the surface of his conscience. He had come to the school hoping to clear up some of the mess. Instead, it was worse than ever. Messier than ever. Jane knew about his affair. Nadine had entirely misrepresented herself. What was he supposed to do now? As his daughter reached for the brass door handle, Stephen lightly grabbed her wrist. "Can you do me a favor, C.G.?"

"What did you ask?"

"Can you do me a favor?"

"What now, Dad?"

He held out the envelope, wrinkled and damp from clutching it in his left fist. "Will you give this to Nadine and ask her to meet me this evening? Just to talk. She'll know where."

"You mean the diner? You think I don't know about the diner? She doesn't want to see you. Don't you realize what you've done? You've ruined her life. She hates you."

"Just give her this and tell her, will you?"

"What is this, a payoff? Give it to her yourself."

"She won't see me. You said that yourself. This is to help with . . ." he cleared his throat, "to help with expenses."

"You mean the abortion? To help with the abortion, Dad? I thought you didn't believe in abortion. You have no idea what you've done, do you?"

"C.G., please."

"I guess it's the least you can do." Jane shook free her wrist and snatched the envelope away from him. She opened the door and slammed it behind her, leaving her father in more complete shock and turmoil.

The next voice Stephen heard was that of Mrs. Stewart. Frizzy-haired, pock-faced Mrs. Stewart. She wanted to know if she could help. She assured him that, by the end of the senior year, all students were stressed-out like Jane. She would get over it. They would get through it together. What an ugly idiot, Stephen decided, looking up into her clueless face. What a slob, he concluded, scanning his confused surroundings before storming out. He practically ran out to his car where he sat leaning over the leather steering wheel, his forehead cupped by his sweaty palms. A high school student. She is a high school student. The same age as my daughter. Stephen could not get over the fact that Nadine had lied to him. Duped him.

This was not entirely his fault. She was a little fibber. He was probably not the first to fall for it. A petulant young lady like that should be on the pill. Jane had asked him what the difference was, but to Stephen there was an enormous differ-ence between an almost twenty-year-old library assistant and an eighteen-year-old high school student. Had he known she was only a high school student, he would never have been tempted to involve himself. She must have known that. Well, he had done his part. There were ten one-hundred-dollar bills in that envelope. Surely that would cover most of the cost of an abortion. If she needed one. She may well have been lying about that too. Either way, the money was hers.

His straightforward mission to find Nadine convoluted into a tight angry knot of sickening revelations, Stephen needed desperately to find some way of redeeming the afternoon. All he could think to do was to buy some fresh glue for the broken frame. Stopping at the hardware store, he bought the most expensive wood glue they had. A store associate recommended wide staples to secure the corners once they were glued. And, of course, he would need a special staple gun. Stephen left with an impressive bag of equipment with which to repair the frame. If he could just put that damned frame back together, he would have accomplished something. Fixed something.

UNDER THE BRIGHT FLUORESCENCE of his workbench, a form of light that reminded him too much of Mrs. Stewart's horrible office, Stephen uncovered the waiting lengths of wooden framing. Carefully, with a small flat brush, he painted a thin coat of the fresh expensive glue on the inside angled corners of each piece. The glue smelled slightly musty and sweet. Like cheap perfume. Using the breadth of both hands from his thumbs to his pinkies, he attempted to hold the pieces together so that the glue could set a tight seal in each corner. This did not work, however, because one corner or another kept popping out of alignment. Over and over again, he tried to hold the pieces together. Over and over again, when he applied even the smallest amount of pressure, the unruly corners disengaged. He tried stapling the frame together first with his pricey new staple gun but this unsatisfactory approach left too much space between the pieces. Frantically, he worked at the frame for nearly an hour until four-thirty when, frustrated by failure, he gave up and threw the rag over the whole project once more.

While Stephen was already beginning to realize some closure with Nadine, he felt obliged to go back to the diner and wait for her again. He owed her that much. Assuming Jane had relayed his message, Nadine might be ready to meet with him. She might well show up. She could be ready to talk. In addition to establishing an unambiguous end to the relationship, Stephen was looking for some assurance from Nadine that she would terminate the pregnancy without delay. This would not be easy. Nadine was behaving as if she were obsessed with him. Why else would she have called him at home and taken the risk of speaking to one of his family members? Why else would she suddenly have lunch with Jane? Nadine might have told Jane that she hated him, but she was acting in a way that suggested preoccupation. Possibly, the baby was part of the fixation. He knew she would not take the breakup well. But it had to be done. He had just enough time to clean himself up and get over to the diner before five.

STEPHEN WAS NOT PLEASED THAT ONE of the same waitresses to serve him last night was right there at the double glass door to greet him this evening. "Back so soon?" she asked, "Haven't had enough of our good java, huh?" She winked in a way that made him feel slightly exposed. He could smell meat cooking. There appeared to be many more customers this evening than were there last. Stephen asked to be seated in a different section tonight. All the way in the back right-hand corner. Last night, as he sat close to the cash register, it occurred to him that, if he and Nadine got into a heated argument, nearly everyone in the diner would be able to see and hear them. Back in the corner, there was a little less visibility. He settled into the more private booth. Ordered a cup of coffee and a corn muffin. Prepared himself for another potentially worthless wait. But hoped Nadine would show. As thorny as this might be, it was important to settle the matter.

Stephen was somewhat surprised when, at exactly five o'clock, Nadine came gliding into the diner with the confidence and poise of royalty. She looked gorgeous in a pure-white sleeveless cotton shift that set off her darkening tan. Something was different. She looked more exquisite than ever. What was it? Stephen watched as Nadine looked around the diner for him, finally training her striking gaze on the corner booth where he would end their relationship forever. No makeup. As she approached the booth, he could see that Nadine was not wearing any makeup. That was the difference. Oddly enough, she looked even more dazzling without it.

They had not seen one another since last Wednesday and, Stephen had to admit to himself, he missed her. As displeased as he was with her behavior, he missed those incredible eyes. He missed those long slim legs. They had not spoken since Monday morning. Yesterday morning. Was that just yesterday? For all that had transpired since yesterday morning, it felt to Stephen as if that explosive phone call had taken place a week ago. He was relieved that she did not appear to be angry now. Tired, especially around those remarkable green eyes, but not angry. Nadine's rage would have made this difficult task even more challenging.

Stephen invited her to take a seat across from him and told her right away that he had contacted a doctor who could take care of the problem. But she did not sit down and did not seem to be listening. She opened a small fringed purse, removed the envelope Jane had clearly passed on to her, took out the money, and placed the imposing pile of bills, green side up, in the middle of the white scallop-edged paper place-mat in front of him. She spoke calmly. "Steve, it's all here. Thanks, but I don't need it. I guess it was just a scare." She took a deep breath and continued, "Steve, it's over. Please don't try to contact me again. I leave you alone; you leave me alone. Deal?" He was stunned. He felt his brow furrow. He heard himself clear his throat and reply in a whisper of a voice,

"Deal." He watched her elegant form march out of his life. The waitress delivered his muffin and coffee.

Nadine walked out on *him*. She dumped him. He was astonished. He gripped the hot mug of coffee tightly with both hands and began to heat up inside. He should be pleased. He knew that. She had made it easy for him. There was no demonstrative yelling. There were no embarrassing tears. It happened quickly and calmly and, for Nadine, it appeared to take place painlessly. This was not at all what he expected. Furthermore, she was not pregnant. He should feel enormously relieved and personally liberated. But he was not. He was angry again. He began to think about how ungrateful Nadine was. He had taught her how to make love. He had made her ache. He had taken her places most women would love to have ventured. He had spent a lot of money on her. She ought to be thanking him, not dumping him. What nerve. If he had known when they first met, right here in the bar of this very diner, what a crazy kid she was, never would he have allowed himself to get sucked in. "My God!" he said out loud.

"Did you say more coffee?" the waitress asked from across the room.

Stephen put down the unsipped coffee, loaded his wallet with the stack of hundred-dollar bills, tucked a five-dollar bill beneath the untouched muffin plate, and removed himself from the booth. He walked past the waitress, beyond the cash register, all the way to the back of the other side of the diner, to the bar. He ordered a Bloody Mary. Without horseradish. Breaking his customary "one drink" rule, a rule he had not abandoned since their fateful first meeting, he ordered another. Halfway into the third drink, his anger toward Nadine abated and he began to feel profoundly homesick. At this point in the evening, at this point in his life, he wanted nothing more than to be in his own home with his own family. The party was over. It was time for a return to normal.

As STEPHEN DROVE THE SHORT DISTANCE between the diner and his house, he felt thoroughly drained. His mind now fully on his family, he thought about his baby girl, hoping again that she had not heard anything over the phone early yesterday morning. He assumed Nadine had been the one to tell Jane. He never imagined Helen was the source. He rubbed his dry groggy eyes just for a moment. And in that instant, in that moment which could never be erased or altered once it passed, he drove right through a stop sign near the deli. He had paused at this corner at least twice a day, every day, for nineteen years. Ever since he first moved into the neighborhood. But today, in his emotionally exhausted, vodka-dimmed state, he simply did not notice it. Nor did he see the little blue car coming, the car that crumpled as freely as an aluminum can when he hit it broadside.

The noise of crunching metal and shattering glass was inconceivably loud. The air bag was suddenly everywhere around him, making it impossible to see and difficult to breathe. His glasses were forced up onto his forehead. The space between his eyes stung as if hit full force with the flat side of a brick. His chest felt like a punching bag had been launched into it. His ears were ringing. After the first few seconds of shock wore off, he was eager to get out of the car, to escape the yards of engorged plastic. He checked himself, his chest, his arms, his legs. Everything seemed to be intact. He was, thank God, still in one piece.

Looking toward the crushed blue car, he noticed an older man slumped over. Blood was dripping from his forehead as it rested motionless on the steering wheel. Stephen was appalled. He shouted desperately to a young boy on the street, "Call an ambulance! Call an ambulance!" The frightened child, who witnessed the whole awful scene, ran into the deli, presumably to use the phone. Stephen just stood there. He knew he should be doing something. He should try to talk to this poor fellow. He could not, however, stand the thought of getting so close to the man's injured head. Blood bothered Stephen. It made him feel queasy. He could not bear to look, nor could he erase the grisly image from his mind's eye. He returned to his own relatively unscathed car and sat sideways in the back seat.

The first few minutes after the crash seemed an eternity. He left the car door wide open even though people had gathered and were ogling. He did not look up. Instead, he stared down at his feet, feet that now seemed stuck to the pavement. Just to the left of his shoes, he noticed a mound of ants nesting in a crack in the asphalt. They were so orderly, these creatures, so task-oriented, a quality he admired. Impulsively, he stepped on one of the ants, squashing it to death. Why did he do this? What had the ant done other than witness his disgrace? Although he knew it was probably part of the shock that follows an accident like this, he felt a sudden imposing empathy for these tiny comrades and was very sorry about the one he had just crushed. Then, as he sat there, something happened to Stephen Quintal that had not happened since he was eight or nine years old. Something that had not happened when his sister succumbed to cancer or even when his own parents died. Stephen James Quintal wept. A torrential downpour of tears soaked his face, dripping onto his tailored shirt. These were not cleansing tears. They were tears that shook and melted some interior part of himself. He felt he was dissolving.

The police arrived first, followed closely by a screaming ambulance. Lights were flashing all around him. He could smell escaped antifreeze baking on the exhaust manifold. An emergency medical technician raced over to Stephen. Quickly checked for injuries. Handed him a cold pack to hold on his bruising face. Asked a few questions about his condition. She was not with him for more than twenty seconds. Not wanting her to stare at his tear-streaked face, he hid behind the cool white plastic of the cold pack. She instructed him to remain perfectly still and left him to help Alexander Dolby, the man in the battered car who had regained consciousness and was clearly very much alive.

The police officer on the scene asked to see Stephen's license and registration and began taking notes. In a very businesslike tone of voice, he asked Stephen if he had been drinking. Stephen aimed a temperate "of course not" at the officer. This declaration was, apparently, unconvincing to the eager young officer who asked Stephen to please touch his finger to his nose.

"You're kidding," Stephen complained mildly. "Can't you see how upset I am? My nose is probably broken."

The officer looked at his driver's license and repeated his request. "Mr. Quintal, can you touch your finger to your nose?"

Stephen complied. He was startled to feel his index finger hit the side of his nose instead of the very tip. It was still his nose, however. He passed the test.

"Will you please get out of the car, walk straight over to the streetlamp, turn around, and come back?"

"Is this really necessary, officer?" Stephen asked as respectfully as he could, given the awful circumstances.

"Yes, sir."

"I'm feeling a little shaky from the accident," Stephen pleaded honestly.

"Okay, sir. Just stay where you are. I'll be right back."

Stephen assumed the police officer was leaving to get help for him. The young man returned, however, with a high-tech contraption and asked him to blow into an intimidating tube that was affixed to one side of it.

"What is that thing?" Stephen asked, although he knew full well what it was.

"This is a breath analysis tool, sir."

"Do you actually think I'm drunk, officer?"

"Please blow into the tube, sir."

"What happens if I refuse?"

"You do not have to take this breath test, sir, but I have to warn you that, if you refuse the test, your license to drive will be revoked for a period of six months."

Stephen grudgingly blew into the plastic tube. He queried, "Am I allowed to know the result?"

".13, sir."

"What does that mean?"

"That will be up to the judge, sir. Could be better. Could be worse."

Stephen was never so disturbed by being addressed as a "Sir." The word was a joke. A condescension in the guise of civility. He could tell people on the street were listening to every word, every question, every answer. Undoubtedly, some of them knew him. They were neighbors. The only one he recognized with certainty, out of the corner of his eye, was the bosomy hairdresser who, everyone suspected, offered more than simple hairdressing. He felt nauseous and anxious but his distress was quickly adding layers of provocation to the base of anger that had been building since yesterday morning.

As if to save him from the embarrassing attentions of the Nassau County police force and the humiliation of being treated like a criminal in front of the whole neighborhood, a second howling ambulance appeared. Stephen removed a few things from the car: his keys, his wallet, and his indispensable business planner. He was rushed to the emergency room at Grace Memorial where one of the physicians soon declared him to be "a very lucky man" and nonchalantly took a blood sample. Stephen asked a nurse if the other guy was going to be all right. She told him she was not at liberty to discuss any of the other patients.

After what seemed to Stephen to be a ridiculously long wait, he was told that his blood alcohol level was .08. That seemed better than what the breath test indicated. But what did it mean? Were there two different scales, one for breath and one for blood? Or was it lower in the hospital because more time had elapsed? It was so confusing. He was quietly read his rights, arrested for driving while impaired, led off to a waiting police cruiser, and placed in the bulletproof back seat where there were no door handles. He could not believe what was happening to him. Two drinks. That was all, really. He had hardly touched that third one.

FROM THE HOSPITAL, STEPHEN WAS TAKEN to the Seventh Precinct Station, a plain brick municipal building that housed a small jail. Fluorescent lights swept over his gray eyes for the fourth time in this long dreadful day. A different police officer, an older man this time, explained to him that, by law, he would have to spend the night in jail. In the morning, he would be transferred to the First District Court. What happened after that was up to the judge. He was offered a phone call. With an open business planner, which they allowed him to keep, in his lap Stephen called home. Helen answered.

"It's Dad. Can you get your mother for me?"

He could tell Helen sensed a problem when she asked thoughtfully, "Dad, are you okay?"

"Fine. I'm fine. Get your mother please, would you?"

"She's right here, Dad."

Stephen looked at his watch. It was nearly nine o'clock. Where had the time gone? Where had the day gone? One minute he was sitting in the safety of his office and the next minute he was sitting in the confusion of the Seventh Precinct. Corinne got on the line.

"Stephen, is that you?"

"Yes. Listen, Cory, there's been a little accident."

"What? Are you okay? Stephen, what's happened?" He could hear the shock in her voice.

"Cory, let's not upset the girls. Everything's going to be fine." He certainly hoped everything was going to be fine. He stared up at the watchful police officer and said, "I'm at the police station, but it's all a mistake. By tomorrow morning, it will all be straightened out. The important thing is that I'm fine. I have to stay overnight. I can't give you all the details now but I had a couple of drinks with a business associate on the way home and ran into another car. I failed the goddamned alcohol test so I have to spend the night in jail." In what Stephen often referred to as "the good old days," he would have been released on his own recognizance but in this "time of excesses," a phrase he often used with his clients, the law demanded at least one night in jail. It was absurd.

"You what?" asked Corinne in whispered astonishment, struggling to balance her distress, he guessed, with a desire not to alarm the girls.

He did not respond to her frightened and demanding question. Looking at the list he created on the trip from the hospital to the station, he said in a very cut-and-dried manner, "Call Frank Pagrini and see what he can do to rectify this situation. And give Florence a call. Tell her I'm sick with the flu. Tell her to reschedule my appointments tomorrow. And see if Al's Body Shop is still open. Tell him the car is going to need some front-end work."

"It's nine o'clock, Stephen. What are you saying?" Corinne asked in disbelief. He could tell she was not hauling his state of affairs on board. Well, it was pretty unbelievable. Stephen could easily imagine his wife popping another Xanax following what must be a mind-boggling telephone call to her. He backed off on his requests. He could make those calls in the morning.

"Cory, I have to stay here overnight. Look, I'm sorry about this. Don't worry about me. Don't worry about anything, Cory. I'll call you in the morning."

"What?"

"Cory, don't frighten the girls. Tell them everything's okay. I'll talk to you tomorrow."

"Stephen?"

"Yes, Cory?"

"Did you get hurt? Was anyone hurt?"

Stephen could hear Helen's anxious voice in the background asking, "Where's Dad? Is he all right?"

"I'm fine. Tell Helen I'm fine. Not a scratch on me. I've had a bad day, that's all. Listen, Cory, I've got to go now. I'll call you first thing in the morning. And, Cory . . . "

"Yes, Stephen."

"I love you."

"I love you, too." He was not simply throwing her an emotional bone. In that moment, he meant it absolutely. Over the course of nearly twenty years, they had grown to count on one another. Stephen knew he could count on Corinne now.

CHAPTER THREE
Wednesday / *Jane*

———

BOMBARDED ON EVERY SIDE, as if everything dear to her had become a weapon and was now being turned against her by forces beyond her control, Jane felt completely over-whelmed. The strain of the last few days was nearly unbear-able. Without all that had transpired in the last forty-eight hours, there would have been enough stress in simply readying herself to graduate from high school. Without her father's unforgivable behavior, there would have been enough dis-appointment to last a lifetime in the fact that she would be attending the community college in the fall. Not Juilliard as she had dreamed. Not even one of the good state colleges. She would be attending a community college. It was not a bad school. In fact, it had a pretty good reputation. But it was about as far from her aspirations as a pennywhistle from a flute. It was not any of the places her teachers had encouraged her to consider. Vassar. Wesleyan. Skidmore. It was not any of the places where her friends would soon matriculate. Penn. Carleton. Colby. "You can get a great start closer to home for a much smaller price tag," her father said. At this point, Jane asked herself, what does it matter if I get a B or a C in chemistry?

Two days ago, the school musical was the center of her life. She had secured the lead female role in *The Wizard of Oz*. The sets were coming along beautifully. The director had custom-ordered a pair of glittering silver shoes that were now sitting in her closet. This should be one of the most thrilling times of her life. The Dorothy script ought to be a primary focus of her attention. She was now wishing, however, that she had never tried out. She no longer had the energy for a big production. She did not want to have to explain her sudden exhaustion to anyone. Or her sketchy attitude. She skipped last night's rehearsal, offering the director a "stomach ache." She wanted out. Out of Oz. Out of this crazy house. Out of the horrendous tension that was eating her alive.

Jane opened her private journal. In the tenth grade, she started keeping a daily journal as part of an English project. She discovered that putting her thoughts on paper helped her to think more clearly, to process what was happening within her and around her more effectively. Life seemed a little more grounded when significant pieces of it were suspended in prose. Like flowers trapped in amber. She wrote a simple question: What should I do? She wrote it three more times, underlining different words for emphasis: *What* should I do? What *should* I do? What should *I* do? And then, responding to her own question, she wrote in capital letters a word that filled her troubled heart, almost as if some outside force were speaking this word to her: Go.

Go. It was a commanding little word. She thought about it all night. She could simply leave. Get on a bus. Get on a train. Leave all the troubles to simmer here without her for a few days. Running away would probably make her mother sick. Her mother would not understand. It would break her father's heart but he would at least know why she had left, even if he never admitted it to anyone else. Running away would make a statement to him. While Jane was worried about her father, she was also angry and baffled. Intuitively, she knew not only that there was more to the jail situation than her mother was telling, but that there was more to the story than her mother would ever know. It was all too much. Jane knew she had to get out of the house, to remove herself physically from the unpacked madness there. The hard part was leaving Helen. Helen would fret continuously until she returned. Nevertheless, Jane felt she had to go.

She took a large backpack from her closet and threw a few things into it. A toothbrush. A stuffed kitten named Trigger that her father gave her when she was four or five years old. A little makeup. Her hair dryer. A brush. Her journal. The good Cross pen she won in an essay contest. Two pairs of underpants. One bra. Jeans. A T-shirt. A sweater. The $87.52 she had squirreled away in the back of her bottom desk drawer behind an unused sewing kit. What else, she wondered? How much does a person need in order to run away from home? She spun around the room slowly taking stock of what she was leaving. Things. A pressed-glass penny jar in the shape of a starfish. A framed photograph of her mother surrounded by prizewinning dahlias. A giant stuffed panda her father gave her for Christmas the year they traveled to Washington, D.C., and visited the National Zoo. Souvenirs of what now felt like a bankrupt childhood. She wrote a simple note. It said in big red letters: DON'T WORRY ABOUT ME. Her words were unavoidably hostile. She put the note under her pillow. Before she left, she would place it on top of her dresser propped in front of a balancing porcelain ballerina figurine.

Jane could not run away without at least trying to explain herself to Helen. Helen was probably still asleep. It was very unusual these days for Jane to be awake and up before her sister. Often, in fact, Helen was the one who made sure Jane did not sleep through the alarm. This morning the roles were oddly reversed. Jane went the back way, through the shared bathroom, into Helen's room. She was sleeping remarkably soundly. The soft black-and-white paperback photography of *The Bell Jar* stared up at her, its pink title seeming to accessorize the room. Helen must have fallen asleep reading. Good for her. Jane wished she could have slept so well. For much of the night, unalterable facts kept her awake. Nadine was pregnant. Her father was in jail. Wondering what might happen next, she would not have thought she had slept at all last night but for the fact that she was awakened by a dream. A nightmare really. She could not remember the details, but in the dream, she could feel walls closing in on her.

Jane lightly tapped Helen on the shoulder. Without moving, Helen opened her eyes. "What is it?" Helen asked.

"How's the book coming?" Jane spoke softly, picking up the open book, careful not to lose Helen's place in it.

"Morning, Jane," Helen spoke in drowsy timbre. "The book," she repeated. Coming to, she focused her attention on her sister's question and sluggishly inquired, "Did they really do that to people back then? To mental patients? I mean that whole shock thing?"

"My English teacher said they mostly did it to women back then."

"Jesus, I'm glad they don't use shock therapy anymore."

"I think they still use it sometimes but not so much. They don't have to. There are all these drugs now to help women deal with their lives. That's what Mom does, anyway."

"Shut up," Helen retorted, half-laughing, half-lamenting. She rolled over and let her face fall directly into the well broken-in pillow.

"Helen, we need to talk."

"What time is it?" Helen asked.

"I don't know." Helen rolled back around. They both looked at the clock. It was just past six.

"Helly, I have to get out of here."

"What do you mean?"

"I have to leave, I mean, get out of here for a few days."

"You mean like run away?"

"I guess so."

"Why? It's not because of me, is it? I shouldn't have told you about the phone call. That's it, isn't it? This is all my fault."

"Helen, this has nothing to do with you. I just can't take it anymore. I feel like I don't even belong in this house."

"But what about Dad? Aren't you worried about Dad?"

"Dad will be fine. I'm not worried about Dad. To tell you the truth, I'm more worried about Mom. She has no idea what's going on. She'll never understand why I'm leaving."

"But you'll only be gone a few days, right? You have to graduate, Jane. You have to. Mom is already planning a party. And what about the play? They need you. I need you. You can't just leave."

"I have to, Helly. I'm going crazy here. My whole life I've been trying to live up to everyone else's expectations, espe-

cially Dad's. Now I find out he doesn't live up to them himself! I have to get out of here." Helen was struggling not to cry.
She was so sensitive, Jane thought, so vulnerable. Like a baby
bird with its mouth wide open. Well, Jane thought, right now
I have nothing to give her.

"When did you decide to do this?"

"Last night. After we heard from Dad. I actually called
Nadine and told her what happened."

"Why? This is none of her business."

"It is her business, Helly. Like it or not, Dad is her business. But I mostly called to let her know I was going away for
a few days, because I told her I would go with her, you know,
to the abortion. Now I won't be here to help."

"Where will you go?" Helen asked, sniffling.

"I don't know. Maybe the city. I'm not sure. I'll call you."

"Promise?"

"Promise. Cross my heart and hope to die; stick a needle
in my eye." She drew the expected cross on her chest with her
right thumb and aimed the familiar imaginary needle at her
right eye. "Will you do something for me?"

"What?"

Jane disappeared and returned with a shiny white cardboard shoebox. She put it on the bed next to Helen and
asked, "Can you take this to the high school and put it on
the stage? If you go right after school, I don't think anybody
will see you." Helen sat up. Removed the lid from the box.

Peeled back the unbleached tissue paper. Stared at the sparkly shoes.

BREAKFAST WAS TENSE. Jane, Helen, and their mother shared cereal, toast, and anxiety. She apologized to her mother for leaving the breakfast table so hurriedly yesterday morning. "There's a lot going on right now," Jane said.

"Of course there is," her mother replied with predictable empathy.

"Are you okay, Mom?" Jane asked

"Oh, sure," her mother answered, without even seeming to consider the weight of the inquiry. Jane stared deeply into her mother's soft eyes, searching for the truth. Sensing Jane's concern, she reiterated, "I'm fine. Really. Your father said this would all be straightened out this morning and I'm sure it will be." Her mother could be exasperatingly optimistic. Jane was not going to be the one to burst her bubble, however. Not this morning anyway. As if there were nothing at all unusual happening in their lives, her mother launched into a story about a little boy at the hospital named Mickey who, unfortunately, did have rather large ears and had, to the dismay of his parents, swallowed a large round magnet. The objectionable magnet would have to be surgically removed this morning. "But," she said, "I may take a personal day to help your father, so I don't think I'll be seeing poor little Mickey this morning."

Helen was very quiet throughout the strained breakfast. She observed carefully. Nodded appropriately. Steered clear of the conversation. Kept her mouth filled with crunchy things. Tried not to look as upset as Jane knew she was. If there were any good reason for Jane to stay, it was Helen. Helen, her baby sister. Helen, the gentle giant. Helen, who was so insecure, so easily frightened. Perhaps, Jane considered, struggling to rationalize her decision, this departure would be good for her sister. Like pushing her off the end of a dock, not out of any malice but because she had utter confidence that her sister could swim. Helen can do this, Jane reasoned. If she were headed into a more normal college experience, she would be leaving home in a few months anyway. She could not be responsible for her sister forever and felt she would lose her mind if she stayed an hour longer.

Jane acted as if she were leaving for school. As if nothing at all were different. She was wearing normal school clothes. A pair of jeans. A white T-shirt. Old brown sandals. She was carrying an oversized backpack but, for all her mother knew, it was filled with props. Or school projects. If she noticed the size of the pack at all, her mother did not say a word. Jane did not know whether she would be gone for a day or a week or maybe even longer. She was not sure she was well enough prepared. Or that she could be. But she knew she had to go. She had to get out from under the heavy pile of expectations that were suddenly unacceptable.

APPREHENSIVE BUT EXCITED, Jane walked directly to the train station. As a family, they used to take the train into the city once or twice a year. To catch a show. To window shop. Today, however, she was headed in the opposite direction. East. East to the Hamptons. East to famous beaches. If she had to leave, she might as well go somewhere wonderful. A place with potential for fresh dreaming. A rack of folded paper train schedules stood near the ticket windows, arranged in sections like petite greeting cards. She pulled out a schedule. Found the eastbound section. Discovered the next train would not be leaving until 7:43 and that she would have to change trains at Babylon to keep going. She purchased a one-way ticket. Not wanting to be conspicuous in any way, she bought a newspaper and buried her face in the cheerless tidings of the world. Theft. Murder. Earthquake. Big storm coming.

At last, Jane stepped onto the first train that would carry her out as far as Babylon. There were not many passengers on board. Most people headed west in the morning and east in the evening. She was glad to discover an alcove of sorts, two rows of seats facing each other, all to herself. She fashioned her backpack into a makeshift pillow and leaned her left shoulder and head into it. She felt as if she had been awake for days. As if today and yesterday and Monday were all one sleepless crisis. Once aboard, she slept at last. For a few short minutes. Until the conductor yelled, "Babylon. All change in Babylon."

Without too much trouble, hoping all the while that nobody was taking note of her uneasiness, her unfamiliarity with eastbound train travel, Jane followed a small crowd to another platform. There was nearly an hour before the 8:55 was scheduled to board, the train to Southampton, her intended destination. She shared a concrete bench with two older women, both clad in linen and gold. Their meticulously pedicured and already tanned feet were surrounded by shopping bags from New York's retail giants. Saks. Bloomingdale's. Macy's. Their conversation delighted in purchases. Jane looked down at her own calloused, unpainted toes and wondered if she could possibly make a place for herself in the select social order of the Hamptons. A girl her age would not be expected to dress up like these women, would she? Jane wished she had thrown something more elegant into the backpack.

She tried not to listen to the fancy women. Returned to the newspaper. Studied the job market. The two biggest sections were health care and education. Jane could not imagine herself in health care. A nurse like her mother? Never. She would rather be fed liver and onions than have to administer an injection. The very thought of needles turned her stomach. She could teach, however. She could be a great teacher, an inspiring teacher, the kind students look up to, not only with respect but also with great admiration. Like Mrs. Mallory, her English teacher. Or Mr. Shin, her math teacher. When Mr.

Shin found out she had run away, Jane knew he would be shocked. A lot of people were going to be shocked.

Relieved when the train pulled in, she watched the women board a car and deliberately selected a different one. She was pleased to find another private seat and attempted, once again, to make herself comfortable. This time, however, an older couple came and sat directly across from her. With all the empty seats on the train, why could they not give her some space, she wondered? There must be two dozen empty seats in this train alone. They were very friendly, too. Too friendly. Introduced themselves. Mentioned they were going to visit their son in Montauk. Told her she looked an awful lot like their granddaughter. Asked her where she was headed. "To visit a friend," was all Jane revealed. "Where you from?" they pressed on. It was clear that they were not going to leave her alone. Jane did not wish to be rude, so she forwarded a lie. "I'm a student at Juilliard," she said, adding, "studying music."

She wished this last part were true. Jane was an accomplished flautist, having started lessons in the third grade and practiced three times a week or more ever since. She had played first position in the flute section since the seventh grade. She enjoyed floating melodies that lifted her into another realm, to a place where words and pretense were unnecessary. She loved her flute. Wished she had thought to bring it with her. Juilliard was her fantasy school, a dream her father had shot down authoritatively. He believed that all girls should start out with practical skills. Accounting know-how. Computer proficiency. His girls needed real skills that would help them get good jobs in the real world. Until they were married, of course. Flute playing held no rank in his hierarchy of real-life values. She could get everything she needed at the community college.

Jane removed her journal from a backpack that was feeling smaller and less adequate with each mile. Finally, the couple seemed to catch on that Jane had things to do and they quieted down. She read through the last few pages of entries, listening carefully to each stop as it was boldly announced. Then, against her wishes, the steady metrical advancing of the train coerced her into a hard sleep. Jane was startled an hour later to hear, ". . . hampton." She had missed the first part and jumped out of her seat in the kind of panic that is unique to those surrealistic moments that follow a sudden awakening. She scurried off the train, while the older couple watched with surprise. The sign on the little station wall read Fairhampton. Where was she? Had she missed the Southampton stop or jumped off too soon? Jane spent a few seconds composing her thoughts. Took out the little paper train schedule. Muttered, "Shit," as she realized she had stumbled off several stops too soon. According to the schedule, it would be a long wait before another train came from either direction. Not wishing to sit around in yet another train station, she found a waiting taxi and asked to be taken to the beach.

"Which one?" the driver wanted to know.

"The main beach," she answered after a pronounced and embarrassing hesitation. She tried to sound like she knew what she was doing and where she was going when she, in fact, had no earthly idea. Jane felt like an idiot and hoped that feeling was not too obvious. Her face felt warm as if it had been requisitioned by an unruly blush. She assumed that any town ending in "hampton" must have a nice beach, but the taxi driver was staring at his watch unresponsively. "How about if you just take me to the middle of town," she said. "You got it," he responded. It did not take long to get there.

As they approached what Jane thought must be the town center, her heart swelled a little. It was so cute. So welcoming. Small upscale shops lined the main street. As she emerged from the air-conditioned taxi, she could smell salt in the air. The beach could not be far. Deciding to explore the town first, she took her time looking in the shop windows on the south side of the street. One window displayed a velvet case full of expensive gold earrings. She saw a pair in the shape of seagulls and wished for them earnestly. A woman inside could see exactly what she was coveting. She smiled and held out the box so that Jane could see them better. Jane smiled and mouthed a "thanks" at the woman. Another shop offered gauzy earth-colored clothing hung on one-dimensional, black-silhouette manikins. A small drugstore had a display of sunscreens, sunglasses, and straw hats in the window. Crossing the street, she could smell something cooking. Bacon. It had to be bacon. The lovely smell was coming from a white clapboard cape with a yellow-and-white striped awning over the entrance that, in elegant filigree letters, read KATE'S. The building might have been someone's home, once upon a time. The food smelled good but what she was more interested in right now was a bathroom. Would she need to be a paying customer in order to use the restaurant's bathroom?

Kate's, Jane could see, was quite busy. She read a menu that was posted in the window. "Jesus!" she said out loud, since she did not think anyone was listening. "Eight dollars for scrambled eggs with a muffin! I can't afford this town." As she scanned the rest of the menu, she became aware that someone was staring at her. From inside the restaurant, a tall, big-boned older woman with dark hair braided in pigtails on either side of her head glared at her, as if assessing a new product. Feather earrings hung from her ears and she wore an orange-and-white striped apron. With an irresistible authority, the woman waved Jane in. Red-faced, Jane opened the door, hearing a little bell ring as she did so. The woman grinned and asked, "Are you here about the job?"

"No," answered Jane, "I mean yes," she amended, thinking on her feet, astounded by the question and the good fortune it might represent.

"Well, are you or are you not?"

"I guess I am. Well, to be honest, I was just looking around town for a bathroom but I'm also looking for a job."

"You're in luck. We have both. I just put the sign in the window this morning." The tall woman pointed to a corner of the window Jane had somehow missed. "To tell you the truth, I was surprised to see anyone here so soon. The girl I hired two weeks ago left yesterday for another job. Bigger restaurant. Size-wise, we're pretty small, as you can see. And we're only open for breakfast. The job's thirty hours a week, five hours a day, six days a week, six dollars an hour, off the books, no benefits, you keep all the tips, and the leftover pancakes are on the house. Take it or leave it." The speed with which this woman rattled off the terms of employment made Jane wonder how many times this speech had been offered.

Arms folded confidently across her chest, her right front toe almost tapping, the woman was waiting for an answer. "I'll take it," Jane replied with audible hesitation. She would be a fool not to take it, right? There might be something better out there. Something more lucrative. But this would give her a place to start. Without having to comb through the Help Wanted section. Without having to explain why she had no work history whatsoever.

"You sure?"

Jane nodded enthusiastically.

"What's your name?"

"My name?"

"Yeah. You know, the usual collection of consonants and vowels people use when they are trying to get your attention.

You do have a name, don't you?" There was no unkindness or sarcasm in her voice. She was, Jane suspected, simply trying to move the process along on a very busy morning.

"Yes, of course," Jane said, attempting to focus her thoughts. She needed a good hiding name. Something completely different. She had never liked Jane all that well anyway. It was too plain. Too boring. She needed a new name for a new life. "Cleopatra," Jane said, and when the woman gave her a funny look, she added, "but my friends call me . . . Cleo."

"Huh." The woman nodded hesitantly, acknowledging the curious moniker.

Jane was pleased and amused by her own creativity. She liked the name. It was exotic. Romantic. This big woman, hopefully her first employer, did not seem to share her satisfaction with the name. Jane was amazed by the size of her. She stood well above six feet. Taller than Helen. She had large, long muscular hands, unlike any she had ever seen on a woman before. Her fingernails were clipped as short as possible. Jane looked down at her own hands. Hands that looked much like her mother's. Soft and average.

"Cleo," the woman said, still struggling to accept the sound of it. "Welcome to Kate's. I'm Kate, in case you haven't guessed already. The big question is this—can you start tomorrow? I need the help." The woman waved around the room and Jane could see that only one waitress was scurrying around to all the tables. "You have waitressed before, I take it."

Jane decided she had better be honest. It would become clear soon enough that she did not have any waitressing experience. "No. But I'm a fast learner. I'm a hard worker. You won't be sorry. I promise." She was, apparently, convincing enough for Kate.

"Hang around out until the crowd thins out. It won't be long. Then I'll show you the ropes, Cleo. But I gotta warn you. If you can't keep up, I can't keep you. You understand, I'm sure."

"Yes. Kate? Should I call you Kate?" she spoke nervously.

"If you call me Sue, I won't know who you're talking to. Oh, and the bathroom's down there in the back. On the right. After that, you can sit and have a cup of coffee while you wait, if you want."

Jane was so glad for the toilet at Kate's. The minute she stepped off the train in all her confusion, she found herself wishing she had used the horrible one on the train. Then, when the taxi dropped her in town, it occurred to her that, probably, there had been one right there at the station. Kate's porcelain was a welcome sight. In a much more comfortable state, Jane sat off in a corner, waiting and watching so that when Kate was ready to teach her the fine points of the job, she would have some sense of it. To that end, she observed carefully as a petite dark-haired waitress sprinted from table to table taking orders, delivering plates, connecting with customers. Kate helped the young waitress from time to time. It was abundantly clear that one waitress was not enough. Jane paid close attention as a tall, slim young man bussed the tables. Throughout her observations, she sat there wondering how she could be so lucky. Just like that, she had a job. She got off at the wrong stop yet seemed to be in the right place.

It was not until all but two customers were left that Kate came and sat down with her new employee. First, she showed Jane a list of abbreviations: BC for black coffee, SSB for short stack of blueberry pancakes, and so on. Jane asked if she could take the list with her to review before tomorrow morning. Kate handed her the scribbled list and warned Jane that she had better write legibly. Next, she showed her eager new waitress how to work an antique but perfectly functional cash register. Then Kate gave her a rundown of the menu, which was pretty simple. It was a breakfast restaurant. That was all they served. Kate said, "The good news is that breakfast is the meal with the fewest culinary options. And the better news is that most people who walk through that door order pancakes." She told Jane that she would either have to pull her hair back, wear a hairnet, or get it cut. She could pull it back for now but the idea of getting her hair cut intrigued Jane. Kate handed her a silk-screened orange and white apron from a pile of three or four freshly laundered ones that were hanging from a row of wooden pegs. Again, Kate offered her a cup of coffee. Jane had not yet developed a taste for coffee but decided "Cleo" would have to be a coffee drinker.

"Help yourself. Pot's still fresh. The mugs are all lined up on the shelf up there. You see 'em?"

"Yup." She would never have offered a "yup" at home, where the only proper affirmative answer was a carefully enunciated "yes." Kate brought out the "yup" in her. She liked it.

The newly christened Cleo tried on the apron, satisfied with the look. She poured herself half a mug of the coffee and took a deep whiff. It smelled nutty. She took a small sip. It was strong, bitter, and tasted much as she had expected. She added what probably amounted to a quarter cup of sugar, pouring a long stream of it out of a glass container with a stainless-steel spout. Kate went out back to take a delivery. Jane took another sip. Better, but maybe it needed some cream. Her father always put real cream in his coffee. She went to the refrigerator, found a quart container of half-and-half, and poured quite a bit into the mug. Much better. She could become a coffee drinker. Maybe. Noticing a clock on the wall for the first time, she saw that it was already after noon. The morning had flown by. She wondered if her father was out of jail by now. She hoped so. She wondered if anyone had found her note yet. She hoped not.

Jane had wanted a job for several years now. Many of her friends had part-time jobs but her father said, "under no circumstances." Her father always said, "You have a job. You're a student. You'll have your whole life to work." In her mind's eye, she could see the sincere look on his face when he said it.

While Jane partially understood her father's reasons, she was a good student and probably could have handled a small job better than most. And she was almost eighteen, after all. Now "Cleo" had a real job and was determined to be great at it, to be the most outstanding waitress Kate had ever employed. Kate would not be sorry to have hired her.

"We open at seven, not a minute before. Bill usually comes in first." She pointed to the tall boy who was now busily scrubbing out pans. "He's my combination busboy, floor-mopper, dishwasher, hash-slinger, and pancake-batter-maker. A real renaissance man." He was tall, leggy, blond, and, like the women at the Babylon train station, already heading for a great tan. He wore long baggy shorts and a plain white T-shirt. He had beautiful chiseled features on his long face. The best parts were his almond-shaped eyes, very unusual in color, blue-gray around the outside of the iris and a golden brown on the inside.

"Gee thanks, Babe," he said, winking over his shoulder at Kate to let her know he had heard every word.

"Don't call me Babe."

"I'm Bill, by the way," he said, this time looking in Jane's direction.

"Bill, this here is Cleo. Cleo? Bill. Bill? Cleo. Bill's my right-hand man."

"Left-hand," he objected, "I'm left-handed, Kate," he said walking over to where Jane stood. Extending a long well-tanned arm, taking her hand in his, he said, "Charmed," and lifted it for a kiss. Jane said nothing. It was a warm, gentle kiss that sent shivers right down her seventeen-year-old spine. She curtsied and tried not to look as embarrassed as she felt. Jane did not believe in love-at-first-sight but this was as close to the experience as she had ever come.

"Why don't you chop me some onions, dear?" Kate said, in an obvious attempt to send her over-attentive employee back to his duties.

"Don't call me dear," he said smiling slyly at Kate. "Excuse me, dahling," he said to Jane in a posh British accent, "my onions await." He retrieved a cardboard box of Vidalias from a low cupboard. Picked out five. Placed them on the chopping block section of the counter, next to the sink. Replaced the box. Called across the room to Jane, "Where are you from?"

"New York City," she answered.

"Oh, where in New York?"

"Downtown," she said as politely as she could, while making it clear to him she was not about to supply details.

"Just asking."

"I don't feel like answering questions right now, that's all." Jane felt a little threatened but did not want him to feel that she was, in any way, rejecting him.

"May I ask where you're staying out here?"

"No. Sorry." She tried to answer sweetly.

"Okay." He backed off. She was relieved. Jane did not wish to be rude but she was certainly not yet ready to hand out personal information. Kate interjected, "You need a place to stay?"

She was further discomfited by Kate's question and answered, "I'm going to look this afternoon."

"Won't be easy to find a place by tonight. Did you just come out here on a whim? No job? No place to stay?"

"Something like that." She felt very self-conscious. She knew Bill was staring at her. Perhaps even feeling sorry for her. If she looked over at him, their eyes would undoubtedly fix a gaze. She could not, therefore, look.

"I think I can help you. Excuse me a minute." Kate went back behind the counter. Jane could see her placing a phone call. She tried to listen in but could only hear a word here and there: "Ev . . . Kid . . . Yeah, real nice . . . Maybe." She wondered who Kate could be talking to and hoped, whoever it was, would not be charging her too much.

Released from his good-natured taskmaster, Bill left his onions to join Jane where she sat with her unpersuasive coffee. She stared down into her nearly full coffee cup, pretending not to notice him. He asked, "You trying to see into the future? I have a funny cousin who says she can tell the future from the way the coffee swirls." Jane shrugged and continued to scrutinize the coffee. He persisted, "Here, let me have a look." Like a teacher relieving her of the burden of a science experiment gone badly, Bill gently took the cup from her and looked down into it. He said, "I see mystery, intrigue, romance. I see . . . coffee with way too much cream in it."

"Very clever," she responded, daring to look up at him again. Big, beautifully shaped eyes. Kate came back over to the table.

"You're all set for tonight. This woman charges a five-dollar donation for the room. You got five bucks?"

"Five bucks? Sure. Why the donation? Is this place safe?"

"Oh, yeah, it's safe all right. It's a house. Well, actually, the church owns it but the Rev lives there and she lets people stay."

"The Rev? It isn't a convent, is it?" Images came to mind of small stony cells and scary quiet women dressed in black from head to toe.

"This is nothing like a convent. It's a big house owned by the Presbyterian Church where the minister lives. They call it a manse."

"Oh, I don't think I can stay with a minister. I've only been to church twice in my life, I think, and those were special occasions. I'm not really religious or anything."

"Don't worry about it. She won't hold it against you."

"She? Did you say the Reverend is a she?"

"You got a problem with that?"

"I guess not." Jane had never met a woman minister before and while it sounded strange, she did feel more comfortable staying with a woman.

"You can walk from here, but I'm headed out that way. I'll give you a ride if you like."

HAVING FINISHED THE BREAKFAST CLEANUP at the restaurant, Kate took Jane in a shiny, red Ford pickup truck to the Presbyterian manse. It was right across the street from a lovely old church, a one-story white-shingled church with a small bell tower. While she knew next to nothing about churches, she sensed the importance of them. Her father once said that church architecture defined a town. The manse was a big Victorian house with a spacious front porch, probably built to accommodate a pastor and his family when American families were much larger. It was a bit run-down, needing a spot of paint here and there, but was impressive nevertheless.

When Kate pulled into the manse driveway, a slim woman who looked to be in her early forties stepped out on to the porch to greet them. Nervous about meeting her, anxiously wondering what this was going to be like, Jane thought this woman did not look much like a Reverend. The Rev. Evelyn Burns, or simply "the Rev" as most town residents knew her, was wearing jeans and sneakers and a navy-and-white striped oxford shirt with the sleeves rolled up. She had short salt-and-pepper hair and walked right up to Jane. As if she did this sort of thing everyday, the woman said, "Hi there. I'm Evelyn. Cleo, is it? I hear you need a place to stay. You're welcome here. You're more than welcome. Come on in." Jane felt like a long-lost cousin being welcomed back into the family.

"Can't stay—gotta go," said Kate and, with a dismissive wave of one hand, started to leave.

Jane stopped her to say, "Thank you. Thank you for everything."

"Just show up on time tomorrow morning. You may not want to thank me after tomorrow morning." Kate laughed out loud and took off in the pickup. Jane was amazed. When she started out this morning, she had no idea where she would end up. Unexpectedly, people were taking care of her. Looking out for her. Taking her into their homes. So far, everyone she met was nicer to her than her own neighbors. On her street at home, not only did most people keep to themselves, they were considered suspect if they were too affable. The only homes in her neighborhood she had ever actually been inside were the ones that housed kids her age.

The Reverend Evelyn Burns led Jane into the manse. She showed her the parlor and the living room, the kitchen and the dining room. It was a huge house and would have been magnificent but for the slightly tattered furnishings. Once, Jane and her family stayed in a bed-and-breakfast in Vermont. Every stick of furniture in that place, every lamp, every knick-knack, was chosen to blend with the style and period of the house. Not so here. The floors were all hardwood but needed attention. Most rooms were wallpapered but, clearly, not recently. The manse had been maintained but not well maintained.

With a graciousness that sounded something like her mother but with more layers, the Reverend said, "It's nothing fancy, Cleo, but I want you to make yourself at home. The kitchen's down here. There's a washer and dryer in the basement if you need to do laundry. Feel free to use anything as long as you clean it up when you're done. Your room is upstairs." Looking at Jane's small backpack, Evelyn asked, "Is that all you have with you?" They glanced at one another, each looking into the eyes of the other for character clues. Signs of trustworthiness. Jane would discover that Evelyn had put up and sometimes put up with a growing number of young transients who needed a place to stay along their uncertain and sometimes dangerous journeys. When Evelyn was invited to be the pastor of this historic congregation, she felt guilty about living in such a huge and spectacular house all by herself. She enjoyed sharing it, even with strangers.

Jane would also learn that Evelyn had been married for three years, once upon a time, but like a bad pie, it simply had not set. She wanted children. He did not. She was not interested in climbing the corporate ladder. He was. It was a friendly divorce. No fighting. No contests. Just the sad realization that they were heading in separate and altogether different directions. While Evelyn dated occasionally, and there were always plenty of parishioners ready to introduce her to "someone special," she had not met anyone with whom she believed she could settle down. She was attractive enough in her own way. Interesting enough. With a magnificent sense of humor. But her vocation often frightened others away.

Evelyn led Jane upstairs and opened one of three doors along the right side of a central hallway. "This will be your space for the night, Cleo." It was beautiful room with an old, four-poster single bed, covered with a patchwork quilt. Two windows, treated with tea-dyed lace curtains, overlooked a gravel driveway. Cream-colored wallpaper dotted with tiny rosebuds covered the walls. A well-worn oak desk and chair were pushed up against the left wall and there was a small closet in one corner. A big, longhaired yellow cat was curled up in a sagging chair that was fitted with a goldenrod slipcover.

"That's Samson. He's very sweet but if he bothers you, just throw him out. He's very accommodating. Oh, and the bathroom is down at the end of the hall. Any questions?" Questions. Jane had plenty of questions. What was the catch, she wanted to know? How did this woman know she could be trusted? Why would anyone give her the run of the house without knowing anything about her? Jane shook her head. The Reverend continued, "I'll let you get settled. If you need me, I'll be across the street in the church office. Alright?"

"Excuse me, Reverend," Jane said meekly, uncertain what she should call this bewilderingly kind woman. She dug around the bottom of her backpack and came up with her folded stash of money. "Here is the five dollars."

"Thank you very much," the Reverend said, taking five wrinkled bills from her overnight guest. "By the way, this is not a fee, Cleo. It's a donation. I send all room donations to a family crisis shelter in Riverhead."

"Oh," she answered, not knowing how to respond. Letting the words "family crisis" sink in. She had just left a family crisis. She hoped her little donation would help some other confused person sort things out. "That's great."

"And please call me Ev."

"Okay. Thanks." Jane thought it would be very difficult to call this woman, who was probably a little older than her own mother, by her first name. But she did not say so.

Samson looked up at Jane with wise jade eyes. Ascertaining that she was no threat, he closed his eyes again. Went back to doing one of the things cats do best. Sleep. She stroked his silky head but he did not move. He did, however, begin to emit a low rumbling purr. Jane sat on the edge of the bed. Took off her sneakers and socks. Massaged her traveled feet. Thought about where those feet had started this morning and where they were now. So much had transpired within a few short hours. It was as if she had clicked her heels together and landed in a dream. She bounced on the edge of the mattress a few times. Decided to search the rest of the second floor.

On the second floor of the manse, there were four other rooms similarly decorated with flowery wallpaper and lace curtains and filled with old furniture. The biggest room was in the back of the house. It had a queen-sized bed that was covered with books and papers. It looked like the most lived-in room. Jane surmised it was the Reverend's. She stepped in for a closer inspection and found that the end wall was covered with small paintings, all of the Virgin Mary. Some looked quite old while others were very contemporary. This odd wall of Marys, some who seemed to be looking straight at her, seemed spooky to Jane. She hoped the Rev would not try to convert her like the young men in cheap suits who sometimes show up at the front door wanting to talk about salvation. Goose bumps ran down her arms and she left the back bedroom without further explorations.

Jane returned to her assigned room, to her "guest" bed. She lay on her back on top of the neatly placed quilt, hands tucked behind her head. She thought about everything that happened since Monday morning. Helen's awful discovery. Nadine's disturbing confirmation. The way her father came to her school and pulled her right into his deplorable behavior. The fact that, when she left the house this morning, he was in jail. The idea of her mother finding the note on top of her dresser. The knowledge that Helen would be fretting already, looking for more gummy bears to quell her fears. It was all too much. Too much. Within a matter of minutes, her survey of troubles and worries led to the welcome escape of slumber.

JANE WOKE UP IN A MUDDLE. She could hear a doorbell ringing downstairs. It took her a few seconds to remember where she was. Who she was. A yellowed, plastic alarm clock sitting on the desk near the bed read 2:18. Must be afternoon. It felt peculiar to wake up in the middle of the day. Seldom did Jane sleep during the day. That only happened when she was sick and Jane was almost never sick. The doorbell continued its persistent old-fashioned ringing. The bright ring of an antique, brass turn doorbell. Should she answer it? This was not her home. It was, undoubtedly, someone looking for the Reverend. But what if it was someone looking for her? Jane felt like a fugitive. Her family could not possibly have tracked her down this quickly. It was more likely that they had not even found the note yet. Whoever was standing there ringing that doorbell must be for the Reverend. Eager not to do the wrong thing, she padded downstairs in her bare feet. With some trepidation, she answered the door. There, on the front porch, stood Bill, a face that nearly took her breath away.

"Sorry, did I wake you up?" he asked.

Jane thought she must look as confused as she felt. She confessed, "I guess so but I really should be up anyway."

"Sorry. I don't want to bother you, Cleo, but you're obviously new around here and I thought you might want the grand tour."

"Grand tour?"

"Yeah, you know, I could be your tour guide. Show you around town. It's not the nicest day, sort of gray and all, but I could take you to the beach."

The beach was where she had hoped to start her explorations this morning. She was eager to get there, to see it, to plant her sojourning feet in it, to wrap herself snugly in the sound and the smell of it.

"The only thing is . . . I don't have a car." Bill pointed to an old black bicycle with a wooden box fastened to the back of it with bungee cords.

"It doesn't look big enough for two," she commented.

"I already took care of that. The Rev saw me standing on her porch and came over to see what I was doing here."

"You know her?"

"Everybody knows the Rev," he said. "Her office is right there. I've been standing here maybe fifteen minutes, Cleo. You must not have heard the doorbell." Bill pointed almost directly across the street from the front door of the manse to what must have been the church office. There was the Rev, standing at the window of her office, watching them. Waving to them. Giving Jane a thumbs-up. "Anyway," Bill continued, "she has a bicycle she rides around town all the time and she told me you could borrow it. It's yellow. She said you can borrow it as long as you lock it up."

"Well, I suppose I could go for a little while." Jane wanted to get to know the territory. Bill could be a big help in this regard.

"She said it's parked inside the garage on the left-hand side. Believe me, we won't have any trouble finding it."

"Just let me put something on my feet." She ran back upstairs, brushed her hair, put on her sandals, and stepped back out into the cloudy day.

Bill was right. Nobody could miss this bicycle. It was an old three-speeder with the gearshift attached to the handlebars. It had been hand-painted yellow, like a bright ripe banana, and had a big, bulb-driven trumpet horn screwed onto the middle of the handlebars. Jane wheeled the bicycle from the garage and tested it in the driveway. It would be fine. Conspicuous but fine.

"Can we go to the beach first?" she asked with enthusiasm.

"Of course. Of course. Our first stop on the tour will be the beach." He put on the formal voice and character of a tour guide. They took off toward the middle of town. The roads were completely flat. Even flatter than in Alquot. Lovely for riding. There was certainly no need for more than three speeds. The wind coming up off the ocean blew through her fine brown hair, across her willing face, and over the tops of her sandaled feet. It felt marvelous. Therapeutic. As if all the heavy dust of the last few days was gently being blown away. She felt a suggestion of real happiness for the first time since Sunday evening at the play rehearsal. A lifetime ago.

They passed several considerable estates with very large homes planted in the middle of flawless lawns. She tried the funny bicycle horn, which let out an obnoxious honk and made Bill laugh. He had a deep resonant laugh, a movie star laugh. Jane could sense when they was nearing the beach. She could smell it. Almost taste it. Finally she could hear the ocean beckoning. Bill led them into a parking lot that had a long rack made of steel piping where he locked the two bicycles up together. There were not many. Not many cars either. But it was not a great beach day. Overcast. Quite breezy. Jane watched as Bill took a brown bag out of the box strapped to his bicycle, held it up and, returning to his guide voice, said, "A late lunch is included in the tour, complete with M.C.s." When Jane shot him a confused look he added, "Major cookies." She followed him up a set of rough-hewn wooden steps that led through a range of rolling dunes. The beach expanded her horizon of vision as they neared the top of the steps. It was magnificent, a living postcard of sweeping sand and pulsing surf.

Twenty yards or so from the dancing ocean, Bill seated himself in the sand and, with his muscular hands, patted a spot next to him. Jane sat. Studied the ocean. Watched it devour the sand over and over again. Filled her hands with the tiny beige crystals, allowing them to course through her slender fingers. The sand was surprisingly warm given the fact that the sun was so thoroughly veiled by cloud cover. Sand escaping freely through the spaces between her fingers gave Jane the feeling of emancipation. But she knew she was not really free. Try as she did to think as little as possible about home, Helen's dismayed face would not leave her alone. How was it possible to feel so good and so guilty at one and the same time?

As Jane and Bill sat next to one another, rear ends burrowed in cold but reasonably dry sand, Bill opened the brown paper bag. He had packed a small picnic for which Jane was much obliged. Not having eaten much since she got on the train, Jane was ravenously hungry. She watched expectantly as he unpacked the much-appreciated provisions. First, he pulled two small bottles of raspberry juice out of the bag. These were followed by two huge submarine sandwiches, one of which he handed to her. "The choices are turkey or turkey," he said apologetically. "I love turkey," she reassured him. Bill was clearly accustomed to managing unwieldy sandwiches. He made no mess at all eating the behemoth sub, yet she seemed unable to control it. Sliced peppers and olives rained on her lap. Bill laughed at her. Not with her but at her. Humiliating as the scene was, she had to admit it was pretty funny. She felt like a topped pizza. Made it through half of the sandwich. Conceded defeat. He offered her a consolation prize—a cookie, still warm from someone's oven. It was very sweet and gooey. Chocolate chips. Peanut butter chips. Butterscotch chips. Pecans. Macadamia nuts. This cookie had everything in it. It was, as he described, "major." Jane broke off stamp-sized pieces, savoring each one. Her mother made great cookies. Oatmeal with milk chocolate chips. Buttery snickerdoodles. But this. She held the half that was left, lifted it to her nose, and took pleasure in the rich smell of it. This cookie might be the best one she had ever eaten in her life.

They threw the remains of their picnic into a wire trash-can and started walking east down the beach. They moved closer to the ocean, strolling barefoot along the edge of the surf. She carefully selected four smooth opaque stones as she walked. Put them in her pocket. Felt them there with her fingers. She touched them, one at a time and thought: Helen, Mom, Dad, Nadine. The people most on her mind in spite of her best efforts to banish them. As a way of moving them into a waiting room, at least for a little while, Jane invited Bill to talk about himself. He did so readily. She learned that Bill grew up on a farm on the outskirts of town. He graduated from the local high school three years ago and was still uncertain what to do with his life. The only thing he knew for sure was that he would not be farming. "It's a good life," he explained, "but it's really hard to keep a farm going on Long Island these days." They exchanged personal stories. Jane stuck to real-life events, except for the invented part about having already graduated from high school and wanting to "get a life" before she went to college.

"Isn't it early to be out of school? Around here, graduation doesn't take place until the middle of June."

"Well, the actual graduation isn't until June, but I finished all my exams last Friday and I really don't want to go to graduation anyway."

Jane could tell this part of the story sounded strange to Bill. Before he could question her any further, she asked him to tell her more about the farm. Bill told her he did not live there anymore. His parents started out as small crop farmers, with a modest dairy as well. While it was a life he admired and respected, it was not for him. He used to love the taste of fresh, unprocessed milk. He used to love all the earthy smells of the farm. Now these once comforting and pleasing sensory experiences felt dull to him. He told Jane that his parents were utterly understanding. They wanted him to "find himself." If the search process led him back to the farm, fine. If not, they just wanted him to be happy, to "follow his bliss." To Jane's ears, Bill's parents sounded exactly opposite her own. They sounded deliberately uncontrolling.

"I don't think I've ever even been to a farm," Jane admitted.

Bill talked about how nice his parents were. How they respected his desire for independence. How one month after high school graduation, they helped him move into a little apartment in the back of a house on the Quogue Road. He had lived there for almost three years now. Bill continued to have dinner with his parents every Sunday afternoon and he loved them. "They're great parents," he professed. "But I couldn't live there forever." Jane understood more than he could know.

FOLLOWING THE SHORELINE, they passed large beach homes built in odd shapes. Almost all were the color of the overcast sky and stood like mammoth sentries guarding the beach. A handful of people shared the beach with Jane and Bill. Seasoned beach walkers. Most with dogs. Jane would have felt like an intruder had she not been at Bill's side because, clearly, this was not a public beach. An older woman, wearing a whimsical purple hat seemed to be approaching them. Nearby, a beautiful golden retriever galloped along the shore, its well-groomed blond coat flying in the breeze. Jane loved dogs. She loved most animals and had always wanted a pet. The dog ran up to her, wagging its tail gregariously. He sniffed with extreme enthusiasm. She patted his head with both hands, scratching him behind the ears, loving the feel of this soft, warm, friendly beast. The woman with the purple hat picked up the pace. Approaching Bill with agitation in her gait, she said, "Hey, there. You know this is private property?"

"Why, yes, as a matter of fact I do," he replied.

Jane was starting to feel very uncomfortable when the hostile woman came back at Bill, "They'll let any sort of riffraff on the beach these days." Jane left the friendly dog and slowly walked toward Bill again. She was about to suggest they leave, when Bill said, "Let me introduce you to the newest riffraff, Aunt Wally. Cleo, this is my Aunt Wallace. Aunt Wally, this is Cleo. She's new in town. Starts work at Kate's in the morning." Bill flashed the woman a big toothy smile but Jane could tell she did not approve of her. The woman looked her up and down with harsh judging eyes. "You had better get home before it starts to rain," she told Bill and called the dog, whose name was Bernie, to her side. "Good luck," she said to Jane. Aunt Wallace and Bernie marched back the way they had come.

"Aunt Wally's a very private person," Bill explained. "Used to be a teacher. English teacher. But she retired a long time ago. Actually, she retired early because the school board kept increasing the size of her class. She did it to make a statement. She's a real character but she's also a very kind person. Generous too. I always get good birthday presents from Aunt Wally. Last year she gave me a bread machine. It's awesome. Anyway, she doesn't like strangers much. I guess you could tell." They turned to look at Aunt Wally only to find her, from a distance, doing the same. Bill and Jane muffled giggles that quickly escalated into gut-wrenching guffaws, sending Bill rolling in the sand laughing. Bill clutched his stomach. Jane landed on her knees, rocking her head into her chest. They laughed until it hurt. Bill's aunt looked back on the pair and shook her head. Eventually, regathering his wits and brushing the sand from his legs, Bill got serious again. "Aunt Wally's right," he said, "we better get back before it rains." The clouds were darkening.

They turned back. Picked up the pace. As they were cutting back through the dunes, Jane stopped for a moment. She reached beyond the roping placed to keep beachcombers out of the dunes. Carefully parted some of the tall sturdy grass. Removed the stones from her pocket. Placed them gently in the sand, as if they were eggs in a nest. "An experiment," she explained to Bill, although this was not scientific experiment as much as symbolic release. She promised herself she would leave those stones alone until she was ready to go home again. This simple act seemed to free her mind. Provisionally. Jane allowed herself to think of other things, of serving pancakes and owning a cat and what it might be like to live on a beach.

On the way back into town, Bill gave Jane a tour of Fairhampton, adding personal comments as they rode along on their bicycles. Here was the home of a mysterious South American ambassador who was never in residence. There was the home of a well-known political family where Bill had once helped carry manure onto the property for their gardener. He pointed to another house where, apparently, his best friend used to live before going off to Stanford University. He rarely came home now. Jane took it all in, fantasizing that she too had grown up here. That she had known Bill since they were small children. That all of the amazing places he was showing her fell within the landscape of her own memory. When it started to sprinkle, the raindrops felt wonderful on her hands. Jane could not remember the last time she felt this happy. Or this comfortable in her own skin. The irony of her new identity was that it felt more authentic than the real one. What was real? What was imagined?

It began to rain more steadily and Jane, wearing the simple T-shirt with which she had started the day, began to shiver visibly. Bill stopped and pulled a ratty-looking but reasonably clean sweatshirt from the wooden box on his bicycle. He insisted she put it on. She appreciated his thoughtfulness, the way he was taking her under his wing and offering her immediate friendship. She felt extraordinarily lucky. Back on the front porch of the manse, she thanked him for a wonderful afternoon. "See you in the morning," she said. Bill parted with obvious reluctance. Jane watched as he removed a plastic trash bag from the box on his bicycle. Poked holes in it. "Instant raincoat," he said, pulling it over his head. Bill rode out into the rain, leaving Jane to contemplate all the things she liked about him. His sense of humor. His kindness. His muscles. His almond eyes.

Jane had plenty of experience in the dating arena. Not much that her parents knew about but that was not her fault. To bring home every boyfriend would be to create a string of disappointments for her father, a man who held impossibly high standards when it came to boys. It was a good thing, Jane thought, she did not live in one of those countries where the father selects a husband for his daughters because she would never, under those circumstances, get married. No one would ever be good enough for her father. Once, when she was a sophomore, Jane invited Kevin to come home for dinner. Kevin was the sweetest young man, a friend from the drama club who was also a high honors student. There was nothing wrong with Kevin. He was pretty good-looking. He was polite. He was good-natured. Her father, however, hardly spoke to him that evening. His conversation at the dinner table avoided Kevin completely, as if there were no guest sitting right there at the table. Then, once poor Kevin left, her father wanted to know, "Where did you find that mealymouthed loser?" She was certainly not going to subject anyone else to his irrational scrutiny.

EVELYN WAS NOT YET HOME. Jane used this private opportunity to explore the manse parlor more closely. In one corner stood an old glass cupboard full of books, the titles of which sounded totally foreign to her. *Between Two Worlds*, *Jesus of Nazareth*, *God of Hope*, *The Church in the Midst of Creation*, *The Meaning of Revelation*, *The Unreasonableness of Jesus*. That last title caught her eye and she wondered why a Reverend, of all people, would think Jesus unreasonable. She pulled it from the shelf, and read the opening sentence of the first chapter: "There is no end to the forgiveness that is required of us."

It boggled her mind. It made no sense. It was ridiculous. No one could require you to forgive. She closed the book tightly and returned it to its appointed place. Just then, Jane heard footsteps coming up the wooden steps to the porch. Keys in the door. Must be Evelyn.

"Hey there," Evelyn greeted her. "You makin' out all right here?"

"Great," Jane said, meaning it.

"How was your bike ride?"

"It was wonderful. This is a beautiful place. The beach was fantastic."

"It is nice, isn't it?" Presumably because she was standing next to the bookcase, Evelyn asked, "Find anything worth reading?"

"Just looking."

"There's some pretty risky material sitting on those shelves." Jane did not quite know how to react. She smiled courteously. There was a strangeness about the Rev that Jane found puzzling. She had never met anyone like her before.

"Actually, I was hoping to find a newspaper," Jane said.

"That's an easy one." Evelyn pulled a thin newspaper out of the large canvas bag she had brought with her into the house. "I've already read it. Not much news, I'm happy to report. About the biggest thing happening around here is that, after three days of clouds and drizzle, it's becoming clear that we're into the edge of a big ugly storm system. They're saying Friday will be the worst of it. Maybe after that we'll get some sun again. I hope." Switching the subject at hand, Evelyn asked, "You hungry?"

"We had a late lunch. I'm still pretty full of Bill's cookies."

"I'll bet I know where those cookies came from. There's a great bakery in town. Tuttles. They make an incredible carrot cake. I've seen Bill in there. I'll bet he's a regular. Anyway, if you change your mind, there's some leftover chicken in the fridge and I think there might be a little blueberry pie left too."

"Thanks. Maybe later." Jane wished she could think of a better word than "thanks." This woman was being so nice to her. The Rev did not even know her, yet was treating her almost as a family member. Jane took the borrowed newspaper up to her room, spread it out on the desk, and turned to the rentals section in the classified papers. Throughout the course of this amazing day, she began to imagine staying here, not only for a few days, but maybe for the entire summer. Or longer. Of course, the longer she stayed, the more difficult it would be to go home. She had fallen in love, not so much with this place as with how she felt here. Fairhampton seemed a fairy-tale town where people knew and cared about one another. It was almost as if the people of this town had been waiting for her to arrive. Would it not be wonderful to stay? To let the days lengthen and warm her here in Fairhampton? If so, she could not stay with the Reverend all summer. She would have to find her own place. A room would suffice. Someplace with access to a kitchen, a shower, and, of course, a place to sleep. That's all. Nothing fancy. Something inexpensive and private.

In the safety of her quaint borrowed room, Jane reviewed apartment and room rentals. All too quickly, she determined that an apartment would be out of the question. The least expensive were all in the range of nine hundred dollars a month. The cheapest single room rates, on the other hand,

were in the four-hundred-dollar range. She circled two of
them with her beloved Cross pen. She forgot to bring her
flute. She neglected to bring a raincoat. In the next few days,
she would probably compile a long lost of things she wished
were in that backpack. But at least she thought to bring her
treasured pen. Jane calculated close to a thousand dollars of
income per month if the tips at Kate's were steady. If she
rented a room, that would leave her six hundred dollars a
month, more or less, to buy new clothes and keep herself fed.
This seemed doable.

There was a light rapping on the open door. "You know,
Cleo," Evelyn said, standing there, curiously, just as her
mother had stood in the frame of her door at home on
Monday morning, "the rents around here are pretty steep. You
could stay here for a while if you need to. There's plenty of
room. You wouldn't be too far from work. I'm sure we could
work out a fair rental agreement. Perhaps I could trade the cost
of your room for some light housecleaning."

"Well, I was really looking for a place of my own but, if I
could stay here a few nights, that would be a big help."

"Sure. That would be fine. See what you can find. If you
need any help, just let me know."

"Thanks. I really appreciate this."

"You are most welcome, Cleo."

Earlier in the day, Jane had been so pleased with her new
name. Now, it made her feel cheap. She was lying to everyone.

They were all being so nice to her and she was paying them back with dishonesty. Jane told the Rev, "I'm happy to help keep the house clean but I have to pay you something for the nights I'm here. I have to." Jane was adamant. She would not be given something for nothing.

Evelyn assessed her new tenant's words and made her an offer. "How about ten dollars for the week? And do you do windows?"

Jane laughed and said, "Just call me the streak terminator. And let's make it twenty-five." She was accustomed to cleaning windows. In fact, she enjoyed cleaning windows. A crystal-clear view could be very satisfying, her father always said. Jane looked at the woman who had just offered her such generous terms. She liked her. In spite of her strangeness. And, at least in part, because of it. Evelyn nodded, saying, "Sounds good to me." Is she this nice to everyone, Jane wondered?

Setting her housing concerns aside, Jane looked up the personal ads. They always fascinated her. People looking for love. Romance. Fun. Sex. A way out of their own loneliness. Personals ranged from the ordinary to the wildly creative, from the mysterious to the straightforward. They were always entertaining. This evening, they made Jane wonder how Nadine had ever met her father. Nadine and her father were nothing alike. Nadine was outgoing, expressive, wildly creative. Her father was reserved, aloof, largely unimaginative. The idea of the two of them in bed together disgusted Jane.

How could her father have done this, not only to Nadine, but to her, to the whole family? The events of the day transported Jane beyond the mess but not out of the pain.

She set the alarm clock for 5:30 A.M. Took out her journal. After filling in a few details of the day—the train, the taxi, Kate, Bill, the Rev, the beach, the town, Sampson—she wrote:

> Helen, dear Helen.
>
> I'm so sorry to leave you to fend
> for yourself but understand.
>
> Please understand.
>
> I need you to understand.

On another page, she wrote:

> Fast train.
> Wrong stop.
> Right town.
> First job.
> Kind strangers.
> Cleansing wind.
> Purifying rain.
> Fresh start.

JANE HAD NEVER BEFORE, in any conscious manner, prayed. She knew, however, that her mother was an avid subscriber to the power of prayer. She had always thought it was a bunch of crap. Nothing more than wishful thinking. The same number of patients died with or without prayer. Her father needled her mother about religion all the time. God was a crutch, he said. People leaned on that crutch when they did not want to take responsibility for the messes they made. When she went to bed last night, when she left this morning, she agreed. Now however, as she considered the events of the last twelve hours, it did seem that someone was watching over her. Maybe her mother was right. Jane offered a simple thank you to an unknown God.

CHAPTER FOUR
Thursday / *Nadine*

NAUSEOUS AND DIZZY, AGITATED BY THOUGHTS of having the life cut out of her belly but anxious for it all to be over, Nadine met the dreaded morning. Sat up in bed. Perfectly still. Hoped the feeling would pass. Why is it, she wondered, that I did not feel sick at all before I knew? Aware of her pregnancy, she was now suffering all sorts of peculiar changes. The knowledge of her condition changed everything. Not only physical differences like the way her nipples felt against a dry towel after she showered, but psychological changes. Her vision itself was altered. The entire world looked different. Hopefully, the bodily unease would not last much longer. Her appointment was at eleven. Shortly after eleven, it would be done. No more baby. No more physical changes.

She looked out on still gray waters that wholly reflected the hue of the sky but for the way the sea seemed dipped in silver. This indistinct seascape made the brilliant greens of the trees and bushes and grasses pop out at her. The green of all things growing versus the gray that dappled Steve's head. Right from the beginning, she knew he was a mistake. She had not started out that night wanting to be pregnant. She had simply started out not wanting to be alone. Then, when she met Stephen, the idea of a fleeting affair with an older man felt provocatively daring. One night would be the end of it, she told herself. But before the night was over, they had promised to meet again. She swore to herself she would not go to him the next time. But she went. And she kept going, not as much for the sex as for the attention. She kept going because he made her feel so beautiful. So grown-up. She told Steve she was older because she felt that way when she was with him.

Nadine was aware, from the moment she met him, that Steve was married. That fact had never bothered her especially. It should have. But it had not. Steve told her his marriage had been "technically defunct" for years, that he "felt sorry for the aging woman." Those were his very words. Jesus, why did Steve have to be the one sitting at the bar? Why could it not have been some fat, smelly, thoroughly unattractive

man? The very thought of Stephen Quintal left her numb
with resentment and indignity. How could this man have lied
to her like this? Telling her he was sterile. "Embarrassingly
safe" was the exact term. Those two words kept coming back
at her, like an angry hornet that would not stop stinging.
Embarrassingly safe. God, he seemed harmless enough. And
she had trusted him absolutely. He appeared to be conscientious and loving and safe. So much for appearances. The
cheap motel rug that once seemed so sophisticated had been
pulled out from under her. What lay beneath it were the
rotten floorboards of his coldhearted deception and her
harrowing naiveté.

She remembered the night they first met in the bar of the
diner. The Captain's Folly. Well, it may have been his folly but
she was the one who had to cope with the consequences. On
that now unalterable Christmas Eve, while her mother and
father were completing separate last-minute shopping excur-
sions at the mall, Nadine sat in an overstuffed sofa feeling
insignificant and lonesome. When the nagging fear that she
was shrinking into the sofa grew frightening enough, she left
the house. Overwhelmed by the sadness and solitude of
another unfulfilling holiday season, she walked out of her
flawlessly decorated home. As she closed the front door,
Nadine looked back into the living room. Framed by
cathedral-ceiling windows, an eight-foot artificial tree stood
at one end. The ends of each perfectly proportioned branch

were tipped with something synthetic that looked remarkably like snow. It was covered with burgundy velvet bows and delicate Victorian-style ornaments. Impeccably beautiful but uninspiring.

For many years, as a child, Nadine begged for a real tree, an evergreen that would shed real needles and drink real water, only to be given the same "Don't be ridiculous, Nadine, this tree is perfect" response. After a while, she gave up on the request. She still dreamed, however, of the scent of fresh pine needles. She continued to imagine a tree covered with real ornaments. Mentally, she catalogued and hung all of the silly Christmas decorations she had made as a child. The beglittered star cut out of a paper plate. The clothespin reindeer. The elfin drum made out of a bobbin. These unworthy gifts remained in a neglected box somewhere in the attic. Not picture perfect enough for her mother's taste. Her mother was of two minds with regard to Nadine's artistic talents. She was phenomenally supportive of every idea, every project, every creative impulse. But the outcomes, the finished products, were not welcome on her walls. This had the effect of making Nadine feel encouraged but not appreciated.

SHE STROLLED AIMLESSLY AT FIRST. Passed the golf course where her father used to play. Once, when she was little, he brought her along. She got to ride in an electric cart with a white plastic canopy over the top. She remembered feeling like a princess that day. Like the most beloved child in the world. He was too old to play golf now. At least, that is what her father claimed. Nadine kept going. Walked by the deli where her family maintained a well-used account. Passed the house where the fleshy bleach-blonde hairdresser lived. The one with a shop on the first floor of her home that never seemed to have any customers. People in the neighborhood gossiped about her all the time.

Nadine made a right turn onto the shop-lined highway. When she saw The Captain's Folly up on the corner less than a block away, she thought of their wonderful pies. Last year as a junior at Alquot High, she made regular after-school trips there for strawberry cream and deep-dish apple. She shared thick spongy slices of lemon meringue with her friends. Or cheesecake. Sweet creamy cheesecake topped with huge glazed cherries. They had good lentil soup too. A big bowl of hot, savory lentil soup topped with sour cream might sit well on a cool December evening. Nadine was not especially hungry but her mental review of the menu drew her nearer the diner.

By the time she got there, however, she was thinking more of alcohol than of food. She was remembering how warming a Bloody Mary could be. Not having dressed properly for a two-mile walk, Nadine's legs were cold as freshly dug clams. She headed into the bar, not the least bit sheepishly. It was darker than the rest of the diner. The walls were paneled in faux walnut and hung with tacky nautical paintings. The bartender did not ask her for proof of age, only what she wanted. "How 'bout a Bloody Mary," she requested bravely, "with extra horseradish, please." The bartender, a pasty-faced young man with a prematurely rounded belly and slicked-back hair, dove into his calling, having lifted only the shadow of a glance at his beautiful but under-aged customer. That was the first time she saw Steve. A distinguished older gentleman. In fact, the only other person in the bar that night.

NADINE KNEW SHE SHOULD NOT have called him at home. Clearly, it was against the rules of the affair and, even in her sleepless, close-to-hysterical state, she knew there was a good chance someone else would answer. The phone call had likely made matters worse. But, honestly, she had no idea it was so early in the morning. When she called, time was the last thing on her mind. She had kept the news of her pregnancy to herself for three restless nights. She sat on it and sat on it and sat on it until she was ready to burst. She had to call him. She had to. "Damn him," she mumbled, "damn him, damn him, damn him." She tried to shake him from her mind. Free her head of the humiliating memories.

Nadine knew that, instead of allowing her mind to wander back into a veritable forest of regrets, she should be getting ready for school. She should at least show up today, if only for the first two classes, after which she would leave for her "doctor's appointment." That would be the truth. But she could not imagine being there today. She felt so far removed from the infantile world of her friends' petty conflicts and idiotic comments. And she was more nervous about the abortion than she could possibly admit to herself. Now that she had confronted Stephen and pushed him out of her life, she was determined to pull herself together. To get back on her feet. To get through these last few weeks of high school. But she could not go today. She did not want to be in school this morning at all. Someone might see through her. One of her friends.

They were already suspicious. Little by little, Nadine had grown apart from her closest friends. It was not just the lies that stood between them, although she had to admit to herself, she had told many. Her fabrications had hardened into a wall, a barrier that could not be crossed from either side. There was the tale about the lesbian lover. It felt more acceptable to make up stories about a lesbian companion than to tell the truth about having sex with a man old enough to be her father. There was the fib she told about being accepted into the Rhode Island School of Design but deferring admittance. Then there was the secret she could tell no one. The terrible secret about her pregnancy. Nadine's friend Cassie had made the mistake of confiding in others. Suddenly everyone was talking about Cassie's pregnancy. Everyone seemed to know the details of her abortion. Nadine did not want that to happen to her.

Beyond the lies and secrets, Nadine wondered how much she now held in common with her friends. What did she share with them anymore? Everything had changed. In the space of a few months, she had traveled thousands of miles and there was no way to get back to where this had all started. She would have to go back in time to Christmas Eve. She would have to sit home alone staring at that phony Christmas tree all over again. It was simply not possible to get there. Last year, at this time, she believed she could depend on her friends for anything she needed. Now, there was no one she trusted with the circumstances of her life. The one person who knew what was happening and could be trusted to maintain the confidence had run off. Jane Quintal was gone.

At school yesterday, she felt like an alien. Like she was in someone else's world. She listened to her teachers through a fog of disparate thoughts. Where her attention should have been on Arthur Miller, it drifted to the way in which she was so easily deceived by Stephen Quintal. When gene-splicing demanded her attention, she was drawn into imaginative but unwelcome glimpses of the baby in her belly. The clay pitcher she created in pottery class took a rounder, fuller form than originally planned. The entire school day was transformed from the inside out by her new-fashioned circumstances. She could not bring herself to go back to school today. Not even for the first two classes.

However the next hour unfolded, Nadine needed to leave the house. It was essential that her parents assume an ordinary day. It was important for them to think she was going to school. If it were any other day of the week, she could pretend to be sick and that would almost be the truth. But she had already played that card once this week. And today was Thursday. Cleaning day. She could not be home when the housekeeper arrived. The housekeeper had a big loose mouth. One time that treacherous woman found a pack of cigarettes in Nadine's room and went straight to her mother with them. Nadine could not stand her. She shuddered at the thought of being discovered in bed watching television by the housekeeper. No. She would have to force herself to get out of bed. Shower. Dress. Leave her room. Leave the house. What was, only last week, involuntary routine had become a challenge. It would be so much easier to stay right here feeling sick to her stomach in the comfort of her lovely room. But she had to get up.

Nadine's room was spacious. She had decorated it herself last year. It was hand-stenciled with wild dark red roses trellising the windows and doors. There was a queen-sized canopy bed, covered with yards and yards of striped sage green and white chintz. The same fabric was used to create valances over the two large windows that overlooked the bay. She had a large walk-in closet that could have been a small boutique. The closet led to a bathroom equipped with a whirlpool bathtub and separate standing shower. A beautiful white desk with brass fittings stood near the door to her room. On it sat an unusual phone in which the keypad was embedded into a colorful artist's palette. This phone serviced her own private line. Opposite her bed stood a white entertainment center that was outfitted with a television, a personal computer, a stereo system, and shelf upon shelf of movies. Nadine loved watching movies. In fact, it was what she most felt like doing right now.

Compelling herself to push back both the nausea and the desire to remain under the covers, Nadine swung her legs around to the side of the bed. Cautiously stood up. Graham cracker. If she nibbled on a graham cracker, that might help. It worked yesterday. Without changing her short burgundy silk slip of a nightie, she ambled into the kitchen. It smelled of coffee and toasted bagels. Her parents were sitting at the dining room table just beyond the countertop bar. Father's hands wrapped around a large coffee mug. Mother's fingers tapping the rim of an empty juice glass. Crumbs resting on two small pale-yellow plates. Digested newspaper refolded on the floor. "Good morning," she addressed them and went into the dining room to give them each a kiss on the cheek. Normal morning protocol in the Aiuto household. Nonchalantly, so as to convince her parents that graham crackers were as common a breakfast choice as corn flakes, she went back into the kitchen. Reached up into a high cabinet where boxes were stored. As if removing a book from a library shelf.

"You okay, dear?" her mother asked.

"Sure. Upset stomach, that's all. I think I had too much to eat last night."

"You can't make it through the morning on graham crackers. At least have some orange juice."

"I'll have some before I leave."

"You sure you're okay, Nadine?" her father asked.

They seemed to know something was wrong. But how could they? Without thinking, she looked down. Her stomach was still flat as a board. She struggled to maintain her fragile composure as her parents looked on.

"I'm fine." As they continued to stare at her with too much concern in their eyes, she added, "Really." She would be fine. Everything would return to normal. Today. This morning. Her stomach flinched at the thought of what the day held but, hopefully, at the end of it, she could begin again.

"Are you okay?" she turned the question around.

Her mother shared the unexpected answer. "Do you remember your father's friend, Alex Dolby?" When she did not appear to recall the man, her mother continued, "His house is over on Crescent? He used to get your father to help with the fruit sale at the Catholic Church?"

She remembered him. "The guy who carried lollipops around with him?"

"Uh-huh."

"He died yesterday," her father spoke glumly. He was clearly very upset. Picking the newspaper off the floor, he opened it up to a particular page. Folded it flat. Pointing to an article, he handed the paper to Nadine.

"Oh, my God," Nadine said as she read about a drunk driver hitting Mr. Dolby's car. When Jane called her Tuesday night, she told him all about Steve's accident. Jane had explained that the police thought he was drunk. The article did not mention Steve by name but it sounded a whole lot like the accident Jane had described. If so, Steve was ruining lives left and right. The whole situation was out of control. She needed to do her part to get it back under control. To establish at least a semblance of normalcy again. "I'm sorry, Dad." She dropped the newspaper on the table. Wrapped her arms around her father's neck from behind. Gave him a squeeze. Her father could never know she had anything to do with the man responsible for Mr. Dolby's death. Hastily, she left with the box of crackers. Retreated from her parents. Hoped her mother would not follow. Back in the refuge of her room, Nadine ate two of the grainy squares. They did seem to help a bit.

Flustered by the insult now added to injury, she threw herself into getting out of the house. Quickly, she put on a pair of formfitting jeans. Threw on a scoop-necked burgundy top. Added the gold necklace from which a so-called "lucky" crystal dangled. Looked in the full-length mirror. If anything, she'd lost a few pounds in these early weeks of pregnancy. She did look different and it was not simply a matter of weight. Unluckily, her parents seemed to have noticed. The sooner she could get back to the way things were before Steve entered her life, the better everyone would be. She unzipped her backpack. Added a small sketchbook and set of charcoal pencils. Staring at herself in the mirror again, she brushed her short hair back and was generally pleased by what she saw. Stopped in the kitchen. Said, "I'm running late. See you later," as her parents sat nearly motionless at the breakfast table. Grabbed an apple from a fruit bowl that had been arranged so carefully it would have been suitable for a Cézanne still life. Again, gave each of her parents a kiss. Pretended to leave for school. Her mother called after her, "Don't you want anything else to eat, Princess?" Nadine smiled weakly, held up the apple, and walked out the door. It was after seven.

She stuffed the apple into her backpack and meandered through the neighborhood, taking streets her parents would have no reason to travel when they left for their respective days. She passed dozens of familiar houses. The homes of neighbors. The homes of childhood friends. She passed by Crescent Circle where the Dolby house stood, but she did not turn in. She had met him only a few times but she remembered his face. She remembered his lollipops. One minute he was alive. The next minute he was dead. The same would soon be true of the life she carried but she could not dwell on that shocking fact. She could not afford to dwell on it.

As she continued walking in the direction of the canals that bordered the west end of her part of town, she wondered again what she was going to do with the rest of her life. Nadine had no immediate plans for college. She was somewhat envious of those students who were all set to go, not because of the education they would receive but because they appeared to have so much direction in their lives. Nadine's parents took her on an obligatory college search, but both they and Nadine knew she was not ready. Not especially interested. She hoped that, at least on a temporary basis, she could find an interesting job and live at home until she had a better idea of what the future might hold for her. Perhaps flower arranging. Something artistic that also produced a livable income. Someday, she might be focused enough to pursue a college education. Although she hated to acknowledge it, her affair with Stephen Quintal had dampened her interest in going away to school. Stephen had no idea what a thief he was.

At the dead end of a short street, a large rectangle of lush sod edged a canal. Nadine sat down in the damp grass. Took out her sketchpad and a soft charcoal pencil. Started to outline a small sailboat that appeared to be standing at attention. This did not hold her interest for very long, however. She flipped the page and looked around for something else to draw, but nothing spoke to her immediate artistic compulsion. She closed the pad, deciding to walk on until she located a subject interesting enough to merit a page of the splendid drawing paper. Just as she was about to stand up again and move on, along the far side of the canal she caught sight of a mahogany-brown mother duck fastidiously followed by six very young and enthusiastic golden ducklings. She knew they would not sit still for her. They cooperated by not traveling very far from where Nadine sat. Lovingly, with soft downy charcoal lines, she depicted the feathered family. At one point, the proud mother waddled out of the water. Waited patiently for her babies to figure out how to get out by themselves. One after another, they jumped and kicked until they were all on land again. They looked very funny marching in formation along the edge of the canal. Ducks are not made to walk, Nadine thought. They look elegant in the water and exquisite in the air. But on land, their short legs waddle clumsily. As if the mother duck had overheard Nadine's unspoken assessment, she jumped back into the canal and, after some predictable hesitation on the part of the little ducklings, one followed another in jumping to the watery side of their watchful mother.

WITH MORE THAN TWO HOURS TO WAIT until she could get "this problem taken care of," Nadine closed the captured birds in her drawing pad. Ate the apple. Threw the core in the canal and watched it sink. Started walking to the big new bookstore in town. She was anxious and hungry. She needed something else to eat before the nausea returned. The diner was not far but she never wanted to set foot in that place again. Never wanted to see Tuesday evening's waitress again. Or, for that matter, the careless bartender who would have done her a favor if he had checked for ID that night.

The memory of Steve sitting at the table there the other night, as if he were the king of her life, rose to the top of her mind like the full head of a freshly poured beer. When she first walked into the diner Tuesday evening, she could see, all the way across the room, that the knuckles of his left fist were pressed up against his closed mouth. Before she could say a word, Steve blurted, "Nadine, we have to have this problem taken care of. Immediately. I've contacted a doctor who will see you this week. Sit down." The callousness of his words was appalling. Nadine was proud of the way she held her shock in check, banishing her fear long enough to do what she had to do. He spoke to her that night as if he could not even see her standing there. As if her feelings fell outside the realm of his expediency. She recalled looking into those steely blue eyes, eyes that did not return her gaze, and feeling confirmed in her decision to end the disastrous affair with this cruel man. She was amazed to find that she was not even angry with him as she stared into those empty eyes, pools that would never be deep enough. She was not full of anger. She was full of pity. She pitied this wintry man. She pitied his poor "aging

woman." Nadine had been stupid but she would rise above
the insulting mess. She would. She did not need this selfish,
horrible man. And she did not need whatever food they had to
offer in a diner that had a growing menu of difficult
memories.

NADINE RAN THE CHANCE OF RUNNING INTO one of her
mother's friends at the bookstore. It was just the sort of place
where women like her mother meet to chat about their
unsuccessful diets, shopping victories, and occasionally a good
book. However, one of the bookstore's giant pistachio biscotti
with an aromatic cup of chai tea would make it worth the risk.
If she were spotted playing hooky, she could easily explain that
seniors had special privileges and were permitted to leave
during their study halls. That would be true. She wanted so
much to crawl out from under the lies and reclaim whatever
truth was left in her life.

Before sitting down, Nadine called the school to let them
know she was still sick. She found a stimulating coffee-table
book filled with Mary Cassatts. Beautiful children nestled in
their mothers' laps. Exquisite women setting off soft, flowing
landscapes. She took it to a small, white Formica table.
Ordered her biscotti and tea. Then she waited. The minutes
passed far too slowly. Even with Mary Cassatt for company.
Nadine wanted desperately to be on the other side of the
abortion. She wished she had been able to get an earlier

appointment. After a while, she wished she had not consumed two cups of the milky chai. She felt sick again.

Nadine, for all her blustering independence, did not want to be all by herself today. She had known, from the time the test results turned out positive, that she did not want to go through this alone. It was nice of Jane to call and let her know she was running away but it would have been so much better had she hung around another day or two and followed through on her offer to help. Impatiently, Nadine watched a polished regulator clock on the wall until both hands were aimed at the curly, gold-embossed 10. At which point she called a taxi that arrived with incredible speed. As if it had been sitting right behind the bookstore just waiting for someone to call. After a densely slow morning, everything started to fast-forward. She was not sure she was ready for this. Her heart raced. She breathed through her mouth to keep up with its unmanageable pounding. The ten-minute taxi ride was filled with unspoken questions. How much would this procedure hurt? How much bleeding might there be? How long would she have to stay there? Could anything go wrong? Who would she call if something did go wrong? Nadine found herself swallowing air. Tried to stop but could not. With a great knot in her chest, she asked to be let out two blocks from the clinic. She did not want the driver to see where she was going and she waited until he was safely out of sight before beginning the last leg of the trip. She knew this was unreasonably paranoid behavior, but she felt as if she were being watched.

Nadine was early for her appointment and took her time, donning sunglasses and circling the clinic twice before braving its front door. It was like removing a Band-Aid. Better to rip it off all at once. She took a deep breath. Marched up the concrete sidewalk. Pulled open the door. Released the air in her lungs. Let the receptionist know she had arrived. Quietly collapsed into a black leather chair. The knot in her chest was still tight. As if someone had tied a tourniquet around her heart. Defensively, she scoped out the territory. Listened for sounds of pain. Heard none. Looked for signs of peril. Saw none. Struggled to relax.

This was a very plush office. There were six other people in the room. An older woman with straight blond hair swept up into an elegant French knot. A girl who looked quite young sitting with a pimply-faced, stringy-haired kid, presumably her boyfriend. Two young, fashionably dressed African-American women who might, Nadine thought, be sisters. And directly across from Nadine, in an identical leather chair, a short thin woman with dramatic rings beneath her dark eyes. She looked much too old to be pregnant. Old enough to be a grandmother. Nadine sat back. Closed her eyes. Wished the whole nightmare were over already.

Without any encouragement whatsoever from Nadine, the woman with the dark eyes leaned forward. She spoke with an Hispanic accent, asking, "Have you done this before?" The question seemed so strange to Nadine. Have you done this before? As if she were being asked about a bikini wax.

"No."

"This is also the first time for me."

Nadine was not prepared to chat with a total stranger. Especially about such an intensely personal matter.

"My mother tells me God is going to punish me." She pulled at a tiny gold crucifix that hung from her neck. "I am a religious woman, but I can't have this baby."

Nadine was appalled. Whatever the woman believed or did not believe, it was none of her business. She nodded weakly. Looked away.

"I have seven children already. My husband left last week when I told him I was pregnant again. I don't know if I can feed the kids I have now. God will have to forgive me if I don't have this baby."

Nadine was, apparently, completely ineffective at pretending she was not listening. "My mother does not understand," the woman continued. "You do what you have to do. Right?"

Nadine was glad when the receptionist called the name Ana and the troubled woman left. Without being aware of it, Nadine shook her head. Like an old woman with Parkinson's disease, Nadine could not stop shaking her head. She picked up a magazine and skimmed an article about a woman who lost 150 pounds on a diet of spinach and carrot juice. Tried to control her quivering. She could not believe she was sitting in an abortion clinic reading such an article. She felt as if she had been transported into someone else's life. All of this must be happening to someone else. It could not be happening to her. She was not here. Her head continued to wobble from side to side as if she had no control over it.

Twenty-five long minutes passed before her own name was called. A trim woman with short black hair wearing a crisp calf-length navy blue suit invited her into a small office. "My name is Susan," she said. "I am here to explain the procedure to you and to ask you some questions. And if you have any questions, please feel free to ask me. Okay?" Nadine nodded. Susan's voice was unhurried. Almost too peaceful. As if she were on drugs or had just come from her daily meditation class. When she spoke, she looked directly at Nadine, which was, at the same time, both disconcerting and comforting. Nadine wondered how many women had listened to the same speech. How many times in a week did Susan offer it?

Susan took out a spiral-bound book full of simple line drawings that illustrated the procedure. She would be given an intravenous sedative. The drug would relax her. Perhaps even put her to sleep. They would numb her cervix so that it would not hurt. They would suction out the fetus. She would rest here in the clinic for an hour or so after it was over. Then she could go home. She would be given antibiotics to prevent possible infection. There would be some bleeding for several days. If she had severe pain or developed a fever during the next few days, she should call back and the doctor would see her again. None of this information surprised Nadine but, shortly after the instruction started, she crossed her legs tightly and found her arms folded over her belly.

The woman started asking questions. At first, it was the usual assortment of health status questions but then she headed in a distinctly more private direction. How do you feel about this procedure? Have you given this decision enough thought? Have you considered other alternatives? Have you discussed this with your parents? With the father? Nadine tried to sound absolutely convinced of her answers but she was, in fact, no longer certain. The longer she sat there, the less sure she became. No one was forcing her to do this. She had little more than a month of school to go. Surely the pregnancy would not become obvious until much later in the summer. As much as Nadine longed for the ordeal to be over and done with, she was not sure she could go through with this remedy.

When Susan finished her well-rehearsed monologue and question sequence, Nadine excused herself to go to the bathroom. Then she bolted straight for the door. Headed down the street in a different direction. Stopped. Looked back. Put her hands on her belly. What had she just done? What would she do now? Where would she go? How would she live? Her parents would never put up with a baby. Could she possibly support a baby? Needing desperately to sit down, to regroup her thoughts, she stumbled into a hole-in-the-wall coffee shop. The walls were covered with posters. Bumper stickers. Business cards. Paper napkin art. Ten kinds of coffee were on the menu along with a simple offering of vegetarian selections. A waitress with winged glasses wearing a loose-fitting burnt orange tunic took her order. Bread. Just plain bread. And a glass of water. And another taxi.

NADINE NEEDED SOMEONE TO TALK TO. Someone to listen and help her figure out what she had just done. Was it a decision? Was it simply the postponement of a decision? Talking to Jane was helpful, not only because she was an interested listener but also because she had reasons of her own to be discreet. If only Jane were still around. Nadine had already determined that the rest of her friends probably could not give her what she needed. They would offer a measure of support but it would be accompanied by crude shock and blabber mouthing. She needed acceptance. Confidentiality. Who could give her that? She asked the second taxi to drop her off in the middle of town. She could not go home. The nosy housekeeper would still be there. Who could she trust? Standing in the middle of the sidewalk, a recognizable rooftop caught her eye. It was the top of the synagogue, a white brick building with sky blue stained-glass windows, peeking out from behind a row of little stores. She crossed the street, the sacred rooftop drawing her like a magnet.

While the architectural profile of the synagogue had always been a part of Nadine's surroundings, its insides were altogether unfamiliar to her. Her mother was Jewish but diligently avoided the religious part of her identity. She had been to several Bar Mitzvah celebrations but had never attended an actual ceremony. To open the door of the synagogue, therefore, was a big deal. There was something enigmatic and a little frightening about this place. In Nadine's accomplished imagination, this was where God lived. This was God's house. Softly, not wanting to be heard by whoever might be inside this handsome and mysterious building, she opened the right side of large double doors. Stood still. Sheepishly tiptoed in. Quietly looked around.

On the wall directly in front of her, she saw a large and very colorful framed painting of a family celebration. Eight people, two of them children, sat around a table. Each held a raised wine glass. The table was covered with food and the look on each person's face announced the joy of the occasion. The top of the painting displayed the head of the table, where a very old man sat. He appeared to be saying something. The viewer was drawn into the empty seat near the bottom of the painting, so that, as Nadine stood there looking at it, she could easily picture herself sitting there with these happy people. As she looked deeper into the painting, she was startled by human footsteps. A short older man wearing a white shirt and dark red sweater approached Nadine. He appeared to be about the age of her father. Shorter. Rounder. With far more life in his eyes than she had ever seen in her father's. He held out his hand and, clasping hers, introduced himself.

"Hello. I'm Rabbi Weil. You like this painting?"

"Yes. I do." She withdrew her hand. Not knowing quite what to say, she looked back at the painting. She felt embarrassed. Wanted to run back through the double doors. Why had she come here anyway?

"It's called *Toast to Freedom*," the rabbi explained. "It was painted by an East German Jew whose brother was shot trying to scale the Berlin Wall."

"But they all look so happy." She managed a reply.

"Yes."

The rabbi did not add to her comment. He gave Nadine room to contemplate for herself the meaning of the painting. After a moment of silence, he said, "You're welcome to look around. If you need any help, just let me know. I'll be in my office." He pointed down a hallway and started to walk away.

"Wait," Nadine stopped him.

He must have heard the upheaval in her voice. He turned around to face her again, offering an unmistakable look of deep concern.

"Rabbi, do you have a minute?" She needed help desperately and he had offered.

"I might even have two or three minutes," he answered with a gentle smile. "How can I help you? Miss?"

"Nadine. It's Nadine. Rabbi, I have a problem."

"Why don't you come into my office, Nadine, and we can talk about it."

Silently, she followed him down the hall. Their shoes made clapping sounds on the beautiful blue and white tiled floor. Nadine was apprehensive. She felt queasy again. Only the depth of her confusion gave her the courage to step into the stranger's office. He motioned her to have a seat. The rabbi sat behind his desk.

He left the door to his office open, which made Nadine feel a little more comfortable sitting down. A picture of the rabbi with his family, a wife and two sons, sat in a silver frame on his desk. Nadine was not expecting the rabbi to be so human. On the walls, she noticed several certificates. And another painting. This one offered two dark impressions, which could only represent an emaciated woman holding the hand of a sickly child. It held a feeling opposite that of the other painting. This one clearly spoke of suffering. Of a particular kind of hopelessness.

"How can I help you?"

"It's complicated. I'm not sure where to start."

"Start anywhere. What comes to mind first?"

She took a concentrated breath and boldly confessed, "I'm pregnant." She looked carefully into his face to see how he would react to this information. She saw worry in his eyes but did not find any condemnation in his kind face.

"I see. And how do you feel about that?"

"I don't know. I thought I wanted to get rid of it."

"But?"

"But now I don't know what to do." Her furrowed forehead revealed her bewilderment. If she had stayed at the clinic, it would be all over by now. Instead, she was sitting here.

"What happened to change your mind?

"I don't know. I was supposed to have an abortion this morning but I walked out."

"And?"

"And I ended up here."

"Interesting. What do you think that means?"

Nadine pulled at the back of her hair nervously.

"Maybe it means I want to have this baby?" Her question was weighted with uncertainty. For the first time, she allowed herself to say, "I want to have this baby." As terrifying as those words were, it was a relief to have uttered them, to have spoken what she had not permitted herself to think.

"How could you possibly have a baby?"

"Exactly."

"A child is a very big responsibility." It was uncanny. He seemed to be able to read her mind.

"And your parents probably wouldn't be too happy about it either." She nodded in amazement. Truly, he must be reading her thoughts.

They sat in concentrated silence until Rabbi Weil asked, "What would you do if your parents were not a consideration?" When she did not answer, he said, "Let me put it a different way. If you could do anything you want without anyone judging you for it, what would you do?"

"I think I might have this baby."

"And what do think life would be like if you did have this baby?"

"What do you mean?"

"When you imagine having this baby, what do you imagine?"

"I haven't imagined it. I've been afraid to imagine it. But I know I would love her. And I would pay attention to her. And when she gets older and wants to talk, I would listen to her."

"Nadine, do you want someone to love you and pay attention to you and listen to you?"

She did not answer. Instead she looked over at the open door. She stared at the door and changed the subject. "I'm only half-Jewish, you know. My father's Catholic."

"And?"

"And what do you think of that?"

"Does that change anything?"

"You tell me."

The rabbi's eyes seemed to condense, as if the inside of him were traveling somewhere. He took a deep breath and said, "Let me tell you a story." Rabbi Weil leaned back in his chair and began.

"A long time ago, there was a boy whose parents loved him very much. But he didn't know how much they loved him because they forgot to tell him and because, at the time, he was not listening very well. He was not that much younger than you, Nadine. The boy tried very hard to make his parents love him but they did not seem to notice his efforts. He did very well in school, for instance, but his parents did not appear to care. He was a pretty good catcher on the baseball team but his parents did not always come to his games. He tried to be helpful around the house but he thought his parents took his helpfulness for granted. They always seemed to think he could be doing more.

"One day, the boy made a terrible mistake. He was angry with his parents and wanted to do something to hurt them. Now, his parents had a prized possession, a beautiful crystal bowl that held a place of honor in their home. When visitors came to their home, they often admired the lovely bowl. His mother washed and polished the bowl every week so that it sparkled by sunlight or by candlelight. On this particular day, the boy's parents were not home and he was mad that they were not home. So he took that beautiful crystal bowl and dropped it on the floor. It broke into a thousand pieces. When the boy saw the shattered bowl, he was immediately sorry for what he had done. But the bowl could not be put back together again and he knew his parents would never forgive him for what he had done."

"So what did he do?" Nadine asked, sitting up on the edge of her chair.

"He ran away."

"Where did he go?"

"He did not go very far. Only as far as his best friend's house."

"Then what happened?"

"Well, the boy called his parents and told them that he was sorry about what he had done. Then he told them he was never coming home again so they didn't have to worry about him doing anything stupid ever again."

"And he never went home again?"

"Oh, but he did go home. His parents came and got him. But an incredible thing happened."

"What? What happened?"

"They did not scream at him, as he had believed they would. They did not scold him. They were not angry with him. Or, if they were, they didn't show it. They cried a little but they did not yell. They told him the bowl meant almost nothing to them. They told him the worst thing that could happen to them would be to lose their son."

"So he went home?"

"Not only did he go home but he went home knowing how much his parents really did love him."

"So, what are you saying?"

"What do you think?"

"I think you don't know my parents. My parents would not be so understanding."

He nodded and said, "I don't know them, Nadine. That's true. But sometimes we don't know our parents as well as we think we do."

"Maybe." Nadine was convinced that, if she told her parents she was pregnant, her mother would enter into a screaming match like she sometimes did when she thought someone was trying to take advantage of her. Such as the phone company. Her mother was the queen of not letting anybody pull anything over on her. Her father, on the other hand, would simply have a heart attack. When he found out she was pregnant, he would keel over and die. Of this, Nadine was certain.

"Thanks for listening, Rabbi."

"You're welcome, Nadine."

She stood up to leave and started for the open door but then turned back and asked, "Were you the boy in that story?"

"Maybe," he echoed her earlier response. "And, by the way," he continued, "you may be half-Jewish and half-Catholic, but in God's eyes, there is no such thing as half a human being." She almost smiled.

On the long walk home, Nadine pondered questions that would be interesting to discuss with this remarkable man. What would he think of the woman at the clinic? The one whose husband left her? Would God really punish that woman for not having an eighth baby? Did he believe that?

Nadine guessed not. She appreciated the fact that the rabbi did not seem to judge her. He did not tell her what to do. He did not make her feel stupid or ashamed. She thought about the story he told. That boy in the story must have been him. The kind, forgiving parents must have been his. Emotionally, she felt uplifted by the rabbi, but physically, she was entirely depleted. Home again, late enough that the housekeeper was long gone; she made herself a glass of chocolate milk. Yesterday, she might have had a can of her father's beer but today, she felt like having chocolate milk. She watched the dark brown syrup swirl its way into the cold milk as she stirred it. Said "Cheers" to the empty house and drank it down to the bottom of the glass.

Nadine picked up a pencil and pad of paper that resided on the counter below the kitchen telephone and took them with her out onto the deck. The sky was cloudy, as it had been all week, but out back, the bay was still tranquil and soothing. Nadine slid into a deckchair. Stared at the moorings that sat on the still water like plastic play beads on a mirror. She scratched a list of her problems onto the pad of paper and tried to list potential solutions to each:

PROBLEM	SOLUTION
Having a Baby	Make appointment with Doctor
Telling Parents	???
Finding Support	Rabbi Weil

Nadine stared down at the inadequate list. Her heart wrestled with relief, confusion, fear, regret, exhaustion. What a day it had been. And it was not yet over. She tried to keep her tired eyes open. Her lids kept falling, however, and soon, she slid into the sanctuary of sleep. Into a place where anything is possible.

Tiny drops of rain gathering on her face woke Nadine some time later. She had been dreaming but could not remember about what. Was there a crystal bowl in the dream? She moved inside. Out of the gentle rain. Used a paper towel to blot her damp face and arms. Looking at the clock, Nadine saw that it was already after five. Her mother would be home any time now.

As if her thoughts had summoned reality, Nadine heard her mother fumbling with the keys at the front door. She opened the door for her. When Leslie Aiuto walked into the house, she exuded energy. Like an over-aged cheerleader. "Hi, Princess. How are you?" she asked buoyantly. Without pausing for an answer, Leslie said, "I just came from the club. Had a great workout! They finally got the hot tub fixed. You should really come over and give it a try. It is so relaxing." She gave her daughter the habitual peck on the cheek. "Did you make any progress on your project, Princess?" Nadine thought to herself, project—what project? Her senior project clicked into remembrance. "Yeah. I made some progress. A little." "Can't wait to see it," her mother offered optimistically.

She had, in fact, done very little work on it. All seniors were required to complete an assignment that, in some way, helped them to understand themselves better. While some seniors wrote papers, others created projects. Hers was to be an art portfolio of self-portraits undertaken in a variety of media. The charcoal portrait, the most realistic piece so far, was finally finished. It stood in a brown cardboard portfolio sandwiched between a watercolor and a collage. Three more portraits would have to be completed within the next two weeks. She should really be applying herself to it at this point. But her motivation to finish all of that seemed to sit on another planet right now. It was inaccessible.

Nadine followed her mother into the kitchen. Watched her pour organic cranberry juice into a crystal Baccarat wine glass. Braved a question. "Mom, did you ever get in trouble when you were a kid?" Her mother ran her fingers through her hair. Looked at Nadine curiously. There was a very uncomfortable pause before she added her own "Maybe" to the other significant "Maybes" of the day. Her mother turned, looked her straight in the face and asked, "Why? You in some sort of trouble?" How could she ever tell her mother what had happened without becoming the target of her notorious temper? It would be like trying to convince a swarm of angry bees not to sting. Nadine answered, "No. A friend of mine. It's nothing." She escaped into the bathroom. It occurred to her that, lately, she was having to pee a great deal.

When she came back into the kitchen, her mother was gone. Nadine found her sitting in the living room with her right ankle crossed over her left leg. Staring at a tiny little mole on the inside of her right calf. "I think I should have this removed," she said, "What do you think?" Nadine knew this to be a rhetorical question. By tomorrow, her mother would have an appointment to have the offending mole removed. Between the skin peels, the manicures, the electrolysis, the personal trainer, and the tanning salon, it sometimes seemed to Nadine that her mother's greatest goal in life was flawlessness.

Leslie Aiuto was, in fact, the picture of health and beauty. She taught aerobic dancing at a fitness club. Her physical condition was a full-time job. There was not an ounce of unnecessary fat on her trim body. From the back, she looked much younger than her forty-one years but when she turned around, it was obvious that too much sun had added a few years to her face. Her hair was dark and full, loosely permed in a shoulder-length layered cut. Her face was always made up tastefully. In fact, everything Leslie Aiuto did was tasteful. The living room in which she was now sitting with her daughter, for instance, was magnificent in its simplicity. It was decorated entirely in shades of beige and white. The walls were ecru with white trim. The four matching chairs were tan and the two matching couches were upholstered with a tapestry print in light browns with delicate white rose bouquets scattered throughout. The rug was nubby white wool. Leslie had it cleaned frequently. Rarely did she clean anything herself.

"This is delicious," she said, "Would you like some?"

"No thank you," replied Nadine, her stomach turning at the thought of the tart cranberry taste.

She asked Nadine if she would like to have Thai takeout for dinner. Nadine shrugged, cloaking her unsettled stomach with indifference. Then Leslie asked about going out to dinner at the new seafood restaurant. Another blasé shrug. Nadine observed her mother's dark deep-set eyes light up as she tried a third time. "How 'bout the mall? We can eat in the food court. Just the two of us, Princess. We'll leave a note for your father and bring something home for him to eat later. What do you think?" Nadine rarely turned down a trip to the mall and she did not turn this one down either. Going to the mall was like enfolding herself in a security blanket. There was always some comfort to be had from the experience, however short-lived that comfort might be. The mall would also provide plenty of distraction. And distraction could only help this evening.

The mall was only a fifteen-minute drive from home. Although they hit the food court on the early side, it was already packed with industrious grazers. Leslie ordered a shrimp taco salad with spring water. This she followed with a frozen peach yogurt parfait. Nadine ordered a broiled chicken sandwich with melted Swiss cheese and an extra large root beer. She finished her meal with a bag full of tiny, warm chocolate chip cookies. It did not make sense, but the food mitigated the queasiness. Reenergized, they proceeded to stalk the shops, trying on lots of clothes. Her mother bought a red Egyptian cotton blouse with Chinese knots for buttons. She insisted Nadine "find something." Without too much looking, Nadine settled on a little black skirt. Even though she already had two. At least two. And even though it might not fit for long.

The number of babies in the mall amazed Nadine. Everywhere she looked, some adorable little bundle was being wheeled around in a state-of-the-art stroller. Most of the babies were relatively hairless but she noticed one with straight dark hair that stuck up every which way like a baby punk rocker. She was awed by these little creatures. By the very process through which they made their way into the world. She hoped her mother would not catch her staring. She wanted to stop for a closer look at these tiny new persons but did not dare. A year from now, will that be me, Nadine wondered? Wheeling a baby around the bright open spaces of the mall?

Before they left, Leslie called the Thai restaurant, ordered her husband's favorite, lemon grass scallops, and picked them up on the way home. As they pulled into the driveway, her mother asked again, "Are you in some sort of trouble, Nadine?"

"Nothing I can't handle, Mom," she replied, extricating herself from the car and from the importunate question.

Predictably, her father was sitting in his study. Drinking a dark heady beer from a tall pilsner glass. Reading the newspaper. Both Leslie and Nadine greeted him with a kiss on the cheek. Leslie produced the pungent-smelling brown paper bag and told her husband that dinner would be ready in less than a minute. He gestured loosely with his left hand. The hand suggested "okay" and "go away" at the same time. There was nothing mean-spirited in this act. Her father was a proud newspaper addict and his evening time with the paper was especially sacrosanct. The telephone started ringing in Nadine's room. Her father said, "Oh yeah, somebody named Helen called for you, Nadine. She said she'd call back. I gave her your number. I hope that's okay with you. This might be her now."

"Helen?" Nadine asked curiously and ran off to her room. She grabbed the phone, thinking, "Helen who?" and "What now?"

"Hello?" Her greeting was guarded.

"Hi. Is this Nadine?"

"Uh-huh."

"This is Helen Quintal. You don't know me but . . . "

"You must be Jane's sister." Nadine's tone was neither friendly nor hostile.

"Yeah. I was just wondering. Have you heard from her? Do you know where she went or anything?" Nadine sensed antagonism in the girl's young voice.

"Sorry. I have no idea."

"She didn't tell you anything?"

"Nope. Sorry."

"Would you do me a favor?"

"What's that?"

"If you hear from Jane, would you let me know?"

"Yeah, sure."

The phone call left Nadine questioning what kind of father Stephen Quintal was. Nadine thought of the ever-present business planner and speculated that he must view his children as little boxes or dates and times. Or lines on a page. Then she turned on all the lights in her mind, realizing that he had treated her in precisely the same manner. She mistook his regularity for faithfulness, his punctuality for respect. She was nothing more than the cryptic initials N.A., on the Monday and Wednesday pages between 3:30 P.M. and 5:00 P.M. Again, she felt stupid. So stupid.

A life-sized shadow of personal humiliation had been her nagging companion since Friday. The day she went to the pharmacy and bought the telltale pregnancy kit. She ran from the school to the pharmacy to ensure that no one else from school would be there yet. Much to her relief, the only customer was an old woman who seemed to be looking for a birthday card. The cashier did not blink twice as she paid for the formidable little test kit that would tell her fortune. In the privacy of her own bathroom, the kit confirmed Nadine's worst fears.

For weeks, Nadine had known something was wrong. She had not been able to bring herself, however, to consider the possibility of pregnancy because of Steve's self-professed sterility. She remembered this particular conversation in detail. She remembered feeling sorry for Steve because he would never get the little baby boy he seemed to want so badly. She could not imagine him lying to her about something so important. Something that held such obvious potential to ruin her life. How could he have done such a thing? How could he have done it to her? And how could she have trusted him so absolutely?

NADINE TOOK A LONG SHOWER. To wash off what Steve had done to her. To slough off the experience of the clinic. To repel the taxi slime. To try and rid herself of the guilt she felt during that mercifully brief phone with Steve's other daughter. Helen. She felt bad for her but she could not help. She had no idea which way Jane went. Nadine felt her warm wet belly with her hands. Something was growing in there. She could not see it. But she could feel it. And she was glad it was still there. Lovingly, she soaped up the firm skin that stretched tightly across her abdomen. She understood in a totally new way why women had abortions. But she was glad she had not gone through with it herself.

WHILE SHE WAS IN THE SHOWER, Nadine's mother went out into the damp night air. She noticed something on the deck just to one side of a chair and went over to clean it up. It was a small pad of paper and a plain yellow pencil. Nadine's list was right there, scrawled on the top page, soggy from the rain but legible. Leslie Aiuto was not looking for it. She was not snooping. But there it was. At first she merely glanced at it. Then she sat down in the deck chair to read it again. Out loud. She closed her eyes. Tried to make it go away. She had no idea, none whatsoever, that her daughter's problem was this big. She knew something was wrong. There were signs. That question about whether or not she had ever been in trouble when she was a girl. The way Nadine was gazing soulfully at babies in the mall. The graham crackers. She brought the list back into the house and shared it with Vito. Vito reacted with profound compassion. He was not outraged. He was worried. He did not have a heart attack, as Nadine had presumed, but was immediately filled with tender concern.

RELIEVED TO BE BACK IN BED AGAIN, having survived an unforgettably volatile day, with the biggest decision of her life behind her but without a clue as to how to share that momentous determination with her parents, Nadine flipped channels on the television. The canned laughter of a sitcom. The big toothy grins of a game show host. The weather boasting of a huge storm coming. Nothing spoke to her. Nothing addressed her situation. Nothing amused her. Nothing interested her. Unsatisfied with the evening's offerings, she turned the television off again. Just then, she heard a soft knock on her door. "Come on in," she said. Her mother and father were standing together. Her mother's hands were clutching a pad of paper that Nadine recognized immediately. She must have left it outside. Shit. Why had she left it out there? Her mother's eyes were welling up. Her father sat down on the edge of her bed and patted her right hand, the hand that had just put down the remote control.

"Oh, Nadine," he said. She sat up and leaned into him. Nadine's head fell onto her father's shoulder. His long arms surrounded her.

"I didn't know how to tell you," she said through an unrestrained rupture of tears.

For once, Nadine's father did all the talking. Asked all the questions. Gave all the reassurances. He wanted to know, of course, who the father was. She told him the father was a nobody. Just some guy who did not know about the baby. She did not want him ever to know because he was a jerk. As she spoke in plain but agitated sentences, he promised her, over and over again, "Everything's going to be all right, Princess.

Everything's going to be all right. Everything's going to be all right."

Her parents finally left her room, charging her to get a good night's sleep. "We'll talk again in the morning," was her mother's only contribution to a conversation that could have been much, much more difficult. Nadine settled her worn-out, tear-streaked face deep into her down pillow. She thought of the rabbi's story. Miraculously, the rabbi had been right. She could hear his comforting voice saying, "Sometimes we don't know our parents as well as we think we do." The dread was gone. Nadine clung to the scrap of peace she had discovered during the course of the long day and slept better than she had in more than a week.

CHAPTER FIVE
Friday / *Corinne*

"STEPHEN. STEPHEN. ARE YOU FEELING ANY BETTER? Are you getting up this morning? I don't know what I'll do if you don't get up, Stephen." Corinne's husband was curled up in a ball, his knees nearly touching his chest. He was awake but his only response was a slow slight turn of the head. He was atypically disheveled. Wearing his eyeglasses in bed. They were noticeably smudged. Hair puffed up on one side of his head made him look like a scrawny lopsided clown. The top of his silk pajamas was unbuttoned so that a smattering of chest hairs could be seen. He looked like a patient on sedatives. Like one of those immobilized patients on the psychiatric unit who were both frightening and pitiable. Corinne did not know what to do. She felt suspended in space. As if there were no ground beneath her feet. As if she should be falling. This was not the first time she felt this way, but it had been a while. Thirteen years. She felt this way thirteen years ago when Stephen was gone for two weeks at a conference in Las Vegas and did not call. She tried to track him down in his hotel room and kept leaving messages he claimed never to have received.

Something was terribly wrong with Stephen this time. Something that went well beyond the events of this purgatorial week. Stephen had been arrested but, as their attorney told them, the case against him was very weak. Yes, he had alcohol in his system. But his blood alcohol level was only marginally high enough to charge him with the lesser of New York State's drunk driving offenses. He had no prior convictions. Clearly, he was not an alcoholic. Referring to the breath analysis instrument, their attorney, Frank Pagrini, said, "His numbers are right in the margin for error. There's no way they can make this stick."

The man in the other car was dead and that was an unchangeable fact. But, Corinne knew from years of experience, the blood vessel in that man's brain might well have ruptured anyway. It was not that she was without feeling for the man. She was very sorry he died and she felt for his grieving family. But the accident might have had little or even nothing to do with his death. People died every day from aneurysms, arteries weakened and stretched, often without apparent cause. Men the age of Alexander Dolby often died of lesser injuries. Every day in the pediatric unit, Corinne faced death. Death, she knew, was inevitable. It must have been, she reasoned, Mr. Dolby's time. Stephen could not possibly be held accountable for divine timing.

Their daughter, Jane, had run away. But she would be back. Jane had a good head on her shoulders. She would not do anything stupid. Of that, Corinne was certain. The police went out of their way to reassure her that a kid like Jane, an honors student looking forward to graduation, a star in the upcoming school production, would return home once she cooled off. Corinne was sure the police were right. They had lots of experience with runaway situations. Jane must have been enormously upset about something but, given a chance to settle herself, to work through whatever was bothering her, she would soon be home again. Of course she would. Jane would not miss *The Wizard of Oz* for all the world. The director seemed to be very understanding and, he, too, was utterly convinced that Jane's distress would soon dissipate. She would return. Her normally cheerful self would reclaim center stage. He assured Corinne that, while an understudy would take Jane's part during this week's rehearsals, as soon as she came home again, the role of Dorothy was, without question, all hers.

These assurances served to tamp her fragmented mind into place yet Corinne could not help but worry about her daughter. Jane had never done anything like this before. Jane was so conscientious and sensible. Running away was not like her. Furthermore and surprisingly, nobody else in the house seemed to be worrying. Corinne felt she was carrying the concern of the entire family. Helen? It was hard to know what Helen was thinking these days. If she was worried, Corinne could not see it. Under normal circumstances, Stephen would be brimming over with undiluted concern. Under normal circumstances, Stephen would be taking charge. He would be doing everything in his power to get his little girl home. He would be down at the police station making sure the authorities were doing everything in their power to bring her home. But Stephen was not moving. Literally. He had stayed in bed almost all of yesterday and it did not look like he was going anywhere too quickly today. Corinne had never ever seen him like this. He was always the rock steady one. The foundation of the family. What was she supposed to stand on if he forfeited that role? He needed to snap out of it. Quickly. She needed him. They all needed him.

"Stephen, honey, are you gonna go to work today?" No response. "Listen, if this is about Jane, she'll be home. You know she will." Her husband rolled over so that he was no longer facing her. Corinne walked around to the other side of the bed. "Stephen, maybe I should call the doctor. Should I call the doctor?" He just shook his head ever so slightly within the confines of his pillow. He did not speak. She could not even get him to eat much of anything. Yesterday, he ate some pieces of an apple that she brought up for him on a little plate. That was all. What was she supposed to do now? Helen should be up by now, getting herself ready for school. Should she wake her? Should she get ready for work herself? Corinne did not know how to start the day.

She looked out through their front bedroom window. It was early, but the next-door neighbors were already outside preparing their homes for what some were saying could be the storm of the century. What would those neighbors think if they knew what was going on in this house? She watched them carrying lawn chairs in from their front deck. Corinne supposed she, too, could bring in loose objects. The grill should come in, for instance, and the picnic table benches could be secured next to the house. The hanging petunia could come down so that it would not blow around too much. However, Corinne's most immediate anxiety, with regard to the impending storm, was her garden. She had a garden of tall flowers that were coming up quickly. Cosmos. Hollyhocks. Globe Amaranth. The stalks of these lovely plants, however, still needed time to thicken. To strengthen. She had them planted and staked near the back of the fence. That should offer them some protection. But she could double up on the stakes. If the wind grew as fierce as forecasters were suggesting, extra stakes might make a big difference.

"Stephen, honey, please. Everything is going to be all right. Jane will come home soon. She will. I know it's upsetting. She's never done anything like this before. But the pressure was too much. That's what I think. Between the play and school and graduation being so close and all, she just needed to get away. That's all. It's a teenage girl thing. You know how moody teenage girls can be. She needed a break. That's not your fault. You can't blame yourself."

"Let me sleep, Cory." His words were dry as dust. But he had spoken. At least he had spoken. Maybe if she brewed him a cup of coffee and brought it up to him, he would drink it. It was difficult for Stephen to resist coffee. Perhaps caffeine was the answer. Corinne gently rubbed the rounded place between Stephen's shoulder blades and told him she was going to fix breakfast. He did not resist her touch. He did not say any more. He offered no response. Maybe she should bake something. Muffins. Something that would send a delicious aroma wafting up the steps to draw out his hunger. Something. Anything. Like a person lost in the woods, traveling in circles, hoping to spot a familiar landmark, a sign of some sort, Corinne went downstairs.

The kitchen counter was spread with an unusual pile of clutter. Yesterday's mail, as yet unopened. Yesterday's newspaper still opened to the page that held the small but disturbing article about the accident. An unprecedented assortment of dirty plates and bowls, forks and spoons. A mess Stephen would not, as a rule, have tolerated. Corinne plugged in the coffee pot. Zealously popped a Xanax. Downed it with a glass of cool water. Closed her eyes. Imagined the sense of peace she hoped would soon follow. The coffee would take a few minutes. She had time to retrieve garden stakes from the basement.

The worry about her tall flowers pharmaceutically diminishing by the minute, Corinne switched on the basement lights and went down. Located the enormous green plastic bin that held her gardening supplies. Foraged through it. Emerged victorious with seven long wire stakes. Perhaps, she thought, I should buy more of these lifesaving stakes. Corinne was about to head up the steps again when she noticed a large rag flattened on top of Stephen's workbench. She lifted a corner of it and saw the dismembered frame. Had Stephen taken apart a picture frame? Why would he do such a thing? Why was this week so uncontrollably laden with things that did not make sense?

She switched off the basement lights again. Went outside through the back door to stake her plants. To offer her babies additional support in case they got thrashed about too much by the storm. Ever so gently, she twisted ties around the thin tender stalks of the cosmos and thought again about Helen. Helen who was so difficult to read. Helen who should, Corinne knew, be distraught over the events of the week but who, as always, had so much trouble expressing herself. It would be good for Helen to get up and go to school. She allowed her little girl to stay home yesterday but Helen had spent most of it moping in her room. Reading mostly. Emerging only to fetch snacks and ask if there were any word from Jane. It was not good for a girl to spend so much time by herself like that. She should be in school. With her friends. Helen needed to keep busy. To think about other things. The planned activities in the pediatric unit helped sick and injured children to feel normal again. That is what Helen needed. To have as ordinary a day as possible.

Corinne filled Stephen's favorite mug, the plain white one that required regular soaking to bleach out the coffee stains. She took it up to him. "Stephen," she said, nudging his shoulder, "I made some coffee. It's extra strong. The way you like it. If you sit up and drink it, I know it'll make you feel better. Come on, Stephen. Come on. You can do it."

"I'm not one of your patients, Cory."

She changed the subject. "Fred is out next door getting his house ready for the storm. It's already pretty windy. Looks like it's gonna rain any minute."

"Gonna?" he answered, still unmoved.

She took it as a positive sign that he was correcting her pronunciation. Stephen's mother was Anglo-Saxon through and through, but his father was a Mexican immigrant of Spanish descent who made sure his children spoke absolutely perfect English. No one would ever doubt that his children were one hundred percent American. As a result, Stephen corrected Corinne's Long Island slang when it sneaked out. "Drink your coffee. I'm 'going to.' Hear that, Sweetie Pie? 'Going to' check on Helen."

"Cory, call my secretary. Tell her to put everything off." Every word emerged as a thin desiccated murmur. After all these years, why did he not, Corinne wondered, call his secretary by her given name?

"Put everything off until when, Stephen?" she asked.

"I don't know."

"I'll call her, Sweetie Pie. First, let me make sure Helen's up. Try to drink some coffee, would you?" It was late. If Helen was not awake by now, she would never make the bus on time. Maybe she should have saved the plant staking for later. Perhaps she should have attended to Helen first. Oh well, she thought, I can't be in three places at once. Without knocking, she pushed open her daughter's door. Helen was not in bed. She touched the disheveled sheets. Still warm. She saw that the bathroom light was on, the bathroom door, wide open. Quietly, she stepped over to the open door and looked in. Helen was standing in front of a large wall mirror, wearing a bra that was at least one size too tight and a large pair of purple nylon underpants that were imprinted on the back with the word "Friday" in fancy script. Helen was staring at herself. Studying her image. Gripping the extra flesh on her stomach with both hands. Holding two fistfuls of it. As if she were trying to pull it off. It was clear that Helen had not heard her mother approach. Corinne cleared her throat. Helen spun around, unmistakably shocked to learn she was being watched.

"You want something to eat, Pumpkin?"

"Mom! What are you doing?" Frantically, Helen dragged a towel from its rack and endeavored to wrap herself in it.

"It's not like I've never seen you naked before."

"Mom!" Helen looked desperately embarrassed. Corinne realized she should have knocked first. Plants are so much easier, she thought to herself. By now, the Xanax was working its essential magic. It had smoothed a few rough spots from her thoughts but could not remove the thoughts themselves.

"I'll fix you some eggs," Corinne said, excusing herself. What was so bad about a mother seeing her child standing in her underwear? Corinne tried to remember what life was like when she was fourteen. She did not recall very many details but was certain her own mother would not have bothered to check on her when she was running late. Her own mother was preoccupied with the business of enduring her father. I was on my own, Corinne reminded herself. If I forgot to set my alarm clock, that was my problem. If I missed the bus, no one was going to offer me a ride to school. As she fixed an oversized mound of scrambled eggs, sizzling bacon, and thick buttered toast, she considered that Helen was fortunate to have a mother who cared so much.

Corinne was pleased when Helen made it onto the school bus. She had already driven her in twice this week. With Helen squared away and Stephen still unwilling to move, Corinne thought she should probably see if there were any other hatches to batten down before the storm arrived, but what she wanted most was to go to work. Ordinarily, she looked forward to Fridays. On Fridays, the pediatric nurses ordered takeout and had lunch together in the staff lounge. She needed her colleagues today. She needed a few sympathizing ears. She needed to surround herself with people who would treat her like a human being. She might as well be a piece of old cardboard here in the house. Helen, like so many teenaged girls, took little interest in her mother. She made Corinne feel like a foreign presence in her own home. Stephen, on the other hand, made her feel useless. She was sure he did not mean to make her feel this way. Curiously, this was not far from how she felt growing up. Well, maybe she was truly useless. She did not know how to get Jane home any sooner. She did not know how to handle the incoming phone calls from Jane's friends, who, naturally, wanted to know where she was. She did not know how to get Stephen out of bed. He was practically catatonic and was not responding to any of her offers to help. At the hospital she could at least be useful.

Corinne longed for people to talk to. People to listen. She felt starved for meaningful conversation. To that end, and also because they needed her help over there, she would go to work this morning. Perhaps she could stay at the hospital through lunch, then come home early. If Stephen was still in bed when she returned, she would call someone. A doctor. A psychiatrist. Someone. She had to do something. She could not let him lie there in bed day after day. Perhaps the other pediatric nurses at Grace Memorial would have some ideas. Maybe they could give her some direction. That was another good reason to go to work.

Before leaving, Corinne called Florence, Stephen's secretary. It was still early. Florence was not yet in the office. She left a message: "Hi, Florence? This is Corinne Quintal. Mr. Quintal is still not feeling well. I think he has the flu. He asked me to call and tell you to postpone his appointments until next week. I'm sure he'll be better by then. Thanks so much." The phone call made her feel like a little girl all over again. A little girl making excuses for her sick daddy. She felt a twinge of anger. Dismissed it. She could not bear the thought that Stephen was anything like her father. She had always clung to the thought that, while her father could not control himself, Stephen was usually the picture of control. Many times had Corinne consoled herself with the conviction that, unlike her father, who did not seem to care about anyone but himself, Stephen loved his family. There could be no doubt about that.

CORINNE WAS GLAD FOR HER WORK at the hospital, for the brave faces of her little patients, and for the compassion of her colleagues, every one of whom asked her, at some point in the morning, how she was doing. They all knew about the accident because Stephen was brought to the same hospital. So was the guy in the other car for that matter. They knew what happened to him too. And they all knew about Jane by now. Yesterday, when she called in a personal day, Corinne told her friend, Alice, all about the note Jane left. By now, Alice, who was a dear friend and an inveterate gossip, had shared this information with the rest of the pediatrics staff. That was fine with Corinne. In fact, she was counting on it. It was easier to have someone else reveal the bad news.

The morning passed quickly. Too quickly. Corinne loved her job, although it was often difficult. Sometimes the kids there were combating infections from which they would eventually recover. Or they were there just because they had done something dumb, like swallow a magnet so large it had to be surgically removed. But sometimes they were battling more life-threatening demons like leukemia. Whatever each patient was facing, she felt fortunate to be able to help. She adored the feeling of being needed. It gave her life a center of worth. She loved being able to help, whether that entailed pain management or lasting healing. Kids needed adults to care for them. To care about them. To help them feel better.

THE CONSENSUS TODAY WAS INDIAN FOOD. Chicken Curry. Shrimp Vindaloo. Vegetable Biryani. Spicy comfort food. Indian was one of her favorites and Stephen did not like it at all. She was happy, therefore, when she got to have it at work from time to time. The pediatric nursing staff sat around a small round table in the lounge, spooning samples from each warm container onto Styrofoam plates. It smelled rich. Complicated. It tasted soothing. Consoling. Alice, Corinne's best buddy on the unit, sat right next to her. They were close to the same age. Alice had teenaged girls too. Plus one teenaged boy, the same age as Helen. Cindy sat just beyond Alice. She was the new nurse. Young. Bright. Still learning the ropes but fitting in nicely. Everybody seemed to like her, especially the young doctors. Directly across from Corinne sat Henry, a real sweetheart of a guy who wore funny fire-engine red sneakers that always brought a smile to the kids. Next to Henry sat Lisa, already chowing down purposefully on the exotic-smelling curry. Lisa was highly opinionated but she was also very intuitive. She sometimes knew what was wrong with a patient long before any one else, including the physicians, and was not afraid to say so. Rosa sat to Corinne's right. Rosa was the least known of the nurses. She kept to herself, although she usually attended the Friday lunches. When she did speak up, everyone listened. They were all good nurses. Pediatrics tended to draw nurses who brought gifts of patience, understanding, and encouragement. It was the encouragement Corinne craved today.

"Any word from Jane?" Henry dared to break the ice, revealing to Corinne what was, not surprisingly, on everyone's mind.

"No. Nothing yet. But I'm sure she'll be home soon."

"The police are still looking for her, right?"

"They're sure she'll come to her senses."

"But are they looking?" Alice joined in.

"I think so."

"You think so? I'm surprised Stephen hasn't had 'em searchin' 'round the clock," added Lisa.

"Well, that's another problem. Something's wrong with Stephen. He won't get out of bed. He seemed just fine right after the accident but now he won't even get out of bed to eat."

"That's odd," added Lisa, "maybe it's a concussion."

"Could be," Corinne considered, "but he isn't dizzy or nauseous or anything."

"Did they do a CT scan?" Alice asked.

"No."

"Maybe you should bring him back in. Have 'em take another look." Lisa made it sound like a good idea. Corinne ripped a piece of garlic naan from a big flat loaf in the middle of the table. Wedged the soft flavorful bread into her mouth.

"I think he's in shock," suggested Rosa. Everyone turned to Rosa, considering her theory.

"You mean like some sort of post-traumatic episode?" Cindy inquired.

"He has been hit pretty hard this week," Henry added.

"That's true," said Lisa. "That other guy died, right?" Everyone knew the man in the other car had died. Alice shot Lisa a stern glance that challenged her right to mention, in front of Corinne, the dead victim.

Corinne was about to ladle a forkful of savory shrimp into her mouth when Lisa mentioned the man in the other car. She put the untouched food back down on her plate. Alice hurried to change the path of the conversation. "Corinne, I got you a little present."

"Really?" This brought a tear to her eye. Corinne was so grateful for Alice's friendship. Who else would have thought to bring her a gift during this terrible week? Alice took a wrapped package out of her bag. Handed it to Corinne. Obviously the gift was a book. She looked up at the others as if checking to see if they knew what it was. Carefully peeled the tape from the ends. Slid the book from its flowery paper. It was a book of quotes. *Literary Blossoms* it was titled. Flipping through the pages, she could see that there was one thought per page, enough to carry a reader through 365 days. There were sections as well. The first section had to do with roses. Opposite the first page a delicate yellow rose leaned to the right, like an arrow directing the reader to the quote. She read this first quote out loud, pausing to allow the words room to find a place in her mind: "In real life, unlike in Shakespeare, the sweetness of the rose depends upon the name it bears.

Things are not only what they are. They are, in very important respects, what they seem to be."

"Who said that?" asked Alice.

"Hubert H. Humphrey."

"Who's that?" asked Cindy.

"He was a politician," said Alice.

"Good man," added Henry.

"Must have been a Democrat if Henry likes him," said Lisa laughing. Henry scowled.

"You got a rose garden?" asked Lisa.

"Just a small one."

"Don't be modest, Corinne," Alice spoke up, "She has a huge rose garden. She's practically famous for her roses! And you should see her dahlias. They're amazing."

"Stop, Alice," Corinne protested, smiling at the compliment. Corinne loved her rose garden. It was not, as Alice proposed, huge, but it was exquisite.

"One more?" proposed Rosa, spooning a little more curry onto her plate.

"Sure, here goes:

> Gather ye rosebuds while ye may
> Old time is still a-flying,
> And this same flower that smiles today
> Tomorrow will be dying.

By Robert Herrick."

"Why that's lovely, Alice," Cindy commented.

"Thanks, Al. This means a lot," said Corinne.

"Did you read the front? I wrote something in the front." Corinne opened the cover. There on the inside, Alice had written "Blessings to you, my friend, in the light and in the shadows. Love, Alice." "It's a little blessing we do in my women's group. We pass the blessing around to each other. I'm passing it on to you."

ALICE GENEROUSLY STEERED THE DISCUSSION to other matters. They chatted about patients for a few minutes. Then cleaned up lunch. As planned, Corinne left the hospital right after the last leftovers were stowed in the refrigerator. She did not really want to leave. Sometimes Grace Memorial felt more like home than her own house. Sometimes she felt closer to her patients than to her own children. Nevertheless, it was time to go home. Maybe Stephen should have his brain scanned, she thought. Maybe he is suffering from a concussion. Driving home in the steady rain, her head was filled with thoughts of Stephen, so much so that she almost forgot to pull into the supermarket. She always stopped on her way home from the hospital. She liked to shop daily. That way the food was fresh and less was wasted. It was a ritual. Today could be no different. She needed to pick up something for dinner. Her family had to eat. But what? What would be so appealing Stephen could not help but eat it? A steak? Maybe. Lasagna? No.

Enchiladas. Enchiladas were the answer. Stephen adored enchiladas. With cheese melted all over the top of them. And a good spicy rice dish. And refried beans. Stephen did a good job of ignoring his Hispanic roots but he made the grand exception for enchiladas. In the pouring rain and already gusting winds, she ran into the supermarket. Picked out a firm onion, a pound of fresh ground beef, a large can of diced tomatoes and a small can of tomato paste, two cans of refried beans with jalapenos, a block of good strong cheddar, and a package of lovely soft tortillas. She had plenty of rice at home. They would have a good home-cooked meal on this raw blustery night.

When she returned home at nearly two o'clock, she walked straight up the steps to their bedroom. Stephen was no longer in bed but he had not made it up either. It was a mess of sheets and blankets. She was encouraged to find the empty bed but wondered where he could be. Changed out of her rain-soaked clothes. Put on dry jeans and a warm, navy blue hooded sweatshirt. Pulled the covers up onto the bed. Smoothed them into place. Hoped she would not find Stephen in bed again until much later. Checked Jane's room. It was untouched. She dared to open Jane's closet. Still full of clothing. Her eldest daughter would have to come back soon. She had nothing to wear. Corinne poked her head into Helen's room. Helen would not be home for another hour or so. Back downstairs, she checked the kitchen. No evidence of Stephen. The pile of dishes remained just as she had left them this morning. She looked through the backdoor window at her tall flowers holding steady in the gusty rain. So far, so good.

She walked through the kitchen to the living room. For the first time, Corinne noticed the space on the wall where a family photograph should have been, undoubtedly the one she found on Stephen's workbench, its frame disassembled. She walked past the steps and turned the corner to look in the den. Called his name. Could Stephen have gone somewhere? If so, he must have walked. The damaged car would be in the shop for weeks. His license would remain revoked until the attorneys cleared things up. Where could he have gone? Was Stephen deliberately trying to frighten her? From the den, Corinne thought she could hear little noises behind the basement door. The basement was the only place she had not yet looked. She cracked the door. Called downstairs. A voice called back, "Down here. I'm trying to fix . . . this . . . oh shit." She heard something fall on the floor and went flying down the steps. Stephen was struggling to put the frame back together, one corner at a time. Each time he let go, however, it fell apart again. Corinne wondered how long he had been working on it. His face was red with frustration. He was still wearing his pajamas. She watched as he put the pieces together, putting as much pressure as he could bring to bear from the corners inward. Again, it flew apart, two of the sides hitting the floor.

"Can I help?" she asked, certain he would turn her down.

Stephen took a deep breath. He put the pieces back on top of his workbench and smothered the corners in bottled glue. He placed the loosely joined pieces on the newspaper to dry. It looked terribly sloppy. The corners were not quite evenly matched and small globs of glue oozed from the seams. "There," he said, "it's done." His voice did not sound quite right. The frame looked like a kindergartner had put it together.

"Can I help you?" she asked again.

"Can you turn the clock back?"

She shook her head back and forth. What was wrong with him?

"Stephen, I think maybe I should take you back to the hospital. Have them look you over. You may have an injury that they didn't see Tuesday night. Or you may be suffering from some sort of post-traumatic stress thing."

"There is nothing wrong with me that a doctor can fix."

"Who can help, then?"

"I don't know, Cory. A carpenter? A magician? A priest?"

He walked past her. Up the steps. As if she were not standing right there. She turned out the light over his work-bench. Followed him up to the bedroom where he tore back the covers again and returned to a fetal position.

"Stephen? Stephen?" He was not speaking again. Instead he was sucking and chewing his upper lip. He seemed to be tasting the irritating little hairs that had sprouted under his nose during the day. The situation was both frustrating and frightening.

Corinne did not know any carpenters or magicians. And she knew Stephen was juggling sarcasm and desperation when he said it, but she could call a priest. There was an impressive priest who visited the pediatric unit regularly. Father Comfrons. Everyone seemed to like him and he had a way of making people feel comfortable around him. Would Stephen really talk to a priest? He might. She went back down to the kitchen. Looked up the number for the Catholic Church. Our Lady of the Sea. Would Father Comfrons know who she was? Corinne was one of the nurses clergy could always count on to join them in prayer. He might remember her. She dialed the number. Asked to speak to the priest.

"He's not here right now," a woman said. "May I take a message?"

"Yes, please. My name is Corinne Quintal."

"Did you say Quintal?"

"Yes, that's right. Quintal. I'd like to talk to the priest. It's sort of urgent. Will he be back soon?"

"He should be back in a little while."

"Please have him call me. Tell him it's urgent." She left her phone number.

"Will Father Comfrons know what this is regarding?"

"No, he won't. But please tell him . . . tell him . . . this is critically important."

"Yes, Mrs. Quintal, I will. Thank you for calling."

Corinne was not sure what she would say to the priest if and when he returned her call but, with no small amount of apprehension, she hoped he could somehow help Stephen. She sat on the edge of a kitchen chair fretting. Not knowing what to do next. Her insides seemed to be missing. Just then she remembered the groceries sitting out in the car. She had left them out there in the trunk. Forgotten about them completely. If only there were a way to get from the house into the garage and back without going outside. The rain was heavier now and the wind continued to build steadily. She could not leave the meat and cheese sitting out there. Gathering her courage but neglecting to put on a raincoat, she ran out, grabbed both bags from the trunk, and dashed back inside. Corinne was not out in the rain more than a minute or two altogether but, by the time she was back in the kitchen with the groceries, she was thoroughly saturated. The phone rang. She tossed the wet bags up on the kitchen countertop and, still dripping, grabbed the receiver.

"Hello?" she answered, quite out of breath.

"Mrs. Quintal, this is Father Comfrons from Our Lady of the Sea. Is this Mrs. Quintal?"

"Yes, Father. Thanks so much for calling. We . . . " She paused, still struggling to catch her breath. "We've met over at Grace Memorial. I'm a nurse in pediatrics."

"Oh yes," he replied tentatively, leaving Corinne to wonder if he really remembered her or was simply being polite. "My secretary tells me you have an urgent problem."

"Yes. But it's not me. I mean it's not my urgent problem. Well, it's not directly my urgent problem. It's my husband. He's having some trouble. He is a strong man, Father, but he's in some sort of crisis and I think you might be able to help him."

"Can you tell me what kind of crisis?"

"He's had sort of a bad week. He was arrested and then our daughter ran away and now he's, well, he's shut down or something. He won't get out of bed and he's talking funny. Actually, he's hardly talking at all."

"Mrs. Quintal, if your husband is having some sort of mental breakdown, I'm probably not the right person to help. I can recommend a therapist."

"I think he may be having more of a spiritual crisis. He asked for a priest." That was not absolutely correct. When Stephen chose the words "carpenter, magician, priest," the implied futility was thick as home-ground peanut butter.

"Is this something that can wait, Mrs. Quintal? I've had rather a hard week myself."

"I'm sorry. I was just. I was hoping. I was . . . " She did not know what else to say. He was not going to come. He was having a difficult week himself and was not going to help. Standing there, dripping small puddles all over the kitchen floor, shivering like a wet child, Corinne started to cry. Tears rolled down her cheeks, onto the low end of the receiver. Her voice box choked up. She could no longer speak. She tried to say, "Excuse me, Father," but it stuck in her throat like a large hunk of bread mistakenly swallowed whole.

"Mrs. Quintal?" he said, "Mrs. Quintal?" She was sure the priest could hear bits and pieces of her distress. Frantically, she tried to clear her throat. In panic and frustration, she hung up. Sat down on the floor. Allowed herself a big cry. A blubbering, depleting bawl.

CORINNE WAS NOT CERTAIN HOW LONG she had been sitting on the kitchen floor, her back to the wall, when she heard the front door blow open. Helen was home. Helen. She wiped both sides of her face with the backs of her hands and tried not to look as inconsolable as she felt. What kind of home was this for Helen to walk into? Her sister gone. Her father paralyzed by who knew what. Her mother an unmopped spill on the cold, white kitchen tiles. Helen would, of course, come first to the kitchen. Helen's hunger was unfailing. Corinne stood up. Hurried to the sink. Grabbed a towel. Started to blot her wet hair with it.

"Mom, what happened to you?" Corinne splashed some water on her face. Blotted it up with the same towel. Glanced over at Helen, hoping the blotchy tear streaks on her face were not too conspicuous.

"Same thing that happened to you by the looks of it," she answered. Helen was also dripping wet.

"It's crazy out there."

"Yup."

"You okay, Mom?" Helen noticed. Her silly attempt to pretend nothing was wrong had failed. On the bright side, it was kind of her daughter to notice. And to ask.

"Oh, I'm just feeling a little sorry for myself. That's all."

"Hear anything from Jane?"

"No. I don't think so." She looked over at the answering machine. Three blinks. Three messages. Together, they listened for Jane. The first two messages were from Jane's friends, Alex and Crystal. The third was Mr. Bolger, the director of the musical. Did they have the shoes, he wanted to know, the silver shoes? Three calls. Three disappointments. No Jane. The doorbell rang.

"You expecting anyone, Helen?"

"Me? No."

"Here, have a towel." She removed a fresh blue and white checked dishtowel from a drawer and handed it to Helen. Towels in hand, they both went to answer the door. Standing on the other side was another soaking-wet person. Father Comfrons. Corinne recognized him immediately, an imposing figure draped in wet black clothing, a ring of white at the base of his neck, a waterlogged tweed hat on his head.

"Mrs. Quintal, may I come in?"

"Yes, by all means," she answered, stunned. She was certainly not expecting the priest to show up on her doorstep.

"Please, come in. Helen, can you grab another towel for Father Comfrons." Helen was also clearly surprised by the appearance of a priest at the door. Spreading the bottom corners of her mouth out and down and bringing her shoulders up and forward, she threw her mother a "what's up?" look, then obediently went off to fetch a towel.

"You hung up, Mrs. Quintal. I was worried. I looked up your address and came right over. I hope that's alright."

"Yes, Father. Should I call you Father? I know that sounds like a ridiculous question. I've been calling you Father all along. Do you remember me from the hospital?" He nodded and, standing face to face, she was relieved to see he really did seem to know her. Helen returned with a big, fluffy white towel that must have come from the downstairs bathroom. It looked much more adequate than the saturated kitchen towels she and Helen were holding. Applying it first to his face, then to his balding head, he said, "If you feel comfortable calling me Father, that's fine."

"Thank you for coming, Father. Helen, would you excuse us for a few minutes?" Corinne could tell her daughter was extremely curious about the unusual visitor, but she said, "Sure, Mom." Helen went into the kitchen, emerged with a box of cheese crackers, and with manifest reluctance plodded up the steps to her room.

"Let me take your coat and hat, Father." She draped these drenched items limply over the stair railing and led him into the living room where he selected one of the wingback chairs. "Can I make you some hot tea?"

"No, thank you, Mrs. Quintal. Are you alright? When you hung up, I was very concerned."

"I'm fine. I guess I got something caught in my throat. Then I was too embarrassed to call back and I really didn't think you'd come, especially in this horrible weather."

"Well, as you can see, I'm here. How can I help you?"

"In a nutshell, Father, my husband is upstairs in bed and refuses to get up. He hasn't been to work since Tuesday. Like I said to your secretary on the phone, we've had a really bad week and he's very upset about it. He only got up once today. To fix a frame." Her eyes gravitated to the place on the wall where the picture should have been. "He is normally a very meticulous man, Father, but the frame he fixed looks terrible. I don't think he was even looking at what he was doing."

"But you didn't call me over here to repair a frame."

"No, Father, forgive me. I'm rambling. I have a tendency to ramble. Especially when I'm nervous."

"Are you nervous?"

"Well, yes, but this isn't about me. It's my husband."

"What about your husband?"

"Something is wrong."

"On the phone you described this as a spiritual crisis."

"It could be. You see, it all started on Tuesday. Tuesday evening Stephen had a drink with some colleagues from work and then he was in an accident and the man in the other car died, but I don't think the drinking had anything to do with it. Anyway, he was arrested and had to spend the night in jail and our daughter was so upset, she ran away. I'm sure she'll come to her senses and come home soon but he is, well, I don't know what he is, but I think he thinks this is all somehow his fault, which is ridiculous, and I guess that's where the spiritual crisis comes in. Guilt is a spiritual crisis, isn't it?"

"But you don't think he's guilty?"

"Well, he can't be, Father. He's a decent man. Not perfect, but a really decent man. This can't possibly be his fault. If it's anyone's fault, it's mine. If I had a closer relationship with my daughter, she would not have run away. She would have come and talked to me first. That's what I think anyway. So if there's anyone to blame around here, it's me."

"Let me get a few things straight. You have two daughters. Looks like you have a lovely family." He was pointing to the pictures on the wall. "One of your daughters ran away on Tuesday."

"Wednesday morning, actually. I thought Jane was going to school. Instead, she ran away. She left us a note. That's how we know she ran away."

"Jane is your older daughter?"

"Yeah. She's the one with the long light brown hair."

"Okay, so Tuesday night your husband was in an accident and he was arrested. Wednesday morning, Jane ran away.

Now, your husband won't get out of bed because he mistakenly thinks this is all his fault when in fact, it is all your fault."

"Something like that. Would you be willing to speak to him? Explain to him that it's not his fault? He won't listen to me."

"And you think he'll listen to me?"

"Maybe."

"As I said on the phone, Mrs. Quintal, he probably needs to speak to a therapist or a psychiatrist, but I'm willing to meet with him."

"Thank you." Corinne was, for the first time today, hopeful. Maybe the priest could pull Stephen out of the mystifying hole into which he had so precipitously fallen. "Thank you so much. He's upstairs. In bed, like I said. I know he won't come down. We'll have to go up to him and he's not expecting you. He's not expecting anyone so I'm not exactly sure how this will go."

Father Comfrons followed Corinne up the steps and down the hall to their bedroom. Stephen was still curled up, looking even more disheveled than he had this morning. Corinne whispered to the priest, "Maybe you should speak to him by yourself. Maybe he'll talk to you if I'm not here." Corinne tapped Stephen on the shoulder and said, "Sweetie, someone's here to see you." She squeezed the hand of the priest and left the room, closing the door behind her and praying for the best. She listened at the door but heard nothing.

Finally, she heard Stephen say, "I don't need a doctor. I told my wife I don't need a doctor." She pressed her ear up close to the door. In spite of the inch and a half of wood between them and the hard rain falling overhead, Corinne could hear reasonably well.

"I'm not a doctor. I'm a priest." Stephen did not reply. It was a few more minutes before the priest said, "Your wife has the impression you're in the middle of a spiritual crisis. Is she right?" Still no response. Several more painfully slow minutes passed before the priest said, "I'm sorry I couldn't be more helpful and I do hope your situation improves." He began walking toward the door and Corinne backed away, ducking into Jane's room so as not to be caught eavesdropping. When the priest did not emerge into the hallway, she tiptoed back to the bedroom door. She felt she had every right to know what was going on in there. This was her husband. This was her life. Ear to the bedroom door again, she heard Stephen ask, "Do you know who I am?"

"Yes, I know who you are, Mr. Quintal. Alex Dolby's funeral was today."

"Then you know I'm the one who . . . "

"Yes, Mr. Quintal. You were the man in the other car. Is that why you won't get out of bed?" O God. Her heart seemed to stop. An unwelcome chill ran up her spine. Father Comfrons handled the Dolby funeral? This was not fair. He should have been more honest with her. Had he mentioned

Alexander Dolby, she would have ended the conversation right then and there. She would have gone looking for a different priest.

"I can't fix it. I can't fix any of it." She thought she could hear Stephen crying as he spoke. The priest was way out of line. He seemed to be making matters worse, not better. He might even be doing this on purpose.

"No, you can't," said the priest. "You can't fix any of it." Corinne was tempted to push the door open and tell Stephen that the priest was wrong. Don't believe him, she tried to tell her husband telepathically. You can fix it. Whatever is wrong, it can be fixed, she wanted her husband to hear. What had she done by inviting this priest over to the house? He was supposed to improve the situation, not further complicate it.

"You know what Alex Dolby's death reminds me, Mr. Quintal?"

"That you can't trust anyone?" Stephen asked in a voice filled with gravel and indignity.

"No. Nothing at all like that. His death reminds me that life is uncertain. Life is altogether too brief. It's over in a heartbeat."

"Mine is over. My life is over."

"No, your life is not over. Alex Dolby's life is over. Yours is not. And you have no time to waste, Mr. Quintal. You have no time to waste feeling sorry for yourself. No time to waste on pettiness of spirit. No time to lie in that bed punishing yourself for things that cannot be changed. There are people who need you. Your wife, for instance. Your daughters. You may not be able to fix what's already broken but you can try not to break anything else." Now the priest was being more supportive, more of what she had hoped. He was right too. Lying around in bed for no good reason was a waste of time. She needed him back.

"It's not as easy as you make it sound. You don't know half of what's broken." What was Stephen talking about? From behind the door, she could only silently guess.

"What's going on, Mom?" Corinne jumped. Helen had come up from behind her. "Shhh!" Quickly and quietly, like little mice, they disappeared into Helen's room.

Corinne shut the door behind them. Helen had changed out of her school clothes into a baggy pair of athletic pants and an oversized long-sleeved T-shirt that read All of the Voices in My Head Are Saying Chocolate. "I'm just trying to help your father, Helen."

"What's he doing anyway? Who is that priest? Why is he with Dad? We're not Catholic, are we?"

"No, we're not. I don't know what we are. My mother's family was Episcopalian. Some of the time. The Quintal side of your father's family used to be Catholic. I guess that's the closest thing we've got to a religion. If you want to call it a religion. I'm a very religious person, Pumpkin, don't get me wrong. We all are. We just don't go to church."

"So why is the priest here?"

"Your father seems awfully upset. This week was too much for him. It was too much for any one man to handle. The accident. Your sister. I thought it might be good for him to talk to somebody. I know Father Comfrons from the hospital. I thought maybe . . . Oh, I don't know." Helen was looking at her very strangely, as if trying to figure her out. It was not simple confusion that Corinne perceived in her daughter's face. There was insight in those familiar blue eyes.

"What's for supper?" Helen asked after a considerable silence. As if the previous question no longer interested her. As if they had just been discussing the price of onions.

"I was gonna fix Mexican but I'm so exhausted. I know we just had pizza Monday night, Pumpkin, but what do you think?" Corinne asked, effortlessly leaping on Helen's strange disjointed change of subject. "We can save the enchiladas for tomorrow night."

"You mean the order-out kind of pizza?"

"Yup. The plain old-fashioned order-out kind."

"Meat Meister's Deluxe?"

"Sure. Meat Meister's Deluxe." Corinne hated a greasy meat pizza but Helen's delight was unequivocal.

"Thanks, Mom. Is it okay if I read 'til it gets here? I'm close to the end." Her daughter held up a gray paperback book with pink letters on the cover.

"Sure, Pumpkin."

Corinne ordered the Meat Meister's Deluxe. Popped a Xanax. Sat in the living room feeling like one of the family members who occupy the hospital waiting rooms, anxiously killing time until a prognosis becomes available. Telling herself what she had told so many patients and families: "Think positive." She stared at the place on the wall where she now imagined the hopelessly gluey picture frame. Listened to the rain pounding the roof. Picked a magazine from the slim brass rack next to the couch. Flipped through it inattentively.

Father Comfrons was still up there when the pizza arrived. The poor pizza delivery boy was dressed in drenched yellow plastic, which stuck to the clothes he wore underneath as the rain ran down his arms and chest. Fortunately, the cardboard pizza box was kept safely wrapped in an insulated container so that it remained dry and hot. She gave him a larger than usual tip. The pizza smelled surprisingly wonderful. She hugged the warm box with her arms. She had not realized how hungry she was. Why was she so hungry? She had a big breakfast. A very good lunch. Why was she so famished?

Helen must have heard, or more likely smelled, the arrival of the pizza because she was soon down the steps. Corinne found some paper plates and napkins and they dove into the pie. Right there in the living room. Stephen would never approve. But Stephen was not coming down. There would have been no point in slaving over the enchiladas. He would not have eaten them anyway. Perhaps he would be ready for them tomorrow.

As was her custom, Corinne picked off most of the meat bits, redistributing them among the other slices in the box. Two big cheesy bites into her second scrumptious slice of the meatless Meat Meister, Father Comfrons came downstairs.

"How is he?" Corinne asked, struggling to swallow. Helen continued to eat.

"You were right," the priest said, "He is definitely having a spiritual crisis. I think he was due for one."

She wanted to know what he meant by that. Instead, she asked, "Did he talk to you? Did he say anything?"

"I believe he'll be downstairs soon, Mrs. Quintal. He told me he was going to have a shower and then come down. I think he'll talk now."

"Really?"

"I think so. We had a good conversation, Mrs. Quintal."

"Oh, thank God. How can I ever repay you, Father?"

"No thanks necessary. Just take care of each other, Mrs. Quintal."

"Would you like a slice of pizza?" Helen asked the priest. Corinne was embarrassed. She should have done the asking. Where were her manners?

"No thanks. I've got supper waiting for me elsewhere." He put on his soggy hat and coat and went back out into the blustery storm.

Hopeful that Stephen would soon join them in the living room, Corinne looked at the remaining slices. Helen had eaten four. Corinne could not remember ever eating four slices of pizza. Like her father, who could eat a jumbo bag of potato chip in one sitting, Helen had an extraordinary appetite. There were two slices left. Piled high with meat.

"What do we do now?" Helen asked.

"What do you mean?"

"Do we wait for him to come down?"

"No, of course not. You can go watch TV if you want. Or finish your book. You must be close to the end of that book by now."

"Yeah. It's Jane's book, really." Helen looked down into Corinne's eyes and, with the worry Corinne had mistakenly assumed was missing earlier in the day, she asked, "Mom, do you think Jane is ever coming home?"

"Of course she is, Pumpkin. Of course she is." Helen's upper lip was almost completely inside her mouth. As if she were trying to eat her own face. It reminded Corinne of what Stephen had looked like earlier in the afternoon. She tasted her own upper lip. Soft. Metallic. Having been given permission to go back to her book or to do something else if she wished, Helen remained with Corinne in the living room. Watching. Listening to the rain. Until they heard, at last, light footsteps coming down the carpeted steps.

To Corinne's relief, Stephen looked a little better. His face was still pale, his shoulders uncharacteristically stooped, his eyes a bit sunken. A touch of dehydration, Corinne suspected.

Nevertheless, he looked more like himself again. Helen offered him the pizza. To her amazement, he did not say a word about food being in the living room. Instead, he took a plate. Gathered up a piece. Held it ceremoniously. Like a peace offering. Corinne thought she could see Helen visibly brighten. Then, before she could ask about the priest, before she could find out what happened upstairs, Helen asked, "Can we play cards tonight?" Corinne and Stephen looked at one another with some astonishment. Helen added, "Like we used to?"

HELEN, CORINNE, AND STEPHEN combed the house looking for cards. No one was able to locate a complete deck. One deck was missing all of its kings. Another was short the four of diamonds and the ace of spades. "How about Scrabble?" Helen suggested alternatively. Before Corinne could conjure any objection, Helen dashed to the low cupboard in the den where board games were kept. Corinne and Stephen stood watching as Helen approached the kitchen table with a dusty box. Stephen made a contribution to the effort. He wiped the box with a damp sponge, a sign that he was returning to himself. Helen set up the board. "Do you remember how to play?" she asked, shaking a velveteen bag filled with wooden alphabet tiles. Stephen, looking very weary, nodded. Corinne responded with polite uncertainty. "I'm not sure your father is up for a game right now." Helen frowned, looking over at a box top laden with rules. Stephen, in a startlingly gentle voice, said, "Let's play." Helen instructed her parents to draw one tile in order to determine who would go first.

Corinne drew the letter A and, as her husband and daughter both drew consonants, she was required to create the first word. They each drew seven fresh tiles and stared down at their respective lots. Corinne moved the tiles around on the cradle until she came up with a simple word: WANT. Helen made use of the W, forming WAIT. Stephen intersected WANT with MEND. Then Corinne offered what would end up as the biggest word on the board: REMEDY. And the board began to fill. Helen made use of the D in REMEDY to create HIDE. Stephen seemed relieved to see the H turn up and quickly produced HOP. Corinne added an E, transforming Stephen's little word into HOPE. It felt refreshingly normal to be sitting here around the kitchen table playing a game with her family. In the face of all that had happened this week. Despite the wind singing wildly and Jane having disappeared.

Helen took advantage of the I in WAIT to introduce SIN. Up to this point, the threesome seemed comfortable with the relative silence of the game. Now, however, the silence was suddenly unnerving. Corinne watched Stephen turn red when he saw that particular word pop up in the game. It made her wonder what he had discussed with the priest. She watched as Stephen took a deep breath. She witnessed his shoulders begin to droop again. Corinne asked Stephen if he

needed to lie down. He did not answer. Instead, he concentrated on the board. Searched his letters again. And then the
phone rang.

Stephen and Corinne looked at one another, then at
Helen, who was close enough to reach the receiver from her
seat. To everyone's unhappiness, it was not Jane. It was
Helen's friend, Elaine, wanting her to come over for a "storm
sleepover." Politely, Helen declined. Corinne could hear
Elaine pleading at the other end but Helen held her ground.
"We're having a family night," she said, sounding rather proud
of the fact. Corinne was glad. It was nasty outside. She wanted
Helen home. She hoped Jane was snug and dry and secure.
Wherever she was. She wished with all her heart that Jane
would call. If only to let them know she was safe.

Stephen removed three letters from the cradle before him.
Placed them beneath the N in Sin and next to the T in WANT
to form two words: NO and TOMB. When Corinne saw
the words, the image of Stephen in his pajamas in the unflat-
tering fluorescent light of the basement, desperately pouring
glue on the corners of that frame, came rushing back. That
awful feeling that there was no ground beneath her feet
returned.

"Are you feeling okay, Stephen?"

"I'm fine, Cory. Really."

"You didn't really eat anything. Do you want that pizza?"

"I tried a piece, Cory. It was good. Thanks."

The lights flickered. "Do you think we'll lose power tonight?" Helen asked, and before anyone could answer, she said, "I have that big flashlight in my closet." She raced upstairs, presumably to retrieve the flashlight.

"I'll be right back, Cory," Stephen said. He stood up. Went to the basement steps. Had he read her thoughts? She followed him. To his workbench. There were globs of clear hardening glue oozing out from between the seams of the frame. "It seems to be holding," he told her. "It seems to be holding." It looked awful. He did not touch it.

"Are you okay, Sweetie Pie?"

He looked down at the frame again. Without looking up, he said, "I have done some very terrible things, Cory. This is all my fault. I know that saying it doesn't change a thing, but somehow I don't think anything is going to get better until I say it. I have to say it. That man is dead because of me. Jane is gone because of me."

"No, Stephen."

"Yes. Yes, this is my fault. It doesn't help to pretend it isn't. Father Comfrons was right about that."

"What did he say to you, Sweetie Pie?"

Stephen shook his head as he replied, "He told me I have to stop blaming everybody else. He told me nothing is going to change until I take responsibility for what I've done. And he told me I need to make amends."

"What does he mean?"

"He means I have to try to do something to make things right again with the people I've hurt."

"You mean like doing something for that man's family?"

"Yes. And like doing something for you."

"What are you talking about, Stephen? You haven't hurt me."

"Oh, but I have, Cory. I have."

"Listen, Stephen, is this about that woman?" She asked the question as sweetly as she knew how. He just stared at her, trying, she thought, to assess what and how much she knew. "I know about her. I mean I don't know who she is or anything but I know there's another woman out there."

"How do you . . . when did you . . . ? Oh, Cory . . . "

"Stephen, I can smell when you've been with her. I can sense it." Her tone was startlingly conciliatory.

"You . . . you never said anything." He was visibly shocked.

"What am I supposed to say? Did you think I would walk out on you after all these years just because you had a little fling? Whoever she is, I know it won't last. I know you're not going anywhere."

"You mean you know about this and you don't care, Cory?"

How could he ask such a question? I know and I care, she wanted to scream. Thinking of Las Vegas, she thought of declaring, I know this is not the first time but I pray it is the last. Instead, taking a step closer to him, placing her warm palms on his chest, she replied quietly, "Of course, I care. What? You think I don't care?"

"Then what?"

"Then I forgive you. It's over, right?"

"It's over."

"Then I forgive you."

"Just like that?"

"Just like that."

"That's not what Father Comfrons said. He said I need to make amends first and ask for your forgiveness."

"Well, that's not how it works with me, Stephen. I just forgive. You must know that by now. I just forgive. If I'd waited for my father to make amends, I'd have spent my whole life mad at him. I can't do that. I won't do that. I forgive you. For the sake of my own sanity, I forgive you. For the sake of our marriage and family, I forgive you. Stephen, I love you. You must know that." She could tell he was stunned. Stunned to discover she knew about his girlfriend. Stunned to hear she was not going to hold it against him. "You can make amends with me if you want to," she added, holding her arms wide open, intensely hoping he would respond in kind. Of course, it was easy to say, "I forgive you." What Corinne thought of as the worst part of herself wanted to take those words back, to scream, as she had imagined for several months, "How could you do this me? How could you do this to me again?" The best part wanted to repeat those healing words, "I forgive you," over and over again until Stephen believed them and until she meant them absolutely. For Corinne, however, the overarching motivation to forgive Stephen had little to do with what was best in her or good in her. It was largely practical. Emotionally and financially, she could not afford to condemn her husband forever.

AT MIDNIGHT, STEPHEN AND CORINNE were still wide-awake listening to the besieged trees as they struggled, unsuccessfully, to hang onto their branches.

"I like a good storm," he said.

"I know you do," she answered. It was true. She was terrified by storms while Stephen loved them. He took pleasure at the sight of lightning. The sound of thunder. He loved hurricanes. This fact had often been a source of comfort to her. It was impossible to become too anxious about a storm when it delighted her husband so.

Corinne cradled her head in her husband's warm shoulder.

"Are you mad at me for calling the priest?"

"No, Cory." He squeezed her right arm with his warm hand.

"Was he helpful?" She hoped he might share some of the details of their meeting.

"He was. He helped me to see what I already knew. My life has been out of control, Cory. And I'm sorry. I'm sorry about all of it."

"It's all going to work out, Stephen. I know it will. It doesn't look like you'll be charged with anything. They'll probably never know why that man died."

"Maybe. Maybe, Cory."

"And whoever she was, as long as she's out of your life, we'll be fine, Stephen. We will."

"She was nobody, Cory. She meant nothing."

Her heart relieved by the honesty she and Stephen had shared yet thickly coated with worry over Jane, she said, "I hope our C.G. is safe."

"I hope so too, Cory. I hope so too. Jane found out about the affair," Stephen confessed. "I think that's why she left. I don't think it had anything to do with stress, Cory. I think she had me up on a pedestal and I came crashing down so fast this week, she couldn't handle it."

"She'll come home, Sweetie Pie. She'll come home." But those words were no longer accompanied by absolute confidence. It was easier to believe Jane would be coming home soon when she thought her daughter's running away was related to the pressures of school. If Jane's leaving was the result of discovering her father was a flawed human being after all, that was another matter altogether. When Corinne was a teenager, she thought about running away all the time. And she nearly did a couple of times. She thought about starting over somewhere else. In some other family. Where they might appreciate her for who she was, not just for how well she cleaned up after her father. She remembered the despair she felt back then. The anguish. But Stephen was not at all like her own father. Surely Jane knew that.

"I'm going to check on Helen. You want to come?" Stephen asked. She followed him down the hall. Helen was not in her bed.

"Oh, my God," Corinne said as she fell into an immediate panic. Very quickly, however, Stephen located their baby girl. "Look at this," he said. Helen lay on her right side, coiled around a great stuffed owl she had given Jane for Christmas last year. In Jane's bed. Together, they watched their daughter breathing deeply. As they had watched her when she was an infant. Helen looked remarkably peaceful given the upheavals of the week and the threatening noises of the fierce gales that beat on the window over her head.

BACK IN BED AGAIN, snuggled up against Stephen's side, Corinne took a deep breath. Offered a silent prayer: "Dear God, look after Jane. Help her to see clearly. Keep her safe. Amen." She thought about checking her tall frail flowers again. Her beautiful garden was now under full attack from the raging elements. But the night was so barbarous and she was far too spent to go out there again. So she lay there in the dark. Next to her husband. Trying to make room for this evening's revelations. She remembered Alice's blessing, "in the light and in the shadows." Corinne felt surrounded by shadows. She was tired of shadows. There did not appear to be many blessings in the shadows. She preferred the light.

CHAPTER SIX

The Last Saturday of May, Twelve Years Later / *Weaving a Rope of Sand*

ON THE LUMPY COUCH IN THE LIVING ROOM, a very tattered Trigger, Jane's childhood stuffed friend, lounged on top of four-year-old Perkins, who slept soundly in the arms of his drowsy father. As she sat in front of the kitchen window of their home, watching the tide creep toward her in gentle but determined surges, Jane was comforted by the steady presence of her husband and son. She had decided not to go to the funeral the day before yesterday but was still grappling with whether or not this was the right decision. Had she spared her mother and sister the additional shock and pain that her presence would unquestionably cause or had she simply been a coward? Twelve years ago, she decided to make a break from her parents. As a seventeen-year-old runaway, she was not able to reconcile her own health and sanity with her father and mother. As a twenty-nine-year-old wife and mother, she was still having trouble integrating her family history with who she was. Who she had become.

Leaving home was the most impulsive decision of Jane's life. And the most consequential. She could not help but wonder what her days would now be like had she stayed. They would most likely be satisfactory. She would probably have an adequate life. She would undoubtedly be living near her parents. Might even be married to someone very like her father. She could easily have become a teacher there, even as she had become one here. Had she stayed home, however, she would not have Bill. Or Perkins. Or her life out east with its many pleasures and fulfillments. Jane looked away from the window, back toward her husband and son. She would not trade them for anything or anyone else in the world.

Jane assumed that her sister, Helen, had probably planned the funeral service. She could not imagine her mother being able to handle such a daunting task. Helen had plenty of her own fragilities, however. For more than five years after Jane fled, she maintained a secret correspondence with Helen. She called Duke's house at the same time on the same day every week for nearly three years. Throughout that time, Helen was always there. Eager to take her call. Pleading with her to come home each time. But then, halfway through her junior year of high school, there was a noticeable change in Helen's attitude. She was not always at Duke's any more when Jane called. Duke himself was concerned that Helen might be experimenting with drugs. Helen began to disappear into a world of her own.

The last time Jane saw Helen, they were supposed to meet for dinner. Just the two of them. Helen, then nineteen, showed up at the restaurant stoned beyond rational thought with a sinister-looking young man at her side. The man never spoke a word to Jane. He just snickered as Jane tried to convince Helen to come home with her. After that incident, Helen refused to speak with her. Jane reasoned that embarrassment was the greatest obstacle between them but there was more. Helen's hostility ran deep. Jane understood that she had abandoned her sister and her sister, in turn, was abandoning her. From that incident forward, Jane was cut off from the family in which she had grown up. Her mother and father and sister were part of a past that seemed irrecoverable.

Within a few weeks of Jane's running away, her parents knew where she was. Jane had, in fact, with strong encouragement from Evelyn, called home to tell them where she was. She did not want them worrying about her. Imagining her dead in a Dumpster somewhere. Her mother was, not surprisingly, quite distraught. Initially, she was kindhearted, even strangely understanding of Jane's leaving. But when she would not come home, her mother became almost angry. Why, she wanted to know, was Jane doing this to her family? "Especially to your father," she said. It was as if her mother had begun to shift the blame away from anyone else and on to Jane. Her father, on the other hand, seemed to accept her decision in a way Jane never imagined possible. In fact, he did not even seem to be the same person. At the time, it was terribly confusing. She would never forget what he said to her over the phone. "It's your life, Jane. Make the most of it. I hope some day you can forgive me." Back then, she could not understand what had happened or why her father was not more insistent she come home immediately.

To attend her father's funeral would be to disrupt whatever peace her family had assembled in her twelve-year absence. At least that was how Jane rationalized her decision. A good friend who did social work in Riverhead once told Jane that human beings could go without sex for a long time, even for a lifetime, but they could not go a single day without a good, satisfying rationalization. Right or wrong, one had to live with one's decisions, Jane reflected. With every decision, momentous or trivial, something was gained and something was lost. In the case of her father's funeral, what was gained and what was lost were one and the same. She did not have to face her mother and sister. She did not get to see her mother and sister.

She had both faced and seen her father, however. In the hospital. Without Helen or her mother ever knowing. Two weeks ago, out of the blue, a priest called Jane at home. Her father was very ill, he said. He was not expected to live much longer and he wanted to see her. Jane was stunned. She told the priest she would be there. Right away. That very evening, before she could talk herself out of it, she drove to the hospital. She would see him after visiting hours. When she could be alone with him without running into anyone else. The priest said this would be fine, that a man as ill as her father could have an after-hours visitor. He told her he would meet her at the hospital and take Jane to him. There was no time to ponder an approach or to consider her words or to test the waters. Unprepared, she had to go.

Jane had always imagined some sort of reconciliation with her father, however provisional, but thought there would be more time in which to find it or achieve it. Some day, she thought, the perfect opportunity would present itself. It would be like waiting to go into the ocean all spring long, and perhaps even through June and July, for just the right temperature on just the right hot summer day. When that day arrived, the ocean would be refreshing and exhilarating the way it could not be on any other day. But that perfect day never arrived and, according to the priest, her father was now dying. How long had he been ill, she wondered? What would he look like? Would he recognize her? What would he say to her after all these years and what could she possibly say to him?

The priest greeted her at the main entrance. She was the only visitor heading into the hospital at that hour and he was the only priest. "You must be Jane," he said and smiled at her empathically, kind, brown eyes affirming her arrival. He told her he was a longtime friend of her father. That fact seemed about as likely as a crow befriending a cat. Her father was not a religious man. Stephen Quintal would never have a priest for a friend. To begin with, her father did not have real friend- ships. He had golf buddies. He had business associates. He did not have "no strings attached" friends. But why would a priest lie about something like that? Following him down vividly bright hospital corridors, Jane felt like she was inside a pecu- liar dream. Each step took her further into the surreal. Was she actually here? Was her father really in this place that smelled faintly of antiseptic and hopelessness?

"This is it," the priest said, stopping at a door that was cracked a few inches. "He's in the bed by the window. I'll leave you two alone." "Please don't," she wanted to say but found herself nodding. It was a small double room. The man in the first bed was sound asleep. Pale and gaunt, he looked like a ghost. A drawn curtain separated the two patients. Jane took a deep breath. Tried to breathe out some of the anxiety that gripped her chest. Stepped around the other side of the curtain. Like the man in the other bed, her father was sleeping.

Unquestionably, this man was her father. This was his face. This was the frail shadow of his form. She looked into dark rings beneath sunken closed eyes encased in pale skin. She stared down at his bony hands, skin like tracing paper loosely stretched over them, a dreaded needle sticking out of the left one, an uncomfortable but she supposed necessary meeting of flesh and technology. That something awful was taking place beneath that skin was apparent. He had no hair. There was an odd smell in the room. Like bad fruit. A mildly rotten yet sweet scent. Should she wake him? Of course she should. She had not come all this way to watch her failing father sleep. But how? She could say something. But what? After all this time, what would be her first words to her father? She walked alongside the bed and touched his hand. The hospital was uncomfortably warm but his thin pallid hand was cold. He stirred. Opened his eyes.

"Jane."

"Daddy?" His eyes were the same. Those striking gray eyes that she had inherited. Eyes that could judge her like no others. Eyes, however, that seemed to hold no judgment now.

"You look beautiful, C.G." She had not heard or even thought about that nickname in a long time. "You look like my sister did when she was about your age. I'm so glad you came, C.G." He spoke in a whisper. As if he had a great weight on his chest, his words escaped in fine gasps of breath.

"The priest called. He said you were sick."

"Father Comfrons. I'm more than sick, C.G. I'm dying. There's no easy way to say that." He shook his head. "I can't get over how much you look like my sister."

"Daddy, I'm sorry."

"No, sweetheart, I'm sorry. I don't blame you for leaving. I'm ashamed about what happened. I . . . "

"Dad,"

"No, let me finish. I wasn't the best father. I know that. The day I came over to the high school with that envelope for Nadine, that was . . . well, that was inexcusable. And that's the least of it. I was so hard on you. You were hard enough on yourself. I should have . . . well, I wish . . . I wish I had enjoyed you more. I've had twelve years to think about this, to figure it out. I can't undo what's happened, Jane. But before I die, would you forgive me? Would you forgive me, Jane?"

"I'm not the one you should be asking, Dad."

"Nadine is a separate matter. This is about you and me. I always figured your leaving home like that was a kind of retribution. That I deserved it. But at this point, I think it has to be over. By now, my sentence must be complete."

"Dad, I didn't leave to punish you."

This was not altogether true so she was relieved to hear him say, "I know."

"I left because I was confused. I left because I needed to . . . "

"You left because I was standing in your way. I think you left because I didn't give you room to breathe." Jane was astonished. How did he know this? How could he, after such a long separation, understand her so clearly? He seemed to be inside her head, gleaning long-mulled thoughts, bringing them out into the room to be examined. "Jane, I'll never forget what you said to me that day. You said, 'I've never heard you apologize for anything.' Jane, I'm apologizing. I'm sorry. I'm sorry I wasn't a better father. I'm sorry about a lot of things. I know you'll think this is funny coming from me, but I believe God has forgiven me. I could die in peace if I knew I had your forgiveness." Was this the same man? He looked like her father. But he did not sound like him at all. The father she left behind was the center of the universe and knew it. He was not the sort of person who would seek forgiveness. He was the sort of man who, with extraordinary consistency, blames others. He was not the kind of man who grovels. He was the kind of man who extracts groveling from others. She stared at her father long and hard. He did seem a different man. She was not sure how it had happened but he had changed. "Please, Jane," he pleaded.

His heart in her hands, Jane stood over her father and said, "I forgive you, Dad." It was what he wanted. Surely she could give him this much. What had seemed impossible yesterday now felt like a very small request. "I forgive you." She took another deep breath and felt a calm wash over her. "I forgive you." With those three words, words that, in this moment, felt even more powerful and significant than "I love you," a great cloud lifted.

In wistful, whispered tones, her father did his best to make peace with Jane. Again, he expressed his belief that her leaving was the price of his transgressions. She could not imagine how he came up with such an erroneous equation. His strange theory explained a great deal to Jane, who had always wondered why her father did not march right out to Fairhampton when he found out where she was. She understood now why he never even attempted to convince her to come home. Why he told her mother to let her be. To let her get on with her life. She thought it was because he did not care enough or that he was too angry with her. Apparently, that was not it at all. He left her alone because he actually believed her running away was his punishment. It was a ridiculous idea. She told him as much. She told him to let it go.

JANE KEPT A DAILY WATCH for her father's obituary in the *New York Times*. It appeared on Wednesday. Three days ago. The printed summary of her father's life included an impressive list of accomplishments and organizations proud to claim him as their own. Her own name, however, was missing from the short list of family members left behind. Her mother had probably made that decision. Or Helen. Maybe Helen. Jane understood this judgment fully. She was even grateful to be absent from the list. Relieved. Like a squirming fish being released from a sharp hook. Set free to swim in her own private pond again. That was three days ago. How fortunate it was that the priest had called. That he called before it was too late. She hoped her father died peacefully. And she wished like hell that she could have gone to the funeral.

The funeral, according to the paper, took place the day before yesterday. Jane could not help but wonder what her mother would do now. Her mother was always so terribly dependent on her father. Could she form an opinion without him? Could she keep the household finances in order with him gone? Who would take care of her now? Helen? If Jane stepped in to lend a hand herself, would she be turned away? She knew her mother was upset with her. Helen had made this clear in the earliest of their conversations. According to Helen, her mother blamed Jane for her father's unhappiness. Was she still angry? What would happen if she called home? She ran her fingers over the smooth ivory plastic form of the telephone. What would she say? How could she say it without causing additional anguish? Jane never wanted to hurt her family. What she had wanted, what she had needed back then, was to stop pretending. To stop pretending she could ever be the perfect child. Or that he could ever be the perfect father. Or that they had ever been the perfect family.

HELEN SAT AT HER LITTLE KITCHEN TABLE sipping a cup of strong, black coffee. Allowing each swallow to massage the back of her throat. She needed caffeine. The last few days had been exhausting. It was hard to believe her father was really gone. She still half-expected him to call at any moment. Ask her how she was doing. Offer her words of encouragement. While her whole life she wished her father thought more highly of her, he was nevertheless a steady source of support. She knew how much he loved her. Helen was freshly out of her third drug and alcohol rehabilitation program. She and her father had endured briefly overlapping stays at Grace Memorial: hers for alcohol poisoning, his for a batch of strange lumps that turned out to be cancer. When she left for New Hampshire, her father was sick but not desperately so. When she returned, he could scarcely speak.

From Grace Memorial, Helen was moved into a New Hampshire treatment center for addicts. Either it was a better program than the last two or she was more ready for it this time. Probably the latter. She was measurably older, progressively wiser, and definitely more interested in living. She wanted out from underneath the bell jar. She had good help this time too. In New Hampshire, she met several remarkable people. People to whom she now felt extraordinarily close. People who were committed not only to their own recoveries, but to hers as well. She longed to stay sober but it was incredibly difficult. Alcohol was everywhere she went. Everywhere she looked. It littered the countertops and coffee tables of every one of her formerly close friends. It beckoned to her from the pages of nearly every novel she read. She could smell it the minute she walked into most restaurants.

Right now, there was no alcohol in Helen's apartment. Her sponsor, Vivian, had searched the chaotic apartment, throwing away every noxious bottle before Helen returned home from New Hampshire. She even found the ones that Helen had stowed beneath her side of the bed. Vivian also arranged to have the place cleaned up. It was unusually spotless. Without much confidence in herself, Helen wondered how long it would stay clean. And how long she would stay clean. She wanted it to work this time. She knew, however, that sobriety was going to cost her. It would mean abandoning almost all of her old friendships. She had already lost her boyfriend, Charlie. When he would not drive up for any of her support sessions at the treatment center, she called and told him to get out. To get out of her apartment and out of her life. He did not put up a fight. Just packed his bags and left. Without leaving a forwarding address. Charlie had been using her. She knew that. She provided him with a rent-free place to live and to party. He was a pretty good cook though. And he was a warm body. In his own way, Charlie had looked after her. She would miss that. Was there anything else to miss about him? Probably not.

On the other hand, there was so much to miss about her father. Small attentions paid. The surprising ways in which he never ever gave up on her. The many times he had found yet another job for her when she had blown the last one. He was terrifically supportive of Helen's rehabilitation efforts. She took another big swallow of hot coffee. God, how she wanted a drink. It was only eight-thirty in the morning and her body ached for it. There were several people she could call. Should call. Vivian. Rick, her counselor up in New Hampshire. Lynn, another woman from Long Island who ended up in treatment in the same place at the same time. Helen supposed she could also call her mother. Her mother would probably be feeling a related sense of aloneness. The person she most desired to talk with, however, was Jane. The old Jane. The one with whom she once shared secrets and sorrows.

Helen barely remembered the last time she saw her sister. It was the year after Helen graduated from high school. They were supposed to have dinner together but they got into a fight. She had some guy with her. She could not remember which guy. When they showed up stoned, Jane was upset. At the time, Helen thought Jane was angry about the guy. Looking back, however, Jane must have been disturbed and probably frightened by the drugs. With or without the marijuana, however, their relationship as sisters was already in trouble by then. Like an unsightly tree with gnarled branches, with each year that came and went, Helen's resentment toward Jane grew. How could her sister have left her all alone like that?

CORINNE DID NOT KNOW WHAT SHE FELT. Or if she felt anything at all. She thought she must be the one who had actually died because she seemed to be floating in a different realm. Hovering above her sorrow. Nothing looked the same to her. Nothing sounded the same. Or tasted the same. The world kept revolving around the sun as if nothing had changed. Yet everything was unalterably different. Stephen was gone. His car was properly parked on his side of the garage. His tools were thoughtfully arranged in the basement. His clothes hung neatly in the closet, the white dress shirts lined up facing east followed by the blue dress shirts. And so on. His files remained fully organized in their drawers. His laundry sat waiting in the correct hampers. His business planner sat squarely open on the desk in the den where he had left it. But Stephen was gone. He was really gone.

He was a good husband. He was by no means faultless. Like many men, he was easily distracted. But he was, essentially, a good man. He worked hard. He provided well. He was a caring father. He loved her. She knew that. When Jane first left, Corinne was afraid Stephen might fall apart. There were moments, back then, of wondering if their marriage would hold together. They both felt capsized by failure. Interestingly enough, however, once Stephen pulled himself together, he became more attentive. More loving than ever. He was never quite the same man again. He had moments of yawning sadness. Sometimes in those first few years following Jane's departure, she would find him sitting on the edge of Jane's bed lost in remembrance. However hard this was on Stephen, Corinne interpreted it as a sign of great care. Stephen had become more thoughtful, more considerate. Not that any of these transformations excused Jane's hurtfulness. Running away was wrong.

Purposefully, like accident victims determined not to let their injuries hold them back, Corinne and Stephen resumed their marriage. An observer might even remark that the Quintals had managed to achieve a more stable household balance without Jane in their home. In one of the very few conversations Corinne and Stephen suffered regarding their daughter's absence, Stephen suggested that three is a more secure configuration than four. She tried to believe that, to believe, as he did, that Jane's abandonment was meant to be. What she really thought, however, was that Jane had been enormously selfish. Jane had no idea how much she had wounded them all. Particularly Stephen. In fact, it would not have surprised Corinne at all if the cancer that eventually took Stephen's life had started its slow growth twelve years ago. With Jane's departure.

NADINE READ STEVE'S OBITUARY in the local paper. In twelve years, she had neither seen nor heard from him. Now he was forever gone from their lives. She had not been forthcoming with her son on the matter of paternity. She lied to Xander, telling him consistently but tenderly that his father was dead. She spoke of him only on request. Never did she offer details. He was a nice man, she told her son. He was an executive. Nadine could tell that Xander had no idea what an executive was or did but the word appeared to impress him. He believed his father was an important man. Those few thoughts were as much as Nadine felt she could reveal. Now, however, that Stephen Quintal was really and truly dead, Nadine wondered if she should tell her son more about his father. As she poured him a glass of fresh-squeezed orange juice and looked into his verdant eyes, she wondered if Xander deserved to know more about the man he resembled in so many ways.

Years ago, Nadine forgave Steve. Yes, he had taken advantage of her in inexcusable ways. Yes, he had lied to her. Yes, he had been indefensibly awful about her pregnancy. But, in all honesty, she had wanted the affair as much as he had. And the bottom line for Nadine was this: if she had not had the affair with Steve, she would not now have Xander, her beautiful boy, the center and the joy of her life. With the help of Rabbi Weil, Nadine had figured out that a bitter person would not make a very good mother. She had to let go. She had to move on. And she did. She did it for herself and she did it, most of all, for Xander. This self-serving pardon did not mean she wanted to see Steve. She did not. Nor did she wish to share Xander with him in any way. Nadine was fairly certain Steve knew about Xander. Theirs was not a small town but it was small enough.

Xander was, as far as Nadine could tell, a typically inde-
fatigable eleven-year-old boy. He loved to run, to ride his bike,
to play soccer and baseball. He was a highly creative child who
could produce a lively game out of almost anything. A balled-
up hamburger wrapper and a plastic straw became the equipment of the fast-food world series. Empty CD cases were
skillfully constructed into Frank Lloyd Wright–esque struc-
tures. Almost anything round could be transformed into a
wheel in Alexander's pursuit of the greatest, the coolest, and
the fastest vehicle on the planet. He had an unusually well-
developed imagination and an artistic aptitude that readily
breathed life into it.

The shape of his face and the insistence with which he
organized everything in his life, from his baseball card collection to his growing library of antique 33-rpm records,
reminded Nadine of Stephen. But he had her green eyes,
which Nadine considered to be far more magnificent on him,
and he carried both her compactness of physique and aesthetic
flair. For better and sometimes for worse, he also bore his
mother's impulsive nature. Recently, Xander had begun a
semi-clandestine search to figure out who his father was.
When he thought his mother was not looking, Xander rummaged. Looked for secret hiding places. Searched for clues.
She caught him reading and rereading the penned farewells in
her high school yearbook. Carefully searching the faces of her
male classmates hoping for the familiar. Looking for a name

he did not know. As far as Nadine could tell, in his determined quest to find a father, he had, so far, come up empty-handed. Rabbi Weil called to tell Nadine that Xander was pumping him for information. She knew Xander was desperate to learn more about his father but, until now, she did not feel it would do anyone any good to tell.

Bill winked at her fondly, letting Jane know that he was awake again. Clearly he was trying to remain motionless so as not to wake little Perkins. Her husband had been honest with her. He believed she should have gone to the funeral and was sure Jane would eventually regret not being there. "No matter how severe or stupid he was, he was still your father. Some things you don't get to choose," Bill said, "parents among them."

"My father was never stupid," she argued. "And that's not it. That's not it at all. This isn't about him. I've made my peace with him."

"Have you?"

"There are things I can't forget but I'm over them. I know that sounds ridiculous after everything I've told you about him but I really have made my peace with him. I wish you could have been there. If you'd seen him the way I did, lying there in the hospital, you'd know how impossible it would have been not to make my peace with him. The decision about the funeral is all about my mother and my sister. Can't you see I just don't want to cause them any more pain?"

"Janie, you asked for my opinion. I'm giving it. I under-stand why you don't want to go but I still think you should. You say you've made your peace with your father. Maybe it's time to make peace with everybody else." As was his way, Bill made his case and then stepped back. "Listen, Janie, I know you have to do this thing your way. You have to resolve this situation yourself."

When Jane told Bill she could not do it, she could not go, he agreed to be supportive. And so, on Thursday morning, Jane left for work as usual. She opted to skip her own father's funeral. As if it were any other day of the year. As if she could go to school and not think about him every minute of that day. Her head swimming with memories both pleasant and ugly, she survived the day of the funeral. Now, however, she was in agony. Now she was a mess. Bill was right. She wished she could have found a way to be there. She had not slept well since Thursday.

Jane could tell Bill was observing her every move. As if he thought she might collapse if he looked away. He sat there on the couch, cradling their sleeping son, watching Jane rub the receiver of the phone with tense fingers. He, more than any-one else, could sense her grief. With Bill, there was no place to hide. He usually knew what she was thinking, how she was feeling. As wonderful as Bill was though, Jane needed some-one else to talk to. Someone with a few more years, a few more trials and tribulations under her belt. She wished Evelyn could come today instead of tomorrow. She wished she did not have to wait. Evelyn was so good at helping her sort things out. Unfortunately, Evelyn no longer lived out east. A larger church in Nassau County made her a better offer and, much to Jane's disappointment, she left town three years ago.

They were still fast friends, however, Jane and Evelyn. What started out as a temporary arrangement turned into a six-year room rental. Evelyn helped Jane to get her high school diploma. And then to apply to a local community college. And finally, to receive a master's degree in education. Evelyn became like a big sister and, sometimes, like a mother. She officiated at Jane and Bill's wedding almost six years ago. She baptized Perkins. She was there for almost every significant moment of Jane's adult life. Evelyn almost always visited them on Sunday afternoons. She loved their cozy home on the beach. She adored little Perkins, who thought of her as a grandmother. If only Evelyn were here now. Jane turned to Bill and, in an unexpectedly child-like voice, said, "I'm going to take a little walk. Is that alright?"

"Of course," he responded, "you want company, Freckleface?" He claimed to adore the tiny freckles that ran across the bridge of her nose. She looked at him with perplexed eyes, eyes that told him she did not wish to turn him down or hurt his feelings but she wanted to be alone. Without Jane having to say a word, Bill understood. She knew he would. He told her to go on ahead. Perkins slept through the entire transaction. Almost under her breath, she said, "I'll take Toto." She whistled the first half of the construction-worker's catcall, and a small Jack Russell terrier emerged from the bedroom where it was his habit to sleep late in the morning. Especially on Saturday mornings.

Slowly, Jane walked down the cedar steps to the beach. Toto did not wait for her. He scooted to the bottom of the steps and was wagging his little tail expectantly before she reached the second step. "Let's go," she whispered to the dog, but without her usual enthusiasm. This morning, she walked like an old woman. Somewhere in the back of her mind, she had imagined all the time in the world in which to make amends with her family. She had envisioned a point in the future at which a resolution, a family appeasement, would become possible. The priest had created an opportunity for her and for her father. He presented it to her as an unexpected gift. As a rope woven from sand. She wished someone could facilitate another miraculous intervention like that with her mother and her sister. She wished someone would hand her the wisdom and the courage and the maturity she needed to face them too. Then she could say what children are supposed to say: Please. Thank you. I'm sorry. And what grown-ups are suppose to say: Nobody's perfect. Shit happens. Let's not allow this to stand in our way.

When she first left, got on that unfamiliar train, arrived in this old town, Jane had no idea she would end up staying. She had not thought that far out. She was reacting. She needed to get away and she did. But she never imagined she would live out here permanently. She had packed only enough clothing for a few days. She had left people who were important to her, things that were precious to her. She never intended to abandon her family altogether. Her purpose in leaving had little to do with hurting anyone. It had to do with healing herself. Finding herself. And surely she would have returned home, thought Jane as she looked back up at the house, but for the extraordinary way in which this town had received her. As if they had been waiting for her.

She headed east along the beach, putting one leaden foot in front of the other. Along the way, out of habit, Jane looked for beach treasure. She picked out four smooth ocean-tossed stones and placed them in her pocket. When, at last, she came to the place where a new inlet had broken through the barrier beach in that big nor'easter twelve years earlier, she sat down, massaged those small stones with her fingers, and wept. She offered tears for the years she missed with her father and mother and sister. Tears for the way things might have been. Tears for her own stubbornness. Usually, when she cried, Toto licked her face. Today he sat next to her at a respectful distance. With her, he quietly watched the indomitable ocean rushing into the inlet toward high tide.

Helen went hunting for the phone book. The apartment was perfectly clean and organized. The problem was that nothing was where she had left it. Although Helen's place was almost always in a wildly chaotic state, it was her state. She knew how to decode the mess. She was always able to lay her hands on what she needed. The phone book, for instance, was kept on top of the refrigerator. That is where it was supposed to live. That is where it was supposed to hold down all bills and correspondence she did not wish to look at. But it was not there now. In fact, the top of the refrigerator was bare. Sanitized. It still held a faintly lemony scent from the cleanser that had been used to wipe it clean. The untackled mail was arranged in a wicker basket that sat in the middle of her kitchen table. Finally, she found the phone book in a top drawer under the kitchen counter beneath the wall phone. She understood but did not appreciate the logic of its placement.

Helen hated neat rooms. They made her deeply uncomfortable. She preferred a lived-in look, a space that affirmed the disorderliness of life. The messiness of humanity. In her opinion, Vivian had gone too far in straightening up the apartment. Every towel was washed and folded. Every knickknack was dusted and arranged. The only untouched havens of disarray were her closets. She opened up the phone book. Looked up the number for Nadine Aiuto. Wrote it on the back of an envelope from the top of the unopened mail pile.

Obstinately tossed the phone book back on top of the refrigerator where it belonged. She removed a large pack of wintergreen gum from her purse. Opened three pieces. Stuffed them in her mouth. Left the wrappers crumpled on the tabletop in front of her.

Always from a distance, Helen had quietly observed Nadine over the years. From the picture in the school yearbook Jane had left behind, she had recognized Nadine every time. Begrudged her every time. Nadine, on the other hand, had no idea who Helen was. How could she? Why would she? They had never been introduced. The only contact between them was the one futile phone call placed twelve years ago when Helen was eager for any crumb of information about her sister. Helen had Nadine's face memorized and, with that striking red hair, she was easy to spot. She had, apparently, gone ahead with the pregnancy because there was a child next to her most of the time. A boy who had a bit of her father in him. Especially around the mouth and chin. From what Helen could tell, Nadine had not married. She and the boy lived with Nadine's mother in the same house down on the water. Helen was also aware that Nadine made jewelry. Delicate gold wire earrings. Necklaces decorated with elegant bits of smooth beach glass. Helen, in fact, owned a pair of the earrings. A dangly pair with pale blue glass beads. She liked the fact that the glass beads did not match one another precisely. They were similar in hue and form yet each had its own shape.

Each was worn down in its own distinctive way. But she had not bought them for their beauty. She had bought them as a way of staying connected to the person who had, unwittingly, changed her life forever.

Staring at the phone, she recalled that morning twelve years ago. It had all started with a damned phone call. To this day, she regretted picking up the hallway phone on that miserable morning. To this day, she wondered why she had to be the one to hear it first. To stumble into the hall first. To answer it first. Everything might have been so different. Nadine's predicament, however, would have remained the same. As a fourteen-year-old child, Helen did not appreciate a fact she now understood too well. Like a postmodern Hester Prynne, Nadine had been on her own throughout the whole awkward affair.

As far as Helen knew, her father had never offered Nadine an ounce of help. Either he did not know about the boy or had convinced himself he was not the boy's father. Maybe it was not too late. Helen could reach out to Nadine on her father's behalf. She would be getting some money from her father's estate. The amount would not be insignificant. Her father had done well with his business, a business that could now be sold. He had also fared astonishingly well in the stock market. While Nadine did not appear to need money, it seemed appropriate that some of Stephen Quintal's earnings go to her. And,

of course, to the boy. Five years ago, ten years ago, Helen
would never have imagined giving anything to Nadine.
Throughout most of her adult life, Helen hated her. Blamed
her. Imagined saying the worst things to her. One of the
lessons learned in New Hampshire was that a person was
responsible, first and foremost, for her own life. For her own
decisions. It was not Nadine's fault that Jane left. The only
one who could reasonably be held accountable for Jane's running away was Jane. For so many years, Helen hated Nadine.
It was time to dismiss that childhood hatred.

Helen took a deep breath, used her tongue to stretch the
gum in her mouth into a flat disk. Punched the numbers into
the keypad on the phone. Before it could ring, she placed the
receiver back into its cradle. Took another deep breath. God,
how she wanted a drink. She picked up the phone again. "No
time like the present," she said as the phone rang on the other
end. No time like the present. It was the theme song of her
new life. It was the inescapable message of her father's death.
No time like the present. A drowsy young voice answered the
phone. "Hello?" This must be the voice of her brother.
Helen's half brother. She wasn't expecting him to answer.
After a clumsy silence, Helen asked for the boy's mother. She
heard his young voice call, "Mom?" and a woman in the background answer, "Just a sec, Xander." And then she was on the
other end. Answering Helen's call. Saying, "Hello."

"Hi, Nadine?"

"Yes. Who's this?" Her soft yet confident voice sounded far removed from the girl with whom she had spoken so many years ago.

"This is Helen Quintal. We've never met but I'm Stephen's daughter."

"Steve's daughter? So you're Jane's sister?"

"Yeah." Nadine still referred to her father as Steve and it still shook Helen.

"You're the one who called. Back then. You were looking for her. I remember. You were looking for your sister. She took off. Did you ever find her?"

"Well, sort of. You remember me calling?"

"How could I forget?" There was no sarcasm in that remark. It was a matter-of-fact statement. What should she say now? Where should she start? Before she could find her next words, Nadine said, "Listen, I'm sorry about your father. I read about him in the paper."

"I'm not sure exactly why I called, Nadine, but there are some things I'd like to talk about. With you, I mean. Nothing bad." Helen was certain she sounded like a fool.

"Go ahead, then. What do you want to talk about?" At least Nadine did not shut her down immediately.

"I was hoping we could meet, you know, in person. Maybe you could come over for a cup of coffee or something."

"Sure. We could probably do that some time." It was an indefinite response. Perhaps Nadine was blowing her off after all.

"I was hoping . . . " Helen cleared her throat uneasily. Took the gum out of her mouth, resting it on one of the crumpled foil wrappers. "I was hoping we could meet today."

"Today? It's Saturday. I have my son home with me today."

"I could come over there. This won't take long, I promise."

"We usually hang out here on Saturday," she said, "you know, like a family day."

"I don't want to interrupt but you see, if only you knew how hard it was for me to call. I don't mean to sound melo-dramatic. Five minutes. That's all I need."

There was a pause at the other end. Nadine relented. "Okay. You can come here. But I have to warn you, my son knows nothing about your family. Nothing about your father." This last part she whispered, presumably so that her son would not hear. Helen respected that. This confidential approach not only protected her son, it had protected her father. It had protected her. Nadine, as it turned out, was not at all what Helen imagined. As a fourteen-year-old, desperate to preserve her family, Helen thought Nadine was trying to use her father and ruin their lives. Instead, Nadine had made a decision to keep her life completely separated from her father. She had asked him for nothing.

CORINNE DID NOT WANT TO BE ALONE. Her head felt as if it might explode. It did not hurt but it felt so full. There were too many thoughts in there. Too many memories were whirling recklessly inside her skull. Everything held a remembrance. The coffee mug in her hand, for instance. It was just a cheap souvenir mug with a palm tree and a sailboat on it. There was nothing exceptionally lovely about the mug. It was precious, nevertheless. Stephen bought it for her while they were on vacation in the Bahamas. It was an anniversary vacation. Their twenty-fifth. Jane had been gone only a few years. In those days, Corinne was still struggling bravely to put the past behind her. Stephen suggested the anniversary getaway. It would be therapeutic he said. For both of them. And it had been. The trip was marvelous. Stephen was wonderful.

She wished someone would knock on the door and take her someplace else. Anywhere else. The house was unavoidably replete with Stephen. It looked like him. It smelled like him. Every corner spoke of him. Perhaps she should go for a walk. Impose upon herself a change of scenery. Or maybe she should do something altogether out of character. That was Alice's suggestion. Get a manicure. Go to the movies. Dye her hair. Was it madness to be thinking such banal thoughts? Was there really any way to manage sorrow? Or was it only possible to divert one's attentions from it for a moment here and there? The phone rang. Should she answer it this time? Was it one more person calling to check on her emotional state? She picked up the receiver. It was Father Comfrons. What did he want?

Corinne was sure she sounded like a zombie. One of the living dead. He wanted to meet with her. "Can it wait?" she wondered out loud. "Of course," he replied with unsurprising compassion. But then she changed her mind. Yes, she would meet with him. No, he could not meet her at the house. Somewhere else, she requested. Ten-thirty would be fine, she agreed. At The Captain's Folly. All in the same lackluster tone of voice. Corinne had seen enough of Father Comfrons in the past few weeks to last a lifetime. It was not that she disliked the priest. She knew he was a very special person who had been uncommonly kind to her husband over the years. But she had always harbored some concerns about him. Moreover, in her mind he was now inextricably linked to Stephen's death. She could never see him again without picturing him throwing a handful of earth on Stephen's coffin. Without hearing him speak of a comfort that was beyond her reach.

THE THICK GLASS DOOR OF THE DINER was heavier than she expected. It took some effort to open it. He was already there when Corinne arrived. Sitting in a booth near the door. Huddled with a cup of coffee. Corinne could never quite figure out Stephen's friendship with Father Comfrons. Stephen became almost too dependent on him. When she first called him twelve years ago, asking for help, she had no idea his help would extend all the way unto sickness and death. She was never able to connect with Father Comfrons the way Stephen did. He called the priest Joe. As if he were a next-door neighbor or a childhood friend. She could never feel comfortable calling him anything but Father. This formality was mutual. He always called her Mrs. Quintal.

Wordlessly, she slipped into the seat across the table from him. He looked the same. Father Comfrons always looked the same. Same black shirt. Same khaki pants. The only difference was that twelve years ago, he had a little hair on the sides of his head. Now he was markedly bald. Corinne did not apologize for being more than half an hour late. He would have to understand. Surely he would understand. Corinne was un-accustomed to being at a loss for words. She just said, "Hello," in the same emotionless timbre she offered him over the phone. It was the only voice she had right now.

"How are you doing, Mrs. Quintal?"

She wanted to scream, "How do you think I'm doing?" She did not answer.

"Mrs. Quintal, I have something to tell you. Before your husband died, he asked me to give you a message." One tired eyebrow lifted, a feeble expression of surprise. "He wanted you to know how much he loved you. Stephen said he never deserved a woman as good as you. He was thankful for you. He just wanted you to know." What was this about? She knew Stephen loved her. She did not need the priest to tell her.

Father Comfrons handed her an envelope. Inside the envelope was a letter.

> Dear Cory,
>
> If you are reading this letter, I am gone. I'm sorry I had to leave so soon. I love you, Cory. I have not always loved you well enough but I have always loved you. We've been through a lot together. I wish I could say I have no regrets but I can't. I regret the fact that I was not a more faithful husband and a more loving father. Cory, you have carried so much anger toward Jane over the years and you must have noticed I did not share your feelings. It's my fault she left. Please don't blame her any longer. She has turned into a lovely young woman, Cory. She has some of your gracious qualities. I asked her to come see me at the hospital and she did. I am taking some unresolved issues to my grave but Jane, thank God, is not one of them. We have forgiven one another and made our peace. I hope you will do the same. Don't wait. If there is one thing I've learned over the last few weeks, it's that life is short. Jane's new address and phone number are on the bottom of this letter. Whatever happens, know that I love you. I didn't say it enough. I love you, Cory.
>
> Yours forever,
>
> Stephen

At first, she could find no response. Then a single tear fell from the inside of her right eye. She made no attempt to brush it away. She let it fall down in nearly a straight line, the force of gravity revealing one tiny droplet of her anguish. "He wanted to make sure you knew," Father Comfrons added, reaching across the table, covering her hand with his. Stephen was speaking to her from the grave. From the moment Stephen drew his last breath, she had been talking to him in her head but it had been a one-way conversation. Until this moment.

Corinne was genuinely shocked to learn that Jane had visited Stephen in the hospital. In her hospital. They had not spoken of Jane in years. Corinne, of course, could never forget her daughter. But she assumed that, somehow, Stephen had been able to do just that. That he had been able to excise her from his life. From his memory. From his mind and his heart. Apparently, such was not the case. Perhaps he had never stopped thinking about her. She did not know whether to be troubled or simply puzzled by this surprising information. She drank down the glass of water the waitress delivered and asked for another.

"You know," she said to the priest, "the only person I have ever spoken with about Jane since she ran away is a therapist. A shrink. Stephen never wanted to talk about her. I couldn't even mention her name. We kept her pictures up everywhere in the house. We left her room just as it was the day she ran off. It was like she died. Like she became some sort of ghost."

"Did you ever try to contact her?" the priest asked.

"I wanted to at first, but Stephen . . . " She did not know how to end the sentence. But Stephen what? Stephen would not let her? That was not true. Stephen what? "Stephen thought we should leave her alone. Let her get on with her life."

"Why?"

Why? Corinne thought this was a topic Stephen would have discussed with the priest. Two years after Jane left, when it was absolutely clear she was not coming home again, Corinne went to see a therapist. She went only three times. It occurred to her now that the primary reason she discontinued therapy had to do with that grueling little word, "Why?" She could not answer it because, at the time, she was asking it on her husband's behalf. She was trying to answer it for him. Now that Stephen was gone, she would have to take greater responsibility for that question. Why? She would have to answer it for herself. Moreover, Stephen's totally unexpected dying wish was an end to the long-standing self-imposed restraining order. It would be difficult. She had spent twelve years being mad at Jane. Resentment like that has deep roots. A person cannot be pulled out of it in an instant.

Nadine was anxious about Helen Quintal coming to her house. To her turf. Why had this girl called? What did she want? Was she thinking of becoming involved in their lives in some way? Did she know about Xander? Was she, after all these years, interested in him? Did this have anything to do with Steve's death? Maybe she should not have been so quick to allow this Helen person to come over. What if she said something to Xander about his father? What if she leaked some information about Steve, and Xander figured out what it meant? He was a very bright kid. Sometimes too bright, Nadine thought. Well, it was too late now. The girl was on her way and Nadine was not even dressed yet.

She threw on a plain pair of jeans and a black cotton sweater. She shaped her short wet hair with her fingertips. Added a light layer of foundation. A quick sweep of blush. A hint of mascara. A pair of silver wire earrings. Beckoned by the violent video explosions emanating from her son's room, she poked her head inside his door. Watched him honing his technical skills. Decided not to disturb him. She stopped in her mother's room. It was ten-thirty but her mother was still in bed, surrounded by plump pillows, watching a game show rerun. All week long, her mother got up early to exercise but, on the weekends, it was her habit to sleep in. "Like royalty," Leslie Aiuto claimed.

"Hey, Mom. Can I bring you some juice? I just made some."

"Sure, Princess. That'd be super. Where's our little prince this morning?"

"From the sound of things, he's in the heat of battle, Mom."

"Video games again?"

"You're the one who bought him that damn thing," Nadine said, laughing.

"Well, send him in here. He loves this show. Tell him it's time for our show."

"You got it. And, Mom?"

"Yes, Princess."

"Somebody's coming over in a little while. I'd rather not be disturbed if that's alright, Mom."

"Do I look like I'm going anywhere?"

"Thanks, Mom. And one more thing."

"Yes?"

"If you could keep Xander busy, that'd be great." Her mother sat up in bed. Now she was interested.

"Male or female? Am I allowed to ask?" her mother inquired with anticipation.

"Female, Mom. Not to worry."

"Who's worried? Who's worried? But, you know, Princess, male wouldn't bother me. You're young. You're beautiful."

"I know. I know. Let's not get started already this morning. I'll bring you your juice. I'll send in the little man." Her mother had probably reminded her a thousand times how "young and beautiful" she was. How a father for Xander would not be such a bad idea. She was already thirty. Not as young as her mother thought. Nadine had not dated seriously in more than a year. Most of her male friends got married long ago. Some of them were on their second wives already. Nadine's last serious prospect, Eddie the Buick dealer from Lindenhurst, did not feel he could make the commitment to Xander. "I don't know if I could treat him like he was my own," Eddie said. Maybe he just needed more time to get used to Xander. She was afraid, however, that the longer she waited, the more difficult it would be to break up with him. He was a nice guy. Sweet. If only he had said, "I'll try my best to treat him like my own," or "We'll work on growing into a father-son relationship." Something a little more positive. A little less tentative. She wanted to meet a man while she was still "young and beautiful" but she was not willing to sacrifice Xander's happiness in any way. He came first.

Nadine had not thought of Jane Quintal in many years. Steve's troubled daughter had dropped into her life suddenly, offered her confidential support at a time when she welcomed it, then abruptly disappeared. At the time, Nadine was disappointed that she would have to go to the clinic all by herself. Looking back on the situation, however, she was glad Jane left town when she did. Had Jane accompanied her, she might well have gone through with the abortion. She might have felt some pressure to do so.

When some vaguely familiar joggers ran right by the spot where Jane sat on the beach with Toto, she decided it was time to head back. She did not want anyone to see her in this puffy-eyed state and she could not sit there all morning. It was a magnificent morning, nothing like that stormy week twelve years ago. This morning offered a clear cerulean sky. With brilliant sun. And a breeze no more detectable than the effect of butterfly wings. A good day for sitting. A good day for contemplating joys and sorrows. Bill and Perkins, however, were undoubtedly waiting for her. They would be worried about her by now. She told herself that, as terrible as she felt, she had made the right decision about the funeral. What would it have been like for her mother had she shown up out of the blue? Her presence might have sent her mother into shock. And Helen? Helen would, probably, have been outraged.

Perhaps she could write a letter. Put her thoughts and feelings into words. She was an English teacher, after all. A high school English teacher. If she could not articulate herself, who could? She could explain to her mother how hard it had been to leave. She could tell Helen that she had fully intended to come home after a few days but then . . . well then, her life seemed to open up in ways that had never been possible at home. Would they understand? Jane doubted it. Looking back on what happened, Jane wondered where she had found the courage to leave home. It was so unlike her. It was irresponsible, unpredictable, impulsive. Words that did not fit. Then or now.

As they walked back toward the house, Jane commented to Toto, "I wonder if my mother looks the same." As a child, there were many times when she had found great comfort in her mother's face. In those soft blue eyes. In that calming voice. And, of course, Helen must look quite different by now. She was always a little round like their mother. And beautiful. Also like their mother. As a child, Helen did not have a sense of how lovely she was. How special. Jane hoped her sister had, by now, discovered her own unique beauty. And that she had found some happiness. If only she had been able to keep in touch with Helen. The loss of her sister was the most significant of the costs Jane had borne. In many ways, her sister had been her best friend. Her partner in the important work of family commiseration. Her laugh-mate in the realm of the absurd. Her study partner in the discipline of adolescent crushes. Her confidante in matters of secrecy. Toto looked at her as if he comprehended every thought, every feeling. When Aunt Wally's beautiful retriever, Bernie, died almost ten years ago, Jane could not imagine another pet being a better companion. Now she felt the same way about Toto.

Suddenly, Jane remembered an incident that occurred in their elementary school days, when an older boy, a nasty neighbor boy, stopped Helen and Jane on their way to school. His nickname was Winger because he liked to pull the wings off flying insects. Audaciously, he had demanded their lunches. If they ever told on him, he said, he would beat them up. Both of them. Fearfully, they relinquished their lunches, their cream cheese and jelly sandwiches, their Red Delicious apples, their carrot sticks. Then, after they watched Winger dump the contents of their lunch bags onto the ground, and after he had finished stomping on the sandwiches with his big feet and angrily hurling the apples into the side of a tree because there was no candy in the bags, Helen had cried hysterically. Jane tried to calm her but she was terribly frightened. Inconsolable.

Jane took Helen home that morning. It was so cold outside. Fall. It must have been late fall. Home again, in the warmth of their kitchen, she made hot chocolate for her sister. Their mother was, of course, not home. She was already at the hospital caring for other people's children. Jane washed her sister's face and told her that everything would be fine. She promised to protect Helen. Always. She made fresh sandwiches and cut more carrots. They went to school late. As far as Jane knew, Helen had never shared that story with anyone. Nor had she.

The ocean water was still quite cold but Jane removed her sneakers and walked along the edge of it anyway, along the corridor of sand that is so wet human feet form a deep and immediate imprint. She watched her toes sink with each chilly step. When she neared home again, she looked back along the pulsing shoreline to see that every footstep had, indeed, been gobbled up.

ON THE WAY TO NADINE'S HOUSE, Helen stopped to buy flowers and another pack of gum. She did not want to show up empty-handed. She cherished flowers. Unquestionably, this was her mother's influence. Helen never learned to garden but she did learn to appreciate their splendor. Tulips were still in season. She bought a large potted plant loaded with early red blossoms. Influenced by her mother, Helen rarely purchased cut flowers. Plants live much longer. Not that Helen had ever refused a gift of cut flowers. Helen could count on one hand the number of times people had presented her with flowers. Three times her father had given her bouquets of roses. The first time at her graduation. The second two times, while she was in rehab. Sobering up again. Surely, had he been well enough, another big bouquet would have shown up in New Hampshire. Duke sent her flowers once too. The first time she was in rehab. He sent birds-of-paradise, a big, glorious flock of them.

Helen missed Duke greatly. He had a wonderful flair for the dramatic while maintaining an almost supernatural calm. He died the same year he sent her those splendid flowers. Pneumonia. At the time of his death, Helen felt abandoned all over again. She volunteered to adopt Earl, who was quite an old man by then, in dog years. But a friend of Duke's, a tall, skinny man named Gary, about whom Helen had never before heard a word, had already claimed the dog. The man bawled like a baby all the way through Duke's modest funeral service. When Helen dared to approach Gary at the funeral to inquire about the dog, he became angrily defensive. "I told Duke I'd take him and I'm takin' him. You gotta problem with that, Missy?" She could still hear the word "Missy" clearly in her head. When he spoke it, he sounded like a snake. Duke was gone. Jane was long gone. Charlie was gone, and good riddance. Dad was gone now too. Mom was the only one left. Except for her little half brother. If things went well, she might get to meet him.

NADINE OPENED HER DOOR to a woman who looked much older than she expected. This was Jane's younger sister? The years had not treated her well. Helen did not look like her sister, Jane, at all. Nor did she look much like her father. She was tall. More than six feet. She was big-boned. Naturally muscular. The kind of woman who might once have been an athlete. A basketball player. She had long wavy hair that had been dyed blonde. Obviously with a kit. And she was very worn-looking. Like one of those Third World women who live such hard lives, they appear to be much older than their years. Helen looked familiar too. Someone she might have seen around town. A woman you might pass in the mall hundreds of times but never say "boo" to. Nadine thanked Helen for the beautiful tulips and invited her into the kitchen. She pulled an elegant glass plate from a high cupboard. Placed the pot of flowers on top. Added cool water. Nadine motioned

Helen to pull a stool up to the counter. She had laid out a small buffet of bagels, spreads, strawberries and grapes.

"My sister told me about your beautiful kitchen."

"Did she tell you everything that happened in this kitchen?"

"Most of it. She was so sick. Hung over."

"Well then, would you like a mimosa?" Nadine asked, holding up a chilled bottle of champagne. "It's a weekend tradition around here." Nadine hoped Helen did not think she was celebrating anything. Mimosas were standard fare with brunch on Saturday and Sunday in the Aiuto household.

"No thanks," Helen answered, "I don't drink. That is, I can't drink." Respectfully, Nadine put the bottle back in the refrigerator door. "I'll take some orange juice. If that's okay." Helen sounded apologetic.

Nadine filled two tall champagne flutes with juice. "I'm sorry about your father," she offered again.

"Thanks," Helen said, "Look, I know this is funny, me calling you up like this. It just seemed foolish for us not to meet. I know about the boy. Your son."

Seeing Nadine's face take on a worried look, Helen tried to reassure her. "Look, I'm not here to bother you. Or him. If you want to be left alone, I'll leave you alone. It just doesn't seem right. What my father did, that is. I thought . . . well, now that he's gone, you should get something. Out of his estate, I mean. We haven't been to the lawyer yet or anything, but my

father was a good businessman. I think you should have something. That's all."

Nadine was stunned. This was not what she anticipated at
all. She was not sure what she was expecting but whatever it
was, it was not this. Ordinarily talkative, Nadine was startled
into silence. She smiled a mystified but genuine smile. Just
then, Xander came running in. Looked up at his mother, then
at the stranger. Said, "Hi there." A voice called from a room on
the other side of the house, "Xander, get in here. I told you to
leave them alone." He dashed off again, as if running for
cover.

"He's a good-looking kid," Helen said.

"Yeah, he's a real piece of work," Nadine replied proudly.

"I can see my father in him."

"A little," she conceded. "Listen, I appreciate your coming
over here and offering us something from your father's estate
but we really don't need it. We've done just fine without him."

"He should have helped."

"We didn't need his help. Seriously."

"But he should have helped just the same."

"I didn't want him to."

"I'm sorry about what happened."

"Don't be. Don't be sorry. Xander is the best thing that
ever happened to me." She meant it absolutely. As if he had
been listening in, Xander came running back to the table. "Do
I know you?" he asked Helen.

"I don't think so," she answered.

He was studying her face, as if he recognized a connection. It was a curious meeting. Nadine looked at the two of them and while, in appearance, they were wildly different from one another, the fact that they were brother and sister was inescapable. She had been so careful to keep Stephen out of Xander's life but, watching the two of them looking one another over, she thought that, perhaps, the moment of truth had arrived. Before she had time to think about it too much, before she could chicken out or come up with one more clever way to dodge her son's curiosity, Nadine said, "Xander, this is your sister, Helen. Helen Quintal."

"Sister?" he asked. He did not appear to trust her statement.

"That's right," Nadine said.

"Wow! I didn't know I had a sister. A sister!" Helen nodded intently. He seemed to believe his mother now. And he was clearly pumped up about the idea. His whole body was wiggling with delight. Nadine hoped this was the right thing to do.

"Is this okay with you?" she asked, wincing in Helen's direction. "I should have asked first."

"Of course!" Helen was noticeably surprised but seemed, also, to be pleased.

"That means you know who my father was. He's dead, you know."

"Xander!" Nadine was embarrassed by her son's bluntness.

"It's okay, Nadine. Yes, Xander, he's dead," Helen echoed, her voice tinged with sadness.

"You got a picture of him?" This was what he always wanted, Nadine knew. To see what his father looked like. If Helen pulled a picture out of her pocket right now, Xander would think he was the luckiest boy on the planet.

XANDER WAS A CHARMING LITTLE GUY, endearingly bright and energetic. He already had Helen wrapped around his little finger. And he probably knew it too.

"Where do you live?"

"About five miles from here. Not far."

"Can you get the pictures and bring 'em back? The pictures of my father?" He wanted urgently to see what his father looked like. He was so wound up at the prospect of seeing these photographs that, without being conscious of it, he was bouncing on the balls of his feet, nearly jumping up and down. He had discovered there were pictures of his father. Their father. And he was visibly excited. Helen was ready to run right home and make it happen but Nadine threw a little cold water on their growing enthusiasm. "You don't have to go to any trouble, Helen. Really you don't."

"Oh, please, Mom, please," he begged.

"I don't mind," Helen said, "It's not that far."

"Maybe you could come back tomorrow. For lunch or something." Nadine said. She could tell Nadine had had enough. She did not become rude or unkind but her arms were now folded in front of her, a gesture akin to shutting a door. It was enough for one day. Helen understood. These were life-size decisions. Telling Xander who she was. Who his father was. Although meeting her little brother was not her primary reason for visiting Nadine, it was a great thrill to be introduced to him. More importantly, in terms of setting a few things straight in her life, it felt good and right to see Nadine as a real human being. To see her with different eyes. Grown-up eyes that have abandoned black and white, eyes that have learned to put things in perspective, to see things in shades and colors. For so long, Nadine was a two-dimensional caricature to Helen. Now she was more real.

"She wants to come back," Xander reassured his mother. Then he checked with Helen, "You want to come back, right?" Helen allowed herself to smile a little as she nodded willingly.

Helen could see Xander watching outside through the living room window as she left. She imagined him trying to figure out what it means to have sister. His father was dead but he had a sister. This was exactly how she felt. Even as Helen mourned her father, she celebrated her wonderful kid brother. Like Duke, the counselors up in New Hampshire dished out an never-ending supply of pithy sayings. One such oft-imparted aphorism was this: "Where one door closes, another door opens." Today that flat piece of wisdom came to life for Helen.

NADINE DID NOT TELL HER PARENTS much about Xander's father. She told them he was married and that she did not want to have any more to do with him. He was someone she had once cared for deeply. By mistake. And she did not want to talk about him. Ever. They respected her wishes. They did not pry into Xander's mysterious paternity. Her father was clear. "If you change your mind," he said, "or if you want him to take responsibility, you let me know. I'll take care of it." There was no doubt in Nadine's mind that her father would follow through on this promise if she wanted him to. But she never did change her mind. She did not wish to see Steve again. Or talk to him again. Or listen to his lies ever again. She certainly did not want to ask him for anything. Now that the snake was out of the basket, however, she thought she had better tell her mother. Before she heard it from Xander.

Nadine's father died four years ago. When Xander was seven. Her father struggled with congestive heart failure for more than two years. In the end, he seemed to give up. Although he was never really able to keep up with Xander, he thoroughly enjoyed being a grandfather. He shared quieter activities with his grandson. Chinese checkers. Puzzles. The pleasure of sharing a bowl of popcorn. Nadine missed him greatly. She knew Xander missed him too.

Helen was long gone but Xander was still glued to the window. Nadine kneeled backwards on the couch alongside her anxious son. Leaned into him tenderly. Asked, "Are you okay?"

"Yeah." She stared out of the window with him.

"Are you mad at me?" As he looked up at her, she continued, "For not telling you more about your father?"

"I don't know, Mom," he answered candidly. "I don't know him yet." It was a remarkably introspective answer for an eleven-year-old boy. He had a lifetime to figure out how he felt about his father. How angry to be about his mother's concealment. From what Nadine could tell, Xander was, for the moment, totally focused on the photographs that would arrive tomorrow with his sister.

"You know, you look a little bit like him."

"Just a little?"

"Yeah, just a little."

"What did he look like?"

"Well, he was not as tall as Grandpa but he was not short either. He was a handsome man, really. He had a nice face. Gray eyes. A good nose. Better than Grandpa's. You'll see. I have to tell you something else, Xander. This might make you mad." He looked up at her. She held him close and said, "He died only a few days ago. He hasn't been dead all this time."

"Is that why Helen came to see you?" He was such a smart kid.

"I think so, Xander. Your father had another family. That's why he couldn't be your daddy." There was, of course, more to it than that. But this was enough for now. Xander did not say a word. He accepted her embrace. Nadine hoped it was a safe place for him to think about these important matters.

When Stephen was in the hospital, especially when it became clear that he was not going to make it, that, like dominoes falling down, one knocking over the next, his organs were failing, Corinne was upset by the priest's interference. It was her duty to be in that hospital room with her husband while he died. It was not the priest's job. Stephen and Father Comfrons had become good friends over the years but what is a friend compared to a wife? What is a friendship born of trauma compared to a marriage born of love? She was thankful for the priest's help but he did not always seem to know his place. He did not always know when to get out of the way. Nevertheless, by the time she left the diner, Corinne understood better why Stephen had spent so much time with Father Comfrons. Why they had met for lunch once a week throughout these twelve uneasy years. There was a presence about him that was very reassuring. He made Corinne feel that, in spite of everything, all would be well.

Corinne appreciated the fact that twelve years ago, with the priest's help, Stephen started taking spiritual matters more seriously. Before that, he placed his faith, first and foremost, in himself. He believed in certain values like hard work and clear thinking. That was his religion. He used to poke fun of her practice of prayer. He would sometimes ask, when she prayed, "Does that really change the facts?" She could hear his voice so clearly. "Does that really change the facts, Cory?" Yet, she was convinced that a big part of Stephen's attraction to the priest was the idea that this man of God might just be able to change the facts. On his deathbed, with his hand in Father Comfrons's hand, Stephen was still trying to change the facts.

HOME WAS A LONELY PLACE but Corinne did not know where else to go. She thought of stopping by the hospital but her closest friends would not be there on a Saturday and her supervisor had firmly instructed her to take a couple of weeks off. He must have thought his edict was a kindness, a gift, but it left Corinne without an outside focus. Without a diversion from the emptiness. Home was her only option. She looked for a place to sit down. First, she tried her favorite chair in the living room but it felt, somehow, different. The pictures on the walls reminded her that she was now stranded in this house. All by herself. The others were gone. Helen did not live very far away but that relationship had definite boundaries. From the time she was a baby, Helen seemed to resist Corinne's care. She needed more time to herself than other children. Corinne envied the kind of mother-daughter relationship that her friend, Alice, chatted about endlessly.

The kind where confidences are shared and having lunch together is a regular event.

Jane was apparently alive and well. Stephen had opened a door, leaving instructions for Corinne to walk on through. The idea of contacting Jane was extremely intimidating. She wanted to do it but did not know whether or not she had the strength. The nerve. After Jane left, they never had another family photograph taken. Time stood still on the living room walls. Stephen eventually gave up on the broken frame. Threw it away. Quietly, some months after what Corinne referred to as "Stephen's meltdown," she bought a new frame, replaced the photograph, and hung it in its designated location. Stephen must have noticed but he did not say a word. He never went to see a doctor, as Corinne's colleagues suggested. Corinne was not sure, therefore, exactly what happened. It was not really a nervous breakdown. It was more like a temporary response. Like what happens to victims of war when they are overwhelmed by what is happening around them and to them. Changed forever but able to move on.

Perhaps the den would be a better place to sit. Corinne went to the den, acutely aware that the only sound in the house was the shuffling of her own feet on the carpet. There, she found the coffee table next to the couch piled with papers. Papers from the hospital. Papers from the funeral home. Papers from their attorney. And over on the computer desk, sat Stephen's planner. Until he was admitted to the hospital, that planner was always with him. If there were one item in the house that most symbolized Stephen, the planner was it. Corinne felt a little bit like a despondent Goldilocks in a fractured fairy tale, moving from room to room, assessing the furniture for comfort level. She could not stay in this room. There was too much going on in here. She moved to the kitchen. Poured herself a glass of water. Took an antidepressant. Sat at the kitchen table. From here, she could see her untended garden, weeds growing to record heights, flowering plants begging for her benevolent hands. Maybe she could start that vegetable garden she had, for so many years, dreamed about. In the garden, there were no memories of Stephen. It was uniquely her own space. Perhaps it was time to get back to it. Time to put on the gloves and get back to the business of growing.

HELEN BOUGHT A CHICKEN SALAD SANDWICH at a deli on her way home. She ate it in the car, attempting to gather up the chunks of chicken as they fell to her lap. Enclosed with the sandwich were three thick round slices of dill pickle. These she sucked on, one at a time, until there was such little life in them, they had to be swallowed. She chased them with a bottle of cold spring water. The whole way home, she tried to remember where her photographs were stashed. Were they in the storage compartment in the basement or were they tucked away in her bedroom closet? She had always intended to put these pictures into albums. To organize them into a nice chronological collection. Her father was so good at that sort of thing. But her own tendency was to let things pile up. To set projects on the back burner.

Home again, Helen decided to search the closet, daunting though that task might be. There were boxes full of unfinished intentions in her closet. She opened each one. Studied her delinquencies. A needlepoint pillow that never really got off the ground. Blouses in need of buttons. A glass-etching kit she bought with the notion of making a nice glass beer mug for Charlie. With his name on it and everything. It was a good thing she had not started that chore yet. One at a time, she placed the uncompleted projects on her bed, determined not to be overwhelmed by them.

As she neared the back of the closet without having located any photographs, she decided to take a break. Rummaged through the kitchen cabinets. Found an unopened roll of LifeSavers. Tore a red one from one end of the roll. Let it dissolve in her mouth. Helen was not fat anymore. In fact, according to her mother, she looked too thin. She had traded in her food addiction for more titillating and dangerous substances. Her mother never seemed quite able to face the reality of her addictions. When Helen overdosed, which had happened no less than three times, her mother seemed to think everyone was overreacting. One of the counselors up in New Hampshire suggested that, since her mother had grown up in the shadow of alcoholism, she could not cope with the reality that her own daughter was casting the same frightening shadow. Emotionally, her mother could not afford to believe that her own daughter was an addict. In Helen's opinion, however, her mother was just lazy in that way. It was easier to let her husband, Helen's father, deal with the tough stuff. Well, ready or not, her mother was going to have to deal with certain realities. Such as the fact of her father's death. It was not possible, even for her mother, to avoid the power of death.

Helen wished she could have a little more support from her mother right now, not only with regard to her father's death but also because she had just come home again. She was newly sober again. Her father had always been a source of strength for her. If only her mother could take on some of her father's qualities. Instead of receiving support from her mother, Helen was thrown directly into offering it. On Tuesday, she met with the funeral director to discuss arrangements. On Wednesday, she met with the priest to talk about the service. On Thursday, she went over to the house to help her mother dress. Drove her mother to the graveside. Stayed with her mother for the rest of the day. Twice yesterday, she went over to the house to make sure her mother was okay. Helen knew her mother was not functioning well at all because during neither visit did her mother offer her any food. Today, however, she was trying to give herself a break from her mother. She would call her on the telephone. Later.

Removing a yellow LifeSaver from the roll, it occurred to Helen that one of the kitchen drawers might have some fairly recent photographs. Sure enough, in the bottom drawer, she found a stack of pictures wrapped in a piece of stationery, bundled tight with a rubber band. She had not left them that way. They had been cleaned up. Vivian strikes again. She removed the rubber band. These were not such recent pictures after all. They were at least two years old because they were pictures of the Christmas when her parents gave her ice skates. Her mother thought she needed a hobby, a "healthy hobby" were her precise words. To humor her parents, she signed up for ice-skating lessons and, to her own amazement, she actually enjoyed them. Her mother was right. Helen had been a naturally athletic child and took quickly to the ice. But then she had blown it again. She showed up high as a kite for her fifth private lesson and wound up with a dozen or so stitches in her right hand. That was the end of ice-skating. She looked down into the palm of her right hand and traced the scar with her left index finger. Maybe she could try again this winter. Sober.

There was, in that same stack of pictures, a particular photograph she thought Xander might enjoy seeing. It was a picture of her father. Their father. Standing in the living room next to the Christmas tree. Holding a new drill. Some kind of cordless wonder drill that he wanted and she gave him. He was smiling in the picture. Beaming really. An uncommon event for her father, especially after Jane left the house. He looked quite handsome, Helen thought. Her father was a fine-looking man. Unfortunately, Helen pondered, as she looked more closely at the picture, she did not seem to take after him. She took the drill picture with her and threw the rest back in the drawer.

Helen's bedroom looked exactly as she had left it a few minutes before. Cardboard boxes were stacked haphazardly on the bed. The bottom of her closet was littered with scraps of paper and accessories that had been thrown in there over the last few years. Belts. Sandals. Old handbags. Items long ago written off. She pushed them all to one side and there, way back in the corner, sat three shoeboxes stacked on top of one another. The top box was empty. Why, Helen wondered, did I save an empty shoebox? The second box still looked brand new. Inside that long-forgotten box were her sister's silver shoes, the pair she never wore, the ones Helen was supposed to leave on the stage of the high school. What earthly reason did she have for keeping those? Feeling stupid, she tossed the box on the bed with the others.

In the bottom shoebox, Helen hit the jackpot. It was over-stuffed with photographs and papers. She pulled it out. Dumped its contents onto the carpet. There was no sequence at all to the pictures so that they drew her back and forth in time. Finally, she found another good one of her father. Stand-ing on a tropical beach with one of those priceless grins on his face and a wreath of exotic flowers on his head. Clearly, this was photographed by her mother on their big anniversary trip. She set it aside. With single-mindedness of purpose, she sorted through the photographs, looking primarily for shots of her father. She found a striking black and white, probably a business photo of some kind. Yes. She remembered something about a magazine article highlighting her father's business. As she continued to sort through the contents of the box, she found the article itself. It was entitled "Tough Love for Small Corporations." Subtitled "One Man's Strategies for Downsizing." A reduced version of the black-and-white photo was reproduced next to the article. While Helen never completely understood her father's work, it was a good picture. Xander could have it. She collected ten different shots of her father. Left the rest of the mess on the floor.

Jane was glad she and Bill had plans for the evening. She felt stuck in a Möbius loop, an endless ribbon of melancholy. Tonight's Senior Variety Show might just have the power to pull her out of it. Her students would never forgive her if she failed to attend. For that matter, she would never forgive herself if she missed it. She wanted to see her students in action. She longed to spend the evening in a different place, in a different frame of mind, maybe even laughing from time to time as the seniors wove their memories into skits, songs, and adolescent gags. From years of experience Jane knew that, despite the best efforts of the school administration, the Senior Variety Show was often a bit rough around the edges. Perkins would, therefore, get to sleep over with his grandparents on the farm.

Perkins loved it there. The cows were gone. Bill's parents had scaled back considerably. But they still had three black-and-white cats, a corgi named McDuff, a goat named Porky, and several acres of corn and broccoli. It was a place of interesting smells and hard work. Through Bill's family, Jane learned a few things about farming. There was no such thing as a sick day. Or sleeping late. Constant attention was necessary. No wonder Bill felt he could not continue the family business. And, thank heavens, his parents were so accepting of their son's wishes. They were pretty good parents, though Jane deemed them to be a little too relaxed as grandparents. Perkins adored them unreservedly. Therefore, she kept her opinions to herself when they let him stay up too late or encouraged him to eat apple pie and leftover steak for breakfast. Most of the time she was grateful for their presence in her little boy's life. It was good for Perkins to have grandparents who knew and loved him.

IT WAS A PERFECT DAY. Neither hot nor cold. Feathery bands of cirrus clouds dappled the late afternoon sky. The contrast between what Corinne felt inside and what the day had to offer outside was almost too much to bear. The beauty of the

earth wanted nothing to do with her grief. Her lovely children, the Jonquilla daffodils, could not comprehend her loneliness. They pleaded with her to set aside her sadness that they
might be weeded and mulched and fed. After so many weeks
of unavoidable neglect, they needed her. Corinne complied.
What else was she to do with herself? These plants were the
only things left at home that depended on her.

When her mother did not answer the phone, Helen was
concerned. There was so much to worry about when it came
to her mother. She was such a contradiction. An outsider
would see a deeply caring woman and yet, Helen knew full
well that her mother was not deeply available. At least not to
her. Her mother was enormously bright yet so often in the
dark. Over at Grace Memorial, her mother carried on a life
independent of her family. Nevertheless, she was a markedly
dependent human being. Helen considered her father to be
hard evidence that human beings were capable of growth, of
real change. Her father became a new person after Jane left,
not an altogether different man and not a happier one, but a
person with more layers and with greater compassion. Her
mother, on the other hand, was proof that such change was
very, very difficult. How would her mother survive without
her father to direct her? Who would maintain stability, order-
liness, in the household? Helen hated the thought that family
responsibilities might now fall to her. "Domestic" was not her

strong suit. She left the growing disorder in her apartment and drove over to her parents' house.

The car was in the driveway but no one answered the door. Helen used her key, called to her mother throughout the house, and was relieved to find her, at last, out in the garden.

"Hey, Mom."

"Oh, hi, Pumpkin."

Helen was so tired of being called Pumpkin. Here she was, twenty-six years old, and her mother was still calling her Pumpkin. But now was not the time for confrontation. Now was a time for kindness of spirit. "Mom, have you had anything to eat today?"

"Not a whole lot, I guess. I haven't been that hungry."

"I know, but you have to eat. Why don't we go get some dinner? We could go out to eat, just the two of us."

"I'm afraid I'm not very good company."

"If you'd rather be alone, I understand. But if you're willing to put up with me for a little while, we can go get a bite to eat somewhere. My treat." Her mother did not answer. She was probably considering, Helen thought, how else to put her off. "I'm sure you're gonna get sick of hearing this, Mom, but you need to take care of yourself."

"Okay."

"Okay you'll come?"

"Okay, I'll come."

"Where do you want to go?"

"I don't know. You pick." Her mother sounded miserably vacant.

"It's a beautiful evening. Why don't we try that new seafood restaurant down on the water? We can sit out on the deck and eat steamed clams and you can pretend I'm Dad and tell me all about your day."

"It'll take me a few minutes to get cleaned up."

"Take your time, Mom. Take your time."

While her mother went upstairs to get changed, Helen surveyed the house. It was sadly apparent her father had not been home in many weeks. Clothes were strewn about in almost every room. Dishes were piled up in the kitchen. Mail seemed to be reproducing like rabbits in the den. The only room that might have passed Dad's inspection was the living room. There was no clutter in the living room. There was, Helen noticed, a mounting layer of dust that she was in no position to condemn. She was making short work of her recently cleaned apartment. When it came to standards of organization and cleanliness, Helen definitely took after her mother.

THE SENIOR VARIETY SHOW proved an outstanding distraction. It was difficult to be consumed by regret when the most introverted boy in this year's graduating class was up there on stage pretending to be a male stripper. It was hard for Jane to be gloomy when everyone around her was laughing so hard, they were clutching their stomachs. It was impossible to become lost in her own world when, after the successful show ended, Jane found herself surrounded by animated students seeking her approval, eagerly asking, "Did you see me? How was I?" Knowing she would answer, "You were wonderful. You were hilarious."

Home again, Bill asked, "You tired, Cleo?" Within a few days of her arrival in Fairhampton, Jane had confessed that her real name was far more ordinary. After some initial confusion on the part of everyone to whom she had introduced herself otherwise, they began to call her by her given name. For Bill, however, "Cleo" remained a pet name he used playfully from time to time.

"I'm not especially tired, Bill. I'm actually kind of wound up."

"The kids were great."

"Outstanding."

"It was nice to see you enjoying yourself again."

"Well, we'll see how long it lasts." Bill took her in his arms. He was right. It was nice to have a few minutes of normal. She knew, however, that things were not normal. Things were not right. She felt, in her heart of hearts, that something had to shift. Framed pictures that hung cockeyed constantly irritated Jane. She found herself straightening pictures in other teachers' classrooms when they were not looking because she bore so little tolerance for anything askew. That was the feeling she had now.

Xander spent the day vacillating between quiet reflection and bouncing in and around the house. Nadine gave him the obituary from Wednesday's newspaper, which he reviewed over and over again. Nadine thought that by now, at the end of this long, momentous day, he must have every word memorized. Why, Xander wanted to know, did some of the obituaries have photographs with them while his father's did not? His wife must have made that decision, she told him. Her answer did not satisfy him. Nothing was going to satisfy him until Helen came back tomorrow with a picture. Xander was a visual child. He was fixated on seeing his father.

Earlier in the day, before Xander could spill the proverbial beans, Nadine told her mother about Steve. About Helen. About Xander's excited response. Her mother seemed most surprised by the fact that Xander's father was so much older.

"There must have been something good about him if you fell in love with him." Her mother wanted to know.

"I don't know. To tell you the truth, Mom, I think he was probably like most human beings. A mixed bag. Sometimes he was very good to me; other times, he was really selfish. Honestly, I don't think I really knew him. I'm embarrassed to say it was more physical than anything else. At the time I thought there was real love involved but, looking back, I'm not so sure."

"Someday you'll find real love."

"Maybe, Mom. But if I don't, I have the realest kind of love I know, the love a mother has for a child."

"I'm proud of you, Princess."

"Don't be. I did the easy part. You and Dad, you did the hard part. I thought you were gonna kill me when you found out."

"You think you're the only one who ever made a mistake? I've made loads of mistakes in my own time. Your father made plenty too. Mistakes are a dime a dozen. How you face those mistakes, that's what counts, Princess. I'm proud of you. Maybe he never said it, but your father was proud of you too."

As it had been the night her parents discovered, by chance, that she was pregnant, this long-avoided discussion was more painless than Nadine anticipated. She did not think she could ever tell her mother about Steve. Perhaps that was part of what kept her from telling Xander. She went to her mother with embarrassing information about her past and came out with an "I'm proud of you." There were some pieces of the story, however, that she would never share. Her mother did not need to know, for example, that Steve was the man whose car killed Alexander Dolby.

HELEN WAS A GOOD GIRL. Thoughtful. She did not have to come over and take her out to dinner but she did. They were not especially close, Corinne knew. She was not especially chummy with her own mother and the pattern repeated itself with her own daughters. Helen's dinner invitation was probably the child of obligation. It did not matter, however. It did not matter what her daughter's motivation was. It mattered that she cared. They ordered steamers and iced tea.

"Something happened today, Pumpkin."

"What's that, Mom?"

"The priest called."

"Oh yeah?"

"He told me something. I'm not sure I should tell you."

"What?"

Corinne was not sure she should tell Helen but could not help herself. In fact, she wanted Helen to know. "It's about Jane. Apparently, Jane went to see your father before he died." The look of shock on Helen's face was unmistakable. "I know. It's unbelievable. She went to the hospital. Your father wrote me a letter and gave it to the priest and he gave it to me and in the letter, he talks about Jane. He says she's lovely. That's the word he used—lovely."

"How did she find out Dad was in the hospital?"

"She didn't. Father Comfrons tracked her down and told her your father was sick. The priest asked her to come, but it was actually your father's request. He wanted to see her before he died and he wanted to make peace with her and he says he wanted her to forgive him."

"He wanted her? To forgive him?"

"I had the same reaction but, you know, your father always thought it was his fault. You must know that. He had this idea that he did something wrong and when Jane ran away, well, he thought that was sort of his sentence. I think he thought that, since he was dying, he didn't have to be punished any more."

"I don't understand."

"I've been trying to make sense of it all day. All these years he wanted nothing to do with Jane and now I find out he never really stopped thinking about her and, honestly, I don't know how I'm supposed to feel about that. All I can think to do is respect his wishes. He wanted to make peace with her and he did and I have to respect that. But there's more."

"More about Jane?"

"Sort of. I get the feeling he wants me to make peace with her too."

"Did he say that in the letter? Do you have that letter with you?"

"No. But I know what's in it. He wrote, 'We have forgiven one another and made our peace. I hope you will do the same.'"

"Did he mean you, Mom, or did he mean us?"

"I thought he meant me." The letter was addressed to Corinne alone. But maybe his wishes were for Helen too. The steamers arrived, a big bowl of them, fragrant like the tide. Mother and daughter dredged the soft bellies and tender necks in melted butter and let the warmth of them settle in their stomachs.

"So, are you going to do anything?"

"I haven't decided. I'm not sure what I would say to her after all these years."

"You know," Helen said, "Dad had his moments but he didn't make Jane run away. Nobody forced her to leave. She did that all on her own. Life wasn't always great for me but I didn't run away."

"I know," Corinne responded, "I know."

CHAPTER SEVEN
Sunday / *The Fragrance of Violets*

As JANE PREPARED A BIG POT of her celebrated Manhattan clam chowder, her thoughts jumped between conflicting images of last night's hilarity, her father's hospital room, and imagined scenes of the funeral. She wanted more of the joy she tasted last night but her appetite for happiness was diminished by a persistent uneasiness about her mother and her sister. Internal tension notwithstanding, Jane was determined to prepare a nice Sunday dinner. She had acquired some fresh quahogs from a neighbor and, while the weather was almost too warm for soup, clam chowder with warm crusty bread was one of

Evelyn's favorite meals. She put Bill to work slicing onions and Perkins to work on the carrots. He loved to peel carrots.

Jane was relieved that, as usual, Evelyn would be on her way as soon as she finished up at church. She needed Evelyn. Jane wanted to review her options. Process her intense feelings about her parents and her sister. Evelyn knew so much. She was skilled at digging beneath the surface of problems. At seeing what others could not. Way back when Evelyn generously offered to share her home, Jane asked, "Why? Why are you doing this? Why are you being so nice to me?" Evelyn replied that she saw something special in Jane. "A rare integrity," were her very words. Jane was, from that moment on, inspired to live up to Evelyn's assessment. Evelyn was an experienced lifeline.

"How are you doin' there, girl?" Bill asked.

She turned and looked at him. "I'll survive," she said. "Really, I will. It's not just about the funeral, Bill. It's the whole deal. The whole family deal. I guess I figured I would see them all someday. When I was ready. Or when they were ready." Bill wiped his onion-oiled hands on a dishtowel. Moved to the sink where his wife was putting the clams in cold salt water to clean themselves. He wrapped his arms around her and she settled into them willingly. She did not move. She was thinking about a trip her family took to Washington, D.C., the summer she turned thirteen.

They left right after breakfast, she recalled. A big pancake breakfast, not unusual in the early years of the Quintal kitchen.

It was a long drive. Must have been four hours but, at the time, it felt much longer. When they finally arrived, they strolled down the mall, the elegantly long park that spans the distance between the Capitol building and the Lincoln Memorial. She was hungry. In fact, she remembered looking down at her brand-new, shiny gold birthday watch to verify the fact that it was indeed lunchtime. Her father reminded her of the stacks of pancakes they had consumed and told her she could wait. But she went ahead and asked her sister if she was ready for lunch. Helen whispered, "I'm starving." They passed a snack stand where Jane courageously asked if they, she and Helen, could split a hot dog. Her father turned to her and explained, "You can have a hot dog now or you can wait. Chances are, if you wait, you can have something much more delicious later."

Jane could not recall what they had to eat later that day but she could remember clearly how hungry she was for the hot dog. At the time, standing there on the mall, she assumed her father must be right. Surely, if they waited, they could find something better than a cheap hot dog. But maybe he was wrong. Maybe that hot dog would have been the best meal a kid could have eaten that day. Maybe it would have become a memorable part of their Washington experience. Delaying lunch while her father looked for the perfect restaurant, the perfect opportunity, perhaps they waited too long. Maybe waiting is not always the best thing to do, she thought. Perhaps they should have settled for the hot dog.

When Perkins was born, Jane thought of contacting her sister. Her parents. She imagined how thrilled they would be to meet baby Perkins. "Babies have a way of bringing people together," Evelyn remarked at the time. Jane decided, however, that the occasion was not ideal for her. Postpartum hormonal instability had left her feeling especially vulnerable. She wanted to be in top form when she saw them all again. She wanted them to see how well she had done for herself. To witness the benefits of running away. Had she wanted to rub her successes in their faces? Was that what this was all about? She turned around and looked at Bill, his arms still holding her as she pivoted comfortably. "At least I got to see my father before he died." She removed his wrists from her back and checked the time on his watch. Almost eleven-thirty. Depending on traffic, Evelyn would not arrive until one o'clock or so.

CORINNE DID NOT SLEEP WELL. It was strange. She slept soundly throughout Stephen's illness and even on the night of his death. She supposed she was so weary in watching him fail, she could not help but sleep. But now. Now with Jane squarely and intractably in the front of her thoughts, she could not sleep. Supporting Stephen through the loss of Jane had required significant umbrage on her part. Although he insisted otherwise, Corinne could not bring herself to hold Stephen accountable for what happened. She could not think of him as drunk. Could not imagine his philandering as anything but an aberration. Could not see Stephen as a deficient father. She fixed the blame, therefore, on Jane. It was the only way she would permit herself to make sense of Jane's behavior. In life, Stephen had told her she was being unfair. In death, he continued to challenge her assumptions about their eldest daughter. But that would entail setting aside her anger. Could she do it? Could she now swallow that bile for good? Could she make that phone call? She sat at the kitchen table staring at the letter Stephen had written, memorizing the phone number next to Jane's name. Stephen did not offer any details. How long was his conversation with Jane? What did he learn of her life? What was she doing now? The address placed her in Fairhampton, which was where Jane had run off to twelve years ago. Why there? Corinne had always wanted to know, why there?

She drank down another glass of water. It seemed she could not get enough water these last couple of days. With her index finger, she underlined two sentences from Stephen's letter. "She has turned into a lovely young woman, Cory. She has some of your gracious qualities." It was the first time Stephen had ever referred to her as gracious. It was nice to hear but, she wondered, what made Stephen think of me as gracious? Corinne did not feel particularly gracious. Certainly not today. She was annoyed at Stephen today. She had given him everything. Her life willingly revolved around his needs. She cared for him in the light of life and she walked with him in the shadow of death. "Don't wait," he wrote. But she wanted the space to mourn him. She did not want an assignment interfering with her grief.

"Why are you doing this to me, Stephen?"

No answer.

"I'm glad you wanted to tell me how much you love me. I'll take that. I'll take that any day. But what am I supposed to do with Jane? How nice for you that you were able to make peace with her before you died. But I'm not strong like you, Stephen. I don't have that kind of courage. I can't pretend nothing happened twelve years ago and, just like that, call her up."

"Think positive. You can do it, Cory." The steady quiet voice she heard so distinctly took her by surprise. It could not possibly be Stephen speaking. And yet, it was a voice much like his that she heard whispering, "You can do it, Cory." She fled from the kitchen. Ran up to Jane's room. Sat down on the edge of the bed to catch her breath. Closed her eyes. When she opened them, there were no surprises. But for a fine layer of dust, the room looked exactly as it had twelve years earlier. Her own portrait, in which she stood in the garden surrounded by her beautiful dahlias, still hung on the wall above Jane's bed. Stuffed animals: the owl, the panda, many other bears long ago arranged by Helen to welcome her sister home again remained in place. She got up. Opened Jane's closet. It was still full of clothes, now twelve years out of fashion. Up on the shelf sat Jane's black flute case. The flute, more than any other possession left behind, was what convinced Corinne that her daughter would come home any day. Jane worshipped that flute. To leave it behind did more to spite herself than to hurt them. She enjoyed playing that flute so much. Why would she leave it behind? Corinne took the case down, blew the dust from it, opened the case. What a waste, she thought, gazing down at the tarnished instrument.

Corinne sat down again, this time at Jane's desk, a desk that had not been used in years. On the top of the desk sat a stack of books. Thick textbooks. On the very top of the pile rested a book that she had not thought about in a long time. *Literary Blossoms*, the book Alice gave her. When Jane first left and Corinne was having so much trouble sleeping, she would come in here sometimes and sit. And think. And hope. And read. Finally, she could not stand to be in here any longer. Stephen could see how upsetting the room had become for Corinne and he volunteered to dust and vacuum it on a regular basis. The dust testified to the fact that he had not been here in a while. She opened the book to a section titled "Violets." The first page had lovely little stems of violets in the place of musical notes on the lines of a free-flowing staff. The quote was from Shakespeare's *Twelfth Night*:

> If music be the food of love, play on;
> Give me excess of it, that, surfeiting,
> The appetite may sicken, and so die.

> That strain again! it had a dying fall:
> O, it came o'er my ear like the sweet sound
> That breathes upon a bank of violets,
> Stealing and giving odour.

She turned the page to a beautiful watercolor patch of the tiny purple blossoms enlivening a grassy sloping field. An anonymous quote followed: "Forgiveness is the fragrance the violet sheds on the heel that has crushed it."

"Think positive. You can do it, Cory," echoed her beloved's voice.

XANDER WAS HAVING GREAT DIFFICULTY focusing this morning. Nadine urged him to go out and play but he wanted to stay inside with her. She attempted next to immerse him in the morning cartoons and even offered to sit and watch with him, but he was uncharacteristically disinterested. He could not even stick with his new video game for more than a few minutes at a time. He could not wait. Nadine's mother came to the rescue. She got him involved in "luncheon preparations." Xander wanted to know if "lunch" and "luncheon" were the same thing. His grandmother told him they were not at all the same, that "lunch" was what you could put in a bag and take to school while "luncheon" required cloth napkins and hot food and at least one fancy dessert. She suggested to Nadine that if Xander's rowdy anticipation was all about

Helen, why not engage him in the process of getting ready for her to come? While Nadine straightened up the living room, Grandma and Xander sat out on the deck together and came up with a menu.

Turkey. Xander wanted to have a turkey dinner. To Nadine, this seemed uncomfortably excessive. Helen was, undoubtedly, expecting something simple. Xander, however, wanted the works. Turkey. Gravy. Sweet potatoes. Cranberry. Stuffing. Pumpkin pie. The good news was that they could get an entire ready-to-go turkey dinner from a nearby market. The bad news was that pumpkin pie was out of season. The fanciest dessert they carried was a lemon torte. Xander was not sure what a lemon torte was but his grandmother assured him it was sufficiently fancy for a luncheon. Nadine was thankful for the way in which her mother took charge. She seemed to sense how conflicted Nadine was about Helen's return and was willing to take care of the details for her. Most importantly, she was keeping Xander busy. Together, Xander and Grandma called in the order, set the table, freshened the water in the potted tulips Helen gave them yesterday. Nadine was more than a little appreciative. And more than a little apprehensive.

This morning was not the first time Nadine had considered how life can change in an instant. What was happening was akin to allowing Steve into her home. This was the certainly the closest he would ever get to their son now. When Xander was born, Nadine was afraid Steve would find out about him and try to interfere in some way. Much to her relief, he never did. What she did not consider was the idea that someone from Steve's family might show up. From what Nadine could tell so far, Helen was not much of a threat. She was nothing like the Steve she remembered. Steve was confident, sophisticated, decisive. Helen appeared to be quite sensitive, a little insecure, far less refined than her father. And Xander was thrilled. If she had tried to plan a way to introduce Xander to his father, she could never have come up with anything as effective and tender and thrilling. For him.

HELEN WANTED TO GIVE SOMETHING to her brother, something related to their father that would lend depth to the photographs she had gathered. Something meaningful. She dumped her antique jewelry box out onto the kitchen table. Began to sort. It was mostly junk. Inexpensive earrings and necklaces, including the beach-glass pair made by Nadine. She found an old rainbow friendship bracelet given to her by Elaine, her childhood friend. A little ratty-looking but worth keeping. She picked out a silver ring with a cutout image of a horse that Charlie gave her last year and held it up to the light. It was not particularly feminine. Xander might like it, but it had nothing to do with their father. One of Helen's problems was that she had no idea what an eleven-year-old boy would find interesting.

She started to disentangle the necklaces, which took longer than she thought it might. The gold pillow heart was in the jumble. She had not thought about that necklace in years. It seemed different to her now. Whereas it was once a reminder of her own failings, as she held it in her hand, she saw it now as nothing more, and nothing less, than a symbol of her father's love. She put it on. Felt the fine chain around her neck. Fingered the delicate heart as it sat just below her neck. It was too short. A child's necklace for "Daddy's little girl." She kept it around her neck anyway. The child could not even look at it. The adult would wear it with greater understanding.

At the bottom of the metallic pile from the jewelry box sat a small black stopwatch. Her father bought it for her back when she was in elementary school. When she was working on her speed. When she was trying to improve her ability to get to the ball on the soccer field. Her father suggested that she run every day and keep track of her time with the watch. That way she could measure her improvement. It worked too. Her speed did improve as, each day, she bested her last effort. It was a gift that represented her father's high ideals and standards. Xander might not be ready to understand the significance of the gift. But he might like a stopwatch.

Helen scooped up the mess and returned it to the jewelry box. In the process, a gold herringbone necklace made its way to the top of the jumble. This necklace was supposed to be a graduation present for Jane. Several years after Jane left, Helen's mother gave it her. "You might as well have it," her mother said, "I don't want it to go to waste." Her mother's intentions were good, but she had no idea how awful the secondhand gift made Helen feel. She already felt like a phantom in her own home. Now she was a phantom with her sister's necklace. Helen would never understand how her mother could be so tuned in to her patients yet so unaware of what she sounded like to her children. She removed the necklace and placed it in the shoebox with the silver shoes.

THE NEGLECTED GARDEN GLADLY WELCOMED Corinne home. For her, this was a place of undeniable beauty and healing. A place where she could almost always quiet her mind. Corinne's garden was her salvation in the days and weeks that followed Jane's disappearance. Surely, it would be a way to mitigate her grief in the days and weeks to come. It would give her hands something life-giving to do. It would offer her fragrant beauty in the face of harsh realities. And it needed attention. Unlike some of the human creatures in her life, the garden responded to her every effort. She knew how to make it flourish and flower. Corinne turned her face to the sun. Felt the calming warmth of it. Standing there for several minutes with her eyes closed, enveloped by green, growing confidants, she did not feel quite so alone.

With Jane unremittingly occupying her mind, Corinne could not help but recall the storm that swept across Long Island twelve years ago. That noisy night when she and Stephen were so worried about their runaway daughter. Chaos, inside and out. It had taken her weeks to clean up everything in the garden. Some plantings were beyond repair and had to be pulled up. The wooden fence required serious mending where winds splintered it mercilessly. The trees sustained many injuries, losing limbs as if they were leaves. It was necessary to remove one tree altogether. A beloved apple. The whole tree toppled over in the high winds, exposing shallow roots and breaking the largest of its impressive arms. They tried re-rooting the tree but it was not able to recover from the blow. And so this still-living tree was severed into chunks with a chain saw and removed. Corinne could not bear to watch it. The painful memory of this event was still surprisingly fresh. Gray sorrow fusing with green hope, Corinne got down on her knees and set a few homemade traps for slugs. She was engaged in another silent conversation with Stephen about Jane when she was interrupted by Helen's familiar, "Hey there, Mom."

"Oh, hi. You can't stay away, can you?" Even as the question popped out of her mouth, she was sorry she asked it. Her daughter seemed to wince. She did not mean it the way it probably sounded. She was surprised, that was all. Helen was not around for weeks at a time. Now, suddenly, she was turning up twice a day. That was, Corinne knew, an unexpected blessing. She did not wish Helen to stay away. In fact, she intended to spend more time with her. Helen might be all that was left of her family.

"Have you made a decision, Mom?"

"About what?"

"You know, Mom, about what you told me last night. About contacting Jane." She had not made a decision. This dilemma was the substance of her unspoken conversation with Stephen. Corinne had committed Jane's phone number to memory but was not sure she would ever use that carefully stored information. "I don't know, Pumpkin. Do you think I should call her?" She really wanted to know what her daughter thought. Maybe Helen could offer some guidance, although Helen's advice would undoubtedly lean in a safe direction, in the direction of doing nothing. Helen, once Jane's most trustworthy champion, now seemed to want nothing to do with her sister. Corinne had been steadfastly cross with Jane. But Helen was another story altogether. Helen's fury was palpable.

Helen surprised Corinne, however, with her ostensibly impartial position. "That's gotta be up to you, Mom," she said. According to Helen, she was on her own with this one. Stephen could not help. Helen would not help. Unsettling her reflections, Helen handed her another surprise. "Here."

Helen held out a shiny white shoebox. "If you decide to call her up, tell her she can have these."

"What's this?"

"It's those shoes. Those ridiculous silver shoes."

Corinne was puzzled. What shoes? She reached back. Tugged at a remembrance. Then a flood of specific memories came rushing back. The school musical. The silver shoes. Dorothy. A part that another student rushed to learn in the weeks before the play was presented. They did not go to see the musical. It was all so painful. Too many people were asking difficult questions. "Have you had these shoes all this time?" Corinne asked. "That music director. What was his name? I can't remember now. I can see his face but I can't remember his name. Anyway, he was looking for those shoes, wasn't he? He called about them, didn't he? I couldn't find them."

"I guess I should have returned them to the school but I figured if I held onto them, she would have to come home. Like they were really magic or something."

Corinne opened the box. Peeled back old tissue paper. "Aren't they supposed to be red? Doesn't Dorothy wear ruby slippers?"

"Mom, they're supposed to be silver. Hollywood changed the color."

Corinne replaced the lid and said, "Maybe you should return them to Jane yourself."

"Mom, you keep them. If you talk to Jane, see if she wants them. If she doesn't, give them to the shelter." Corinne could imagine some weather-beaten homeless woman walking around in secondhand clothes, carrying a tattered shopping bag full of junk, and wearing what were, for all intents and purposes, sparkling new silver shoes on her feet. It was ridiculous. She would throw them away before she would hand them over to a shelter.

NADINE WATCHED XANDER VIGILANTLY peering through the living room window. He was overflowing with excitement as Helen pulled her old green compact up to the curb in front of the house. "She's here, Mom!" he practically screamed. Nadine could see she was carrying a brown envelope that probably held a photograph or two. Xander was waiting for her with the door wide open. He was bouncing nervously on the balls of his feet. "Let's see! Let's see!" Helen laughed at her half brother, who was bubbling over exuberantly. She looked over at Nadine, subtly aimed the envelope in the direction of Xander and asked, "May I?" Nadine nodded. Helen handed the envelope to the boy and watched his face as, ever so carefully, he removed the photographs and silently, solemnly began to examine them.

"Well, what do you think?" Helen asked after a few minutes.

"Good," he answered, "Old. But good."

"You look a little bit like him."

"Yeah?"

"Yup."

"Except a lot younger, right?"

"Yup."

He continued to probe the pictures. He was probably searching, Nadine thought, for clues as to his own identity. Well, he could look all he wanted, as long as he did not forget who his mother was. As long as he remembered who had raised him. Nadine caught herself becoming a little defensive and reminded herself that Helen was not Steve.

Staring intently at the pictures but without looking up from them, Xander asked, "He's really dead?"

"He's really dead. Sorry."

"Well, it isn't your fault," he answered, finally removing his eyes from the pictures, turning them lovingly to his new-found sister.

"What's his name again?"

"Stephen Quintal."

"Stephen Quintal. What kind of name is that?"

"I think it's Spanish."

"He doesn't look Spanish."

"Well, he was part Spanish."

"That makes me part Spanish! Hey, Mom, I'm part Spanish!"

"That's great, Xander." Nadine had not known that about Steve. She had never given a minute of conscious thought to his heritage. This information was another reminder of how little she knew about this man. She saw only certain sides of him. His passion. His drive. A little bit of his humor. A lot of his trepidation near the end. Thinking back to that time, to the earliest days of her unanticipated pregnancy, she, too, was fearful. Perhaps more so than he.

"Helen, we have turkey dinner with cranberries and potatoes and lemon something for dessert. Come see. Come in here." His enthusiasm unabated, it was now perfectly trained on Helen. Xander took his big sister by the hand and proudly led her to the dining room table. Nadine was amazed. Helen was, clearly, also astonished. Nadine hoped Xander's zeal, topped off by the extravagant spread on the table, did not leave Helen feeling besieged. It was funny. Her greatest fear yesterday was that, somehow, Xander would be overwhelmed. Today, she held the same concern for Helen.

FROM THE START, FROM THE MOMENT Jane confessed she was a slightly under-aged runaway, Evelyn pushed her to contact her family. At pivotal moments, Evelyn revisited the subject religiously. When, for instance, Jane graduated from college, Evelyn suggested Jane send an announcement. Jane was afraid, however, that sending an announcement out of the blue might signal the expectation of a gift. They might assume she was asking for money. Or worse, that she wanted them to visit. When she and Bill were getting ready for their wedding,

Evelyn thought Jane should let her parents and her sister know what was happening. This was a big moment. Ordinarily, a family moment. Evelyn convinced Jane that her family would love Bill. Who would not adore Bill? Jane, however, refused to call them. She would not place an announcement of marriage in the newspaper either. Not even the local paper. Just in case her family found out about the wedding. Jane did not want them to feel excluded, neither did she desire their attendance. She told Evelyn she was not ready for them yet. And Evelyn always respected Jane's wishes. It was her life after all. And it was a good life.

Then there was the matter of the funeral. Evelyn thought the very fact that the priest had contacted her, that her father wanted to see her before he died, was a sign. She should go to the funeral. Her father had started the process. She should have the courage to follow through. But showing up would probably have had the same effect as uprooting her mother's rose garden. It would have torn her apart. Again. However, Evelyn suggested, her presence might also function as a bright light on an otherwise dark day. She had even volunteered to go with Jane. So had Bill for that matter. Maybe Evelyn and Bill were right. Maybe she should have gone. But Jane was stubbornly unprepared to see her mother and sister. She clung tenaciously to her justification for staying away. It would have been too much for everyone, not only for her mother and her sister but also for herself.

Evelyn's visit today felt especially important. Jane always looked forward to Sunday afternoons when Evelyn hung up her preacher's robe, drove out to Fairhampton, and put her feet up in their wonderful house. Some days, Jane scanned the salty horizon in dreamy disbelief. How was it that they got to live here? In this amazing place? With this incredible view? She knew the specifics of how but still could not fully accept their good fortune. Bill's funny old Aunt Wally left the house to them in her will. She died more than three years ago and, with no children of her own, left most of the money in her estate to Bill's parents while bequeathing the beach house to Bill and Jane.

It was a small tenacious house, one of the older beach cottages that had miraculously survived a goodly number of fearsome hurricanes and nor'easters. It had also endured the threat of demolition. Many times had Aunt Wally been approached and pressured by realtors and would-be buyers who wanted to tear down the old cottage and construct another contemporary monstrosity. Aunt Wally was firm in her resolve to hang on to the property, no matter how much she was offered, and to let the cottage be.

Jane had grown on Aunt Wally over the years, spending a fair amount of time with her, especially near the end. She liked Wally a great deal and that fact was mutual, in spite of the ambiguous first impressions they formed of one another years ago. Jane admired the way Aunt Wally was true to herself, true and uncompromising. Jane hoped that, if and when she got up into her eighties, she would be in as good shape, mentally and physically, as was Wally. "The old lady," as Bill called her affectionately, took good care of herself. She remained in excellent health until three years ago, when a particularly vicious flu worked its way across Long Island near the end of winter. Wally never went to the hospital. Obstinately, she refused to go. Received all of her medical care at home, where she died surrounded by her loved ones: Bill, Bill's parents, Jane, and a very little baby named Perkins, which was Aunt Wally's surname.

While the pot of chowder simmered gently on the back of the stove, and Bill and Perkins were busy with a Lego creation, a tall, brightly colored structure with a surprising number of windows, Jane went upstairs to the computer room. The room where she corrected papers from school. The room where she e-mailed friends. The room that was, for her, a private refuge. There, on a special shelf sat her journals. Twelve years worth of journals in different shapes, colors, and thicknesses, lined up in order from earliest to latest. She removed the one on the far right, a silvery blue notebook with a half-moon on the cover. This she opened up to the next blank page, a page marked by a silky blue ribbon. She flipped back and reread yesterday's entry:

> I am not the same person I was twelve years ago,
> thirteen, fifteen, a thousand years ago.

> How dare they beckon me to return?
> How dare they ask me to crawl back into such a choked
>   womb?
> How can I abandon my freedom,
>   even a shackled, self-tortured freedom such as this?

Of course, the only one who was doing any beckoning was Jane herself. She knew that. But that did not lighten the burden. Jane stared at the blank page. Picked up her good Cross pen. Took deep breaths. Made space for the most inward parts of herself to express themselves. She closed her eyes for several minutes. Upon opening them she wrote:

> I claimed the role of Dorothy.
> It could not be given to me.
> I had to exact it.
> I had to leave the plains and understand in my own way
>   what I had left behind.
> I am grateful for the storm that has so generously carried
>   me to this place.
> There's no place like here.
> There's no place like here.

Jane closed her eyes again and wondered if she could ever have both worlds. Both families. She reached into her pocket, felt the smooth stones she had been carrying since yesterday, and tried to imagine her mother at the funeral. Her sister. Did they weep? Would she have wept? If only she could talk to Helen. If only Helen were not so angry. If only she, Jane, had the courage to pick up the phone and call her. She had a number for Helen somewhere. One Christmas a few years back, she found herself longing for her sister and proceeded to look up her address and phone number on the Internet. She never actually called but she did keep the number. Where had she put it? Would she have thought to put it in the family address book? She pulled the book from the top of a file cabinet and turned to the Q section. Yes. There she was. Helen. All grown up and living on her own. She stared at the number, then picked up the phone. Punched in the numbers. Her heart quickened. An answering machine offered her sister's voice. "Leave it here," Helen announced. That's all. Every muscle on her nervous bones wanted to hang up. She forced herself to wait for the beep. To speak into her sister's machine: "Hi. It's . . . it's Jane. Your sister. I know it's been a hard week for you, Helly. With the funeral and all. Um, well . . . you may not want to hear from me. I just want you to know that, well, I'm sorry about . . . "

"Dad," she finished after the machine had already cut off her rueful sentence. Jane was uncertain whether or not she was relieved that her sister was out. She did not know if the message was a good idea. And the message she left was so inarticulate. So very inadequate. But there it was. She had taken a step. It might be the first of many. It could well be the last.

STEPHEN'S LETTER SAT NEXT TO THE SHOEBOX on the kitchen table. The pressure to do something was piling up. Father Comfrons had relayed a mission. Why Stephen had not talked to her about Jane directly, she would never understand, but she could hardly change the situation. Jane had injured Stephen irrevocably. He was never the same after she left. When, with the priest's help, he finally got out of bed two days after Jane left, he was not quite the man he had been. While there were benefits to the new, more considerate Stephen, there was a melancholy that surfaced from time to time. The events of that awful week seemed to stop him in his tracks, the way the death of a loved one sometimes brings a person to a standstill. The Stephen who came downstairs on that stormy night twelve years ago, to join his wife and daughter for a palliative taste of pizza and a curious game of Scrabble, was the Stephen who remained. He was quieter. More pensive. He allowed himself only small bites of joy. Consistently, he claimed none of this was Jane's fault. He reminded Corinne that, while he was never charged with anything, the accident was his fault. He was to blame for everything that happened, including Jane's departure. According to Stephen, all the accountability rested squarely on his own shoulders. Could she ever really believe that?

Helen left her with yet another job, that of returning the shoes. While Helen did not actually tell her to take them to Jane, the request was emphatically implied in the delivery of the shoes. A mounting sense of purpose sat before her on that kitchen table. Along with it, a growing list of questions that, before this, she had not allowed herself to ask. What does Jane look like now? What did Stephen mean by "lovely"? Is Jane married? The name on the bottom of the letter was Jane Cooper. Either her daughter was married or had changed her name. If she is married, Corinne wondered, does she have a family? A job? Is she happy with her life? "Watch this, Stephen." She picked up the phone.

JANE HEARD MAGNIFICENT LAUGHTER coming from the living room, Bill's big movie-star laugh providing a bass line for Perkins's melodic giggles. She emerged from her treasured sanctuary of thoughts and rejoined her spirited family. Bill was sitting on the living room floor with Perkins. Together, they gathered the small bricks needed for the next phase of their important construction project. A parking garage. Bill and Perkins were discussing dimensions when they all heard the familiar knock at the door. Three gentle but firm raps on the front door. It was the not-so-secret code by which Evelyn identified herself. Bill opened the door, gave Evelyn a friendly hug, and took the plastic grocery bag from her hand. He looked down between the flimsy handles of the bag and saw three round cartons of high-test ice cream. His eyes widened in response to the sweet gift. Perkins came running up behind his father and practically jumped into Evelyn's arms. He called her "Aunt Evy." This noble title never ceased to elicit an adoring glow from her. They were entirely committed to one another.

"Come in, come in," Bill declared with gusto, motioning Evelyn into the kitchen area. He made room for the gourmet ice cream in the freezer. Gave the pot of soup a stir.

"It smells delicious in here," Evelyn offered.

"Clam chowder," Jane confirmed.

"Yum. This is the best restaurant on the east end." Covertly, while Jane was helping Perkins move his architectural masterpiece off the floor, Evelyn turned to Bill and whispered, "How's Jane?"

"She's been very quiet this morning. I've decided she's suffering from AMF," he whispered back.

"AMF?"

"Acute Mixed Feelings."

"Well, she's the only one who could make the decision about her father's funeral. You know that."

"I know. I know. I just wish I knew how to help her through this."

"I do too."

"You do too, what?" Jane asked. She knew they were up to something and was eager to stop the murmuring before it went too far. She hated the idea that Bill and Evelyn were feeling sorry for her. Apologetically, Evelyn turned to Jane and gave her a long hug.

"Thanks," Jane responded. "Thanks for coming. You two can stop conspiring now. You are helping me through this. You both are. You can put away the black balloons. There'll be no pity party today."

"Not pity. Love," Evelyn answered emphatically.

"Yeah, just gray balloons," Bill added.

"I don't see any balloons," a confused Perkins spoke up.

"Sorry, Perks, we're just kidding," Jane responded, gathering her little boy in her arms. "It's an expression, that's all."

"Aunt Evy brought ice cream!" he declared to his mother.

"I saw. That's wonderful news, Perkins. Can you help me set the table?"

THE TURKEY DINNER WAS LUSCIOUS but the conversation, strained. Nadine's mother asked Helen far too many questions. She did not, thank God, ask anything about Steve but she was shamelessly nosey about Helen herself. What do you do? Where do you live? Did you go to school around here? Nothing she said or asked was rude but it was just over the line in terms of appropriateness. Helen attempted to deflect the attention by engaging Xander.

"Xander, I see you are an accomplished artist."

"That means you're good," his grandmother translated, "like your mother."

"I know," Xander responded proudly. Nadine had seen to it that her son's drawings and paintings were displayed everywhere. Some of the better pieces were nicely framed. Others were taped to appliances. Recently, she found the courage to hang some of her own artwork on the walls too. The self-portraits she created for her senior project remained in a folder in her bedroom closet but the delicate charcoal drawing of a mother duck with ducklings now hung in the living room.

"How about reading? Do you like to read?"

"Not too much."

Helen seemed disappointed in his answer. She said, "I'll bet I can find a book you won't be able to put down. How about sports? You like sports?"

Xander's face brightened at the question. "Baseball and soccer."

"He's a good soccer player. The coach calls him Xander the Great," Nadine added.

"That's awesome. I used to play soccer too. Xander the Great, huh? You have an unusual name. I like it."

"It's really Alexander but everybody calls me Xander."

"He's named for a neighbor who died the same year he was born. If you grew up around here you might have known him. His name was Alexander Dolby. Did you know him?" Leslie Aiuto wanted to know.

Helen shook her head naively. Obviously, she knew nothing of the matter. Or did not remember. Pulling at the back of her hair fretfully, Nadine tried to give her mother a

"That's enough, Mom" signal but she was relentless. It was as if all those years of curiosity had been bottled up inside and, with the lid removed at last, it was spilling out all over the table. "Do your parents still live around here?" she asked.

"Mom, didn't you get something special for dessert?" Nadine interrupted nervously, trying to pry the conversation away from her mother, who finally seemed to get the message. She stood up and started clearing dishes.

Xander took command again, relieving his grandmother of control. He ran off to his room and quickly returned with a small collection of school photographs of himself. He showed them to Helen in order. Kindergarten through fourth grade. Then he set the most recent picture side by side with the photos of his father. There was an unmistakable resemblance, especially with regard to the shape of their heads and the set of their jaws. In both pictures, there was a look of determination that must, Nadine reflected, have some genetic origins. It felt odd to be looking at pictures of Steve. She thought she never wanted to see him again. She thought she no longer cared one way or the other about him. The photographs that Xander studied so carefully brought back memories of a man who, in spite of the terrible ways in which he had used her, could be winsome. Entertaining. Always, always, interesting. Xander seemed so pleased to have the pictures. Nadine no longer carried a clear image of Steve in her head. These pictures, therefore, became for her irrefutable evidence of her son's resemblance to his father. She did not hate the man. She did not love the man. He was no more and no less than the father of her wonderful little boy. Xander, she knew, deserved to learn more about him.

Nadine was indebted to Helen for bravely showing up at what seemed to be precisely the right moment in Xander's life. For taking on the responsibility of introducing him to his father. She was doing a much better job than Nadine could ever hope to do. The ease with which the two siblings connected was remarkable. They were years apart in age. Yet here they sat chatting easily, as Nadine imagined a sister and brother might. As if they had always known one another. Nadine watched as Helen reached into her pocket. Pulled out a watch. A black pocket watch. Helen gave it to Xander saying, "Your father gave this to me. It's a stopwatch. You can time yourself with it. I'd like you to have it. That is, if it's okay with your mother." Nadine nodded in the direction of the stopwatch. It was so very Steve. She understood the gift immediately and hoped Xander would enjoy it.

AFTER DINNER, BILL, PERKINS, AND TOTO went off for an afternoon walk. Recently, a new family moved in up the street. Bill was certain he had observed a small bicycle and other signs of young children. This was a fact-finding mission for Perkins, who was thrilled at the prospect of another kid living on an otherwise well-aged block. Intentionally left behind,

Jane and Evelyn sat with cups of coffee, their bellies full of fresh vegetable-laden clam chowder that was topped off by a little too much very rich chocolate ice cream. They wasted no time in getting down to business, reviewing the range of feelings that had gripped Jane from the moment she first heard from the priest. Shock. Bewilderment. Regret. Guilt. Anger. Even relief, she had to be honest. There was not enough room in her heart to carry all of the feelings she was experiencing. She had to find other places for them or they might consume her. She told Evelyn her mind was flooded with memories. Some deeply happy. Others outrageously confusing. Enraging. Evelyn asked, "Is there one memory in particular that is haunting you right now?"

"Not a memory really. More like an image. I keep seeing my sister all alone in her room. We were so close as children. She used to come into my room every morning. In fact, the day I left I went into her room for a change."

"What did you talk about?"

"I think it was about Nadine."

"The girl your father was having an affair with?"

"Yes. I wonder what ever became of her? She was all set to have an abortion. I was supposed to go with her but I came out here instead. I've always been curious about Nadine."

"What do you imagine happened?"

"Nadine? She's tough. She's a survivor. You know, when I was a teenager, I used to envy her. I thought she had it all."

"And what was that? What did she have?"

"She was beautiful, for one thing. But, looking back on it, I think what most attracted me was her spirit. Her sense of freedom. Nadine seemed unconstrained, free to be herself."

"Maybe that's what got her into trouble."

"You're gonna let my father off the hook?"

"No."

The two sat there silently. Jane was caught in a clutter of feelings toward her complicated father. "It's so strange, Ev. He asked for my forgiveness and I gave it to him and I meant it. But he still stirs up a lot of pain."

"You can forgive without forgetting. In fact it's a good thing you can forgive without forgetting because those painful memories don't ever go away."

"It's so hard."

"Yeah, it is."

"How do you do it?"

"What do you mean?"

"You've been hurt, right? People have said and done un-forgivable things to you. How do you forgive them?"

"For me, it's a mandate. That doesn't make it easy. But I figure, hey, if I can't forgive people who are just plain mean and nasty, who write ugly letters and speak unkind words just because they disagree with me, what chance does the rest of the world have? If I can't forgive a little name-calling, how is a Palestinian supposed to forgive an Israeli for killing her

father? Or vice versa? I think it's the only way out. Forgiveness, I mean. Otherwise, it's endless. You just keep going
round and round on the same old crap." She paused before
continuing, "You know, Jane, I don't want to sound presump-
tuous, but I think the most difficult part for you is forgiving
yourself."

The telephone cut short Evelyn's observations. At first,
Jane thought she might let the answering machine get it. She
even expressed this out loud. "I'll let the machine get it," she
muttered. But then, she got up anyway. Grabbed the cordless
phone from its couch-side cradle.

"Hello?" There was a silent pause on the other end of
the line.

"Hello?" she repeated. "It must be a crank call." She was
about to hang up the phone when someone said, "Jane? Is that
you?" She knew the voice. It was deeper than she remembered. It had a bit of texture to it that was different. Not as
calm as it once was. Nevertheless, the voice was unmistakable.
"Mom?"

"Oh, my God," her mother said.

"Mom?" Jane was too surprised for tears. She was knocked
off her feet, practically falling back onto the living room
couch. Her mother was calling her? In all of the many
scenarios Jane envisioned for their eventual reunion, she
never imagined her mother calling her. She always assumed
she would have to be the one to make the first move. Oh, in

the first few days and weeks and even months, she thought her parents might just show up. But then she figured it out. They knew where she was and they were waiting for her to come home. It was all up to her. How could she explain to them that, in a remarkable turn of events, things were working out for her as never before? That her life had undergone a sudden shift in emphasis from accomplishments to relationships. As it turned out, she never did have to defend herself. They never pressed her for an explanation. Later, she assumed they must have given up on her, a supposition that dumbfounded her.

Evelyn, straight away understanding the importance of the call, mouthed the question, "Do you want me to leave?" Jane offered Evelyn a confused look, then motioned her into the kitchen. Evelyn, however, grabbed a cotton blanket, wrapped it around herself, and gracefully pointed out the back door to the beach. Jane nodded to her good friend. She appreciated Evelyn's sensitivity, her instant willingness to make herself scarce in this bottomless moment. Sink or swim, she needed to be alone with her mother.

"How are you?" she heard her mother ask. She was having trouble visualizing her mother's face. She knew the features. She remembered the coloring clearly. The pink skin. The blue eyes. The softness. But these pieces were not coalescing into any clear image. Her mother might well be having the same trouble. In fact, Jane was reasonably certain her mother would have a hard time picking her out of a crowd. She wore glasses.

All the time now. Her hair was very short with lovely albeit expensive highlights. In fact, her hair had been short since her second week in Fairhampton. Her second week as a waitress at Kate's. And she was, of course, twelve years older. Her face and her form had traveled far from adolescence.

"I'm well. How are you?" The words seemed too ordinary, too simple, for such an uncommon conversation, but she went along, not knowing what else to say.

"I'm fine. Listen, Jane, I'm calling because, well, because . . . "

"I know, Mom. I read about Dad in the paper." Should she mention the fact that she had seen him, spoken with him, fashioned a significant reconciliation with him before he died?

"The funeral was Thursday."

"I know. How was it?" Having asked it without thinking, the question sounded ludicrous to her ears. How was it? As if they were discussing a new movie or a recently opened pizza parlor.

"It was a lovely service. You would have appreciated it."

Jane was glad her mother did not say, "I wish you could have come." She would not have known how to respond to such a condemning statement.

"Your father told me you visited him in the hospital."

So she knew. That would probably make the exchange less complicated. There would be no secrecy requirement, no need to figure out what could be said and what was off-limits. "He asked me to come. We had a good talk. I'm glad I got to see him, Mom."

"I'm glad you did too." It was an unexpected and much desired affirmation, a gift for which she never could have asked.

The conversation moved almost too quickly into an exchange of facts. A quick twelve-year history course. Just the highlights. For her mother, it was a trip to the Bahamas, Helen's problems, her father's successes, a new car, her father's illness. For Jane, it was high school equivalency, college, teaching, Bill, Perkins. "Are you still at the hospital?" Jane wanted to know. "What does Perkins look like?" her mother wanted to know. It became clear to Jane, as the phone call continued, that she would have to see her mother. And so, she invited her. After all this time. After all this viscous water over the illustrious dam. Thoughtfully, her mother replied that she would love to come visit but hoped Jane might come see her first. Come home. See the house. See the garden, although it was something of a mess right now. Perhaps see her sister. Reclaim her flute. Jane had not thought about her flute in years. If, when she left, she had known for sure that she would not be going home, she would have packed that flute. But one day spilled into another so quickly. Other priorities took hold. Could she still play it? Jane and her mother made plans. Next Saturday the three of them would drive in together. Her mother would love Bill. And Jane was confident she would be crazy about Perkins.

When their conversation was finished, Jane clung to the phone, savoring the event. It had been far less demanding than she supposed. All of the torment she had inflicted upon herself over the years, and especially during the last few days, was needless. She had spoken with her. She had actually spoken with her mother. If she was still mad at her, Jane did not hear it in her voice. If her mother was disappointed in her about the funeral or about anything else, she did not say so. Mercifully, she had kept any such thought to herself. Furthermore, there was to be a reunion. About this, Jane had no mixed feelings. She was suddenly ready for it to happen. The time had arrived. The water was perfectly warm and there was no longer any reason to avoid diving right into it. In an instant. In a heartbeat. In a phone call. The gracious conversation between Jane and her mother possessed the quality of an absolution, a mutual dismissal of charges. Jane felt strangely and gloriously liberated.

HELEN WONDERED IF SHE HAD ANY RIGHT to feel so blissful only three days after her father's funeral. How could a day of such incisive dread be followed so closely by a day of such startling joy? Xander was wonderful. Her little brother was amazing. She had spent, altogether, less than two hours with him and yet, she knew him. Moreover, she would get to know him better in the days ahead. In the years ahead. He wanted her to come back. "Tomorrow?" he asked. Nadine was surprisingly amenable. Under the circumstances, she was being disproportionately kind. Nadine was so unlike the bitchy voice she first met through her ill-fated eavesdropping. Helen did not wish, in any way, to exploit Nadine's generosity. Nadine and Xander would get to know the best of her. Surely, the worst of her was spent. It had to be. Xander had presented her with the most compelling reason yet to stay healthy. To be well. To make the most of her life so that she could share a bit of it with him. Her brother. Her wonderful brother. He was charming like her father. He was creative like her sister.

Helen poured herself a large glass of pink lemonade, the elixir Duke used to claim was so good for the soul. She plopped down on the couch, took a swig, and let the sweet-and-sour blend make its way down the back of her throat. From there, she could see through the open bedroom door to the mess she had left on the floor. She took another long drink and then, leaving the glass half-full, Helen decided to take another look. She sat on the floor next to the bed and started sifting through the pile of photographs and papers, placing pictures in one stack and papers in another. The pictures she would review later. Even try putting them in some sort of order. Perhaps. The papers were a puzzle. There were receipts that seemed to have been kept for no reason. Dated deposit slips. Scraps of paper with old, now meaningless, reminders on them. Pick up tonic water. Return library book. Get shampoo. Mundane instructions. She unfolded a small wad of notebook paper and found Jane's address in Fair-hampton. Jane had given it to her early on in their series of secret phone calls, the calls that came to her over at Duke's house. By now it was, undoubtedly, a worthless address. Why had she kept it?

Not knowing how to manage all of this material, how to sort it, how to make sense of it, she layered the papers back into the shoebox, leaving the photographs in a heap on the floor. One corner of a photograph caught her eye. All she could see of the buried picture was a little leg and on the foot of that leg, a patent leather shoe. Helen remembered those shoes. She pulled the picture from the heap. It was a picture of herself in the fifth grade. Having read more books than any-one else in the fifth grade, she won an award for reading. Her teacher, Mrs. Cohen, must have taken the picture. She stood there, tall and proud, holding her prize, which was, of course, a book. She still loved to read. What was the title of her prize? She looked more closely at the picture and could just barely make out the title. *Little Women*. A book about sisters who are deeply devoted to one another. Did she still have that book?

Helen finished the lemonade and went back for a refill. The waxy cardboard container was nearly empty. She wrote a Post-it note to herself. Buy pink lemonade. This she stuck to her pocketbook. Which hung on an angle from a knob on a kitchen drawer. It was then that she noticed the blinking light on her answering machine. Two blinks between pauses. Two messages. The first was from Lynn, her New Hampshire rehab friend: "Just checking in. I'm fine. Hope you are too.

Thought about you all day Thursday. I'll try you again tomorrow. Love 'ya."

The second message was acutely surprising: "Hi. It's . . . it's Jane. Your sister. I know it's been a hard week for you, Helly. With the funeral and all. Um, well . . . you may not want to hear from me. I just want you to know that, well, I'm sorry about . . . "

"Holy shit," Helen said out loud. Was this a joke? Was this really her sister? The voice certainly sounded like Jane's. Deeper but definitely recognizable. The message was cut off. Incomplete. What was she sorry about? The unalterable fact that Dad was dead? The appalling truth that she had left her sister to drown? Is that what she was sorry about? What did Jane want from her? Was she supposed to call her back? Jane had not left a number.

Helen played the message again. Then she played it a third time. There was a different quality in her sister's voice. What was it? Sincerity? Remorse? She rewound the tape once more. Listened again. It was tenderness, the voice of a broken heart. Is it possible, wondered Helen, to abandon someone and still love the one abandoned? Helen had never seriously considered this possibility. She presupposed Jane left her because she did not care enough to stay. The voice on the tape valiantly challenged that assumption. She listened once more. "You may not want to hear from me," Jane said. Was that true? Last year, last week, even up to this morning, she might have said,

"I don't care if I ever hear from my sister again. If my mother wants to reconnect, fine. Please leave me out of it." But the very sound of her sister's voice softened her resolve. It made her long for one of those brave and sometimes hilarious discussions they used to have.

In the course of the same remarkable weekend, might she gain both a brother and a sister? Was that possible? Could she afford to imagine such abundance? Some of her comrades in New Hampshire spent a lot of time talking about God. Could it be that someone, some force, was watching over her after all? Even as she thought it, she trembled lightly as if gently brushed by angel wings.

Helen felt incredibly hungry. She took a large apple from a sympathy fruit basket that was delivered to her apartment on Friday. That was only two days ago. But for the freshness of the fruit, it could have been delivered weeks ago. Years ago. A lifetime ago. Could a lifetime come and go within the space of two days? The basket was from Charlie. The basket came with a note of regret that he could not attend the funeral. Previous commitments. Helen studied the note. It seemed a sign. Previous commitments. That was her agenda now. Previous commitments. Taking greedy bites of the sweet, luminous apple, she opened the sliding door of her apartment. Stepped out onto the tiny balcony. Stood tall and surveyed the world. The sky was still bright with sun. It was an utterly clear and cloudless evening in a season of lengthening days. Full days, she dared to hope. Full to overflowing like this one. Helen could hear Duke's mysterious voice insisting, "Patience is the key," and "It's not about yesterday or tomorrow. It's not even about today. It's about this moment. This very moment is what's real."